The year is 1968

To Americans at home, the Vietnam war is something to watch on a TV screen, between episodes of *My Three Sons* and *The Beverly Hillbillies*. The jukebox rocks to tunes by the Beatles, Simon and Garfunkel, and Blood, Sweat and Tears—songs about love, about sex, about drugs . . . about war.

Protests sweep college campuses as the children of the sixties set out to reshape the world, fighting for their chance to do their own thing. For today, they must decide whether to go to war in the name of Democracy, or flee the country in the name of Peace.

A half million Americans are already in Vietnam, struggling against heat, loneliness and an unseen enemy. They're counting the days to the end of their tours of duty, pinning their hopes on the Paris peace talks, praying that somehow they will make it back home.

It is a time of conflict, as private soul-searching leads to public action.

It is a time of courage, as young men and women follow the dictates of their hearts.

It is the time of Annie Magill and David Nichols.

Dear Reader,

We're sure you are enjoying A Century of
American Romance, a nostalgic look back at the
twentieth century. These stories give us all a
chance to relive the memories of a time gone by
and sneak a peek at romance in an exciting future.

We've traveled all the way from the turn-of-the-
century immigrant experience through the decades
to the Woodstock Nation sixties, as recreated by
Libby Hall last month. In *Till the End of Time,*
Elise Title tells the poignant tale of a group of
friends whose lives are interrupted and influenced
by the Vietnam War.

Watch for all the upcoming titles in A Century of
American Romance, including next month's book
by Tracy Hughes. *Honorbound* is replete with
emotion and seventies ambience.

We hope you continue to enjoy these special
stories of nostalgia. As always, we welcome your
comments. Please take the time to write to us at
the address below.

Here's hoping A Century of American Romance
becomes part of your most cherished memories.

Sincerely,
Debra Matteucci
Senior Editor & Editorial Coordinator
Harlequin Books
300 East 42nd Street
New York, NY 10017

ELISE TITLE

1960s
TILL THE END OF TIME

Harlequin Books

TORONTO • NEW YORK • LONDON
AMSTERDAM • PARIS • SYDNEY • HAMBURG
STOCKHOLM • ATHENS • TOKYO • MILAN

To the women and men who served in Vietnam,
and to those back home who prayed for them

Published February 1991

ISBN 0-373-16377-0

TILL THE END OF TIME

Prologue

To everything there is a season...

On Thanksgiving morning, 1965, eighteen-year-old Annie Magill was studying her reflection in the mirror and thinking to herself how very grown-up she looked and felt.

The day had begun for Annie with innocence, anticipation and excitement. This particular Thanksgiving was more than a holiday, it was a reunion with the boys.

The boys. Annie smiled. When they were little, the boys had often been called the Three Musketeers. And for a short time in high school they were the Dukes. It was funny to think of them as the boys, still. Turner and David had already turned twenty-one and Hawk's twenty-first birthday was in February.

The boys. Well, really, Annie and the boys. By the time she could walk Annie had attached herself to the three boys, and she'd never fully let go. She was the little pest, their shadow, eventually their mascot, and finally the good kid. In turn, they had been her heroes, her advisers, her protectors. There was her brother, Turner, the dazzling star athlete who'd taught Annie how to hit a ball. He was a senior at Northwestern now. Hawk, a senior at Berkeley, was still the endearing clown who could always make her laugh even when she'd scraped her knee or been stood up on a date for the first time. And there was David, now a senior at Yale. David was the hardest to categorize. No easy adjective fit him. He was so many things.

A daredevil, a poet, a dreamer. He had the most open and engaging smile. Yet there was always something mysterious and secretive about David Nichols. Over the years he'd been a source of curiosity and fascination for Annie. While she adored him as much as she adored Turner and Hawk, she felt a heightened tension around the elusive David that she never felt around the others. She wondered if she would feel the same now. Now that she was all grown up.

"The boys are here, Annie. Turner's car is pulling up the drive," Ian Magill called out from the foot of the stairs.

Nervously, Annie tugged on her brown suede miniskirt and gave her brown-and-white checkerboard print silk blouse and white tights a few final adjustments. "Just a sec," she called back, a note of nervous anticipation in her voice.

Frowning into the mirror with concentration she added a bit more brown eyeliner to her eyelids, then brushed her sunflower-golden hair one more time. Gone was the shoulder-length page-boy flip she'd worn last time they'd seen her. Now, her straight, shiny hair fell halfway down her back. The times were a-changing all right.

She hurried across her bedroom, but came to an abrupt stop at the door. She put her hand on her heart. It was racing. Her breathing was shallow, her palms sweaty. She had to stop herself from rubbing them dry on her skirt. Suede wasn't a very forgiving fabric. But it was sexy.

That was, after all, what the perspiration and the palpitations were all about. What she wanted to do was knock the socks off those boys. Let 'em know in no uncertain terms that "the good kid" had grown up.

"Hey kid, where the hell are ya?" Turner's booming voice cut through her thoughts.

She laughed as she opened the door. Okay, so to Turner she would probably always be the kid. But David and Hawk...that was another story.

She looked down at them from the top of the stairs. Her boys. Her men. All three in a row, standing there at the bottom of the stairs, looking up. Turner, Hawk and David. Annie's eyes lingered on David for an extra moment. Her smile deepened.

As for her boys, their smiles reflected surprise, then consternation. It looked to Annie as if they weren't exactly prepared for the grown-up Miss Magill.

Ian came up behind Turner and placed his large hands on his son's shoulder. "I was goin' to warn ya." When Ian Magill wanted to make a point, his Irish brogue somehow always thickened. "Our Annie's now into doin' her own thing. That is the phrase, girl, isn't it now? Doin' your own thing?"

Hawk laughed. From all outward appearances, he, too, was into doing his own thing. Turner and David looked very collegiate in their conservative sport shirts and well-pressed flannel slacks, their hair neatly trimmed. Hawk, his hair worn Beatle fashion, was dressed in a bright yellow silk shirt over gold and black pin-striped trousers. To top off the mod look, he wore a pair of the Ben Franklin specs everyone called granny glasses, a fad John Lennon had initiated.

Ian scowled as he scanned Hawk's appearance, then gave the broad, burly young man a solid but affectionate thump on the shoulder. "Still the clown, I see." He shook his head. "Well, you four take a minute to say your hellos, then come back to the kitchen and help Nanna with the spread. No use any of you takin' on airs and thinkin' you're guests after all these years."

As Ian started off for the kitchen, Hawk called out, "Hey Mr. Magill, you forgot to remind us to wash our hands before we come barreling into the kitchen."

Ian chuckled. "Right ya are, Josh Hawkins. And ya can add a haircut to that reminder."

"Don't listen to him, Hawk. I think you look hip," Annie said, coming down the steps and pausing on the bottom one.

Hawk laughed. "Looks like Flower Power's hit you, too."

The corners of Turner's mouth curved up. "What's become of my sweet little sister? Don't tell me you hang out at discotheques these days?"

"Didn't Daddy tell you I was working my way through nursing school as a go-go dancer over at Dandy's?" Annie asked.

For a moment it looked as though Turner actually believed her. For all his feigned sophistication, Annie knew her brother had a decidedly gullible streak.

"Hey Annie," Hawk said as he leaned against the banister, his eyes taking an extended survey of her long, shapely legs. "Did you get five inches taller or something since summer?"

Turner flung an arm around his buddy's shoulder. "Watch it, Hawk. That's my little sister you're drooling over."

"Who's drooling over Annie?" Hawk winked. "Can't you smell that turkey?"

Annie sighed. "Still the same clown, huh, Hawk?" she said, echoing her dad's crack.

"Only kidding, Annie. You look good. Great. It's just...well, last time I saw you was at your graduation last summer. You had on that pretty little white dress, your hair was in that cute little flip, your face was all fresh scrubbed. You looked so...innocent. Don't get me wrong, kid, I like the new look."

Annie smiled, then took in a noticeable breath as she turned her attention to David Nichols. David looked especially compelling that day. Not as conventionally handsome as her fair-haired brother, not as brawny and muscular as the robust, rugged Hawk, David Nichols had his own unique appeal with his wavy chestnut hair, his cobalt-blue eyes ringed by lashes so dark and thick as to be the envy of every female. But there was nothing feminine about David. His chiseled features radiated strength, determination and a seriousness that Annie had always admired. And now she noticed a sensuality about him that she found both intriguing and disturbing.

Annie put her hands on her hips. "Okay, out with it, Nickel. What's your hang-up?" She'd nicknamed David "Nickel" when she was in junior high, and in turn he'd nicknamed her "Penny Annie." She hadn't called him Nickel in years.

It brought a faint smile to his otherwise somber visage, relieving the tension between them. "I think, Penny Annie, dear old Florence Nightingale would turn over in her grave if she saw the latest fashions for nurses in training."

"It's Thanksgiving, Nickel. I'm not in training today."

He looked as if he was about to say something more, but stopped himself and held up his hands in surrender. "I give up."

Turner gave Hawk a playful shove in the direction of the kitchen, and said, "We better get in there and help out before Nanna has a bird."

"She better have a bird. I'm starving," Hawk quipped.

They all laughed, Hawk and Turner started down the hall, Annie and David lingering behind.

"So, how's Yale been treating you these days, Nickel?" Annie asked.

"Senior year is a grind. Lots of pressure applying for law school."

"Last summer you said you'd decided not to follow in the Judge's footsteps."

She saw the shadow of a frown cross David's face. "If I don't go on to grad school, I'll lose my deferment."

"What about all the teach-ins on Vietnam. And the student marches against the war? Maybe we'll pull our boys out by then."

"It's going to take more than a few college rallies, Annie."

Annie sighed. "I think this war is crazy. I don't even know where Vietnam is. I'd never heard of it before this whole mess started."

Annie wanted to get off the subject of war. It made chills travel down her spine and made her feel helpless and lost. She searched for a new subject and found a familiar one. "So, it's going to be law then. That must make the Judge happy, anyway."

David gave her a sharp look. "There are all kinds of law. I still don't plan to follow in my father's footsteps."

"Sorry," Annie said softly. She knew David and his domineering father had been at odds for years over which of them would decide David's future.

She knew David didn't like talking about his power struggles with his father. She hoped he'd change the subject and that she'd be happier with his choice of topic than he'd been with hers.

"I imagine your dad must be concerned about Turner's deferment."

Annie sighed. "My dad's too excited about Turner being scouted for the majors to think about much of anything else. But once Turner's out of school he will lose his deferment. He could be drafted. Dad has been thinking Turner ought to sign up with a Canadian baseball team for now and wait things out up there. We've got cousins in Toronto. I know one thing. There's no way Dad will risk losing Turner. It would kill him. We're all he has left of Mom."

"We're all at risk, Annie. Don't you get it? Any one of us could be sent over there. Any one of us could come back in a body bag. I ... I already know a few guys who came back that way."

The air was suddenly thick, and Annie could feel the anguish she saw in David's dark blue eyes. For her the war was far removed from her own personal world. It was something to argue about on moral grounds, something that existed in newspaper headlines and on TV.

"Hey, you two malingerers," Hawk shouted from the kitchen door. "Get in here for inspection. Nanna's orders."

Annie shot David a frown. "Somebody better tell that boy that we're strictly antimilitary in this house."

David's expression remained grim. "I think he's practicing for the future."

"What do you mean?"

"Maybe Hawk was just pulling my leg, but driving over here from the station he mentioned that he was thinking about enlisting. Going to officers' candidate school or something."

"Enlisting? Hawk! Never. He was joking," Annie said firmly. The danger of getting drafted was one thing, but enlisting? She couldn't imagine any of the boys doing that. "Have you taken a close look at Hawk, Nickel? You think he'd shave off that long hair, put on a uniform, march in the mud? I could as much imagine Hawk enlisting as I could imagine Turner giving up baseball."

David's smile resurfaced. "Yeah, I guess he must have been joking. Will you help me come up with some way to get back at him?"

Chapter One

And a time to every purpose under the heaven...

It was 5:00 a.m. on a cold, windy March day in 1968 when Annie arrived for her training shift at the Oakdale Veterans Hospital, thirty miles south of Beaumont. Before heading for the third-floor ward she stopped at her locker to stow her gear.

Jeannie Ryan, a fellow nursing student from night shift came up behind Annie and glanced at the poster hanging inside her door. "Time for a new one, Magill. That one's getting kind of ratty looking."

Annie glanced at the poster which featured a childlike drawing of a red-and-yellow petaled flower with a green stem and the child's message: War Is Not Healthy for Children and Other Living Things.

"It's the sentiment that counts," Annie replied with a smile as she changed out of her boots and into a pair of polished, white nursing oxfords.

"Oh, by the way, Wheeler wants to see you before you go up to your ward."

Annie nodded, taking another look at the poster, reflecting back to the day she'd put it up; the day she'd had her first encounter with head of student nursing, Glenda Wheeler. The meeting had taken place on Annie's first day at the V.A. Although she was nervous and apprehensive about doing her final training stint in a V.A. hospital, she had specifically requested the placement and she felt good about her decision. After being assigned her locker, Annie had dug out the rolled poster from her tote bag and tacked it up. Later that morning, a nursing student who had a locker across from Annie's had complained about it to the head of student nurses. By lunchtime Annie was handed a note ordering her to see Glenda Wheeler that afternoon at three.

She'd been filled with trepidation as she walked down the hall to the head nurse's private office. The last thing she'd wanted or needed on her very first day of duty was a confrontation with a head nurse who had a reputation for being a fearsome, hard-nosed stickler.

Nurse Wheeler had come right to the point. "You have hung a poster in your locker that one of the other students feels is unpatriotic." The head nurse spoke in a nasal voice with a Yankee accent.

"Unpatriotic?" Annie's voice quavered on her one-word reply.

Nurse Wheeler walked to the front of her desk and leaned against it, folding her arms across her narrow chest. "A student whose brother is in Vietnam."

Annie was silent.

"Do you have any family members in the war, Miss Magill?"

"No," she said softly. "I only have one brother and he's 4F. A punctured eardrum. He...didn't even realize it until his army physical."

"Miss Magill, several of our nursing students and quite a few of our nursing staff have family in Nam. Husbands, brothers, cousins..."

"I have a very close friend who enlisted. Josh Hawkins. He's with the First Marine Division in Da Nang." Annie took a breath. "And other friends from high school, and guys I've met since then."

"Then I would think you'd understand why this nurse, and perhaps others, might take offense. If you've chosen this training placement to make some kind of activist political statement . . ."

"No, no, I haven't," Annie said. "Believe me, Nurse Wheeler, I have nothing but compassion and respect for the boys who are fighting over there. That's why I requested this placement."

"And do you think," Wheeler said, her tone slightly softer, "that you can handle the stress, Miss Magill?"

Annie didn't answer immediately, but when she did her voice was more confident. "What I have to learn to handle is nothing compared to what these boys must face. So I will handle it, Nurse Wheeler. I'll do my best."

Wheeler nodded. "I never ask for more from my nurses than their best. That will be all."

Annie turned to go but Nurse Wheeler called out to her before she reached the door.

"Before you leave would you mind getting my briefcase for me. It's in the closet by the door."

"Oh...sure." Annie walked over to the closet, opened the door and stepped in to lift the black case off the shelf. As she turned to close the door she noticed the worn poster hanging on the inside of it. A poster with a childlike drawing of a red-and-yellow flower with a green stem—a duplicate of Annie's.

Annie brought the briefcase over to Nurse Wheeler. Neither woman said a word.

That encounter had forged a special bond between Annie and Head Nurse Glenda Wheeler. While Annie certainly agreed with the other student nurses about Wheeler being stern, demanding, hard-nosed, and intimidating, she also knew that there wasn't anyone more compassionate, courageous and dedicated. Annie not only admired and respected her, she saw Glenda Wheeler as a woman to model herself after.

Jeannie Ryan gave Annie's shoulder a little shake. "Hey, quit daydreaming. And don't forget about Wheeler wanting to see you before you go on duty."

Annie gave one final glance at the poster and closed her locker door. "No, no I won't forget." Then she gave Jeannie a knowing look. "We must have had a busy night if Wheeler stayed on for your shift."

Jeannie sighed. "We had three new admissions. And one of the boys on the psych unit went off the deep end."

"Uh-oh, that means Wheeler isn't going to be in a very chipper mood this morning. I wonder what she wants to see me about."

Jeannie just shrugged and slipped on her coat.

Before Annie rapped on Wheeler's door, she absently smoothed down her starched, white nursing uniform.

"Come in."

"Sit down, Annie. Please."

Wheeler's familiar Yankee voice held an unfamiliar note of tenderness.

Annie's knees suddenly went rubbery. "What is it? What's wrong?" Immediately she thought of Nanna and her dad. Had one of them suddenly taken ill? Or worse? Annie'd been living away from home these past six months—sharing an apartment in Oakdale with two other nursing students. If something had happened to a family member, someone might have tried to reach her at the V.A. hospital.

"It's about one of the boys who was admitted to your ward last night."

A whoosh of relief escaped Annie's lungs as she sat down. "Oh, I see."

Wheeler's steady, sympathetic gaze, however, told Annie that she didn't see. "The boy is someone you know, Annie."

It was funny how denial worked. Annie stared blankly at Wheeler. Blank and resolute. "It is?"

"It's Josh Hawkins, Annie," she said gently.

"Hawk?" Annie's eyes remained blank. "No, there must be a mistake. Hawk's doing short time. His duty's up in less than a week. He's made it through three hundred and fifty-eight days. I've got them crossed off on my calendar. Nobody makes it that far and . . . and . . .''

Annie rose in a daze and started for the door, as if she'd been given a dismissal.

"There's no mistake, Annie."

Annie stopped in her tracks but she didn't turn to face the head nurse. "I got a letter from Hawk four days ago. Four days. He was fine."

"Annie, that letter was probably written weeks ago, maybe even longer. You know that."

Annie finally turned to face Wheeler. The blank look was gone. The denial was gone. "Is it bad?" Even as she asked, Annie knew it had to be bad. Her ward was the spinal injury ward. Paraplegics, quadriplegics . . .

"He's paralyzed from the waist down. An injury to the lower spine. The prognosis is iffy. There's a small chance, over time he might get some limited—"

"Oh, no," Annie whispered. "Hawk paralyzed?"

"He's luckier than some."

Annie let out a sharp cry. "Lucky? Yes, I'll be sure to tell Hawk how lucky he is when I'm pushing him around the ward."

"Annie . . ."

"He was always such a clown, Wheeler. Always laughing and joking. And he was so big and powerful looking. That's what made his acting the clown so funny . . ." The words trailed off and died. Annie was flooded with a sadness so overwhelming she found it hard to breathe.

Wheeler gave her one of her infamous no-nonsense looks. "He's still strong, Annie. Better still, he's tough. I spoke with him last night when he came in. He's going to be okay."

Annie swayed on her feet. Wheeler hurried over and guided her to a chair.

Closing her eyes, Annie murmured, "How am I going to tell the others?"

"His parents have already been notified."

"No, I mean David and Turner, my dad and Nanna. It's going to break their hearts."

"David Nichols?"

Annie looked up. "Yes."

"He's with Hawk now."

"David's here?" Annie hadn't seen David in over three months. Not since Thanksgiving. Their first Thanksgiving without Hawk.

"Your friend Hawk managed to charm his floor nurse into putting in a phone call to Nichols at two in the morning. Then Nichols showed up less than an hour later and he charmed a nurse into sneaking him up to Hawk's ward. Most irregular." Wheeler smiled softly. "Those two friends of yours seem to have quite a persuasive way with women."

Annie was amazed to find herself laughing. "You better believe it, Wheeler. They'll steal your heart away if you aren't careful." The laughter instantly died on her lips and her gaze dropped, thoughtfully. "They stole mine years ago."

Wheeler rose and walked over to Annie. "If you need a little time . . ."

Annie rose, too. At five foot seven she towered over Glenda Wheeler. She smiled wanly down at her. "I'll be okay. I have to be."

Glenda Wheeler took Annie's hand. "About what we talked about the other day, Annie . . ." She hesitated. "You might want to change your mind now."

Tears glistened in Annie's eyes, but her voice was unwavering. "No, I'm more certain now than ever."

By the time Annie reached her ward she'd forced a smile on her face. Not just for Hawk, but for all the boys whose spirits were lifted by the smiles of their nurses.

David was sitting on the edge of Hawk's bed. He stood up when Annie approached.

"I'd stand, too, if I could, kiddo," Hawk quipped from the bed. He was pale and he'd definitely lost a good twenty pounds. But, for it all, he wore that old, familiar clownish grin on his face. Only it wasn't the same, Annie saw. Hawk's wide-mouthed grin couldn't quite make it up to those big brown eyes of his. There wasn't even a hint of the old sparkle there. What Annie saw in Hawk's eyes, what tore her apart, was the same ravaged, haunted, terrified look that she saw in the eyes of every boy at the V.A. hospital. But Hawk was working hard to keep up his spirits. Or maybe it was her spirits and David's spirits that he wanted to bolster.

He gave Annie a broad wink. "Hey kiddo, you're the prettiest looking nurse in the place. What happened?"

Annie's smile was a bit less artificial. Hawk's wisecrack was so typical of the old Hawk. The funny clown who could always cheer her up, even when her heart was breaking. Still, even with the smile curving her lips, she had to fight hard to keep back the tears.

"Thanks a lot," she quipped, coming closer to Hawk's bedside, giving David a brief nod though their eyes met and held for a moment longer.

Hawk caught the look. "Come on, you two. It's gonna be okay. Hey, this is a reunion. All we gotta do is get Turner on down here and we can have ourselves a regular party." He winked at David. "We'll get the kid to sneak up a few pints, what do ya say? There's a couple of cool looking nurses around this joint, man. The kid here can play matchmaker. Fix us all up. Yeah, it'll be groovy, man. Real groovy."

Annie took hold of Hawk's hand. She held it lightly, firmly. He was still grinning as the tears welled up and flowed from his eyes, like a faucet had just been turned on. "Ignore it," he muttered.

Annie put her arms around Hawk and cried into his chest. And then David was holding on to them both, tears running down his cheeks, too, along the shallow grooves beside his mouth.

NEARLY A WEEK LATER Annie sat across from her grandmother in a drab, poorly lit coffee shop near the hospital. The jukebox was playing a new hit by Blood, Sweat and Tears. A couple of tables away a group of teens, all clad in bell-bottom jeans and tie-dye shirts, were singing along.

Nanna, who'd flown in to see Hawk, seemed oblivious to the noise. She nibbled daintily on her grilled cheese sandwich, then dabbed at her lips with a paper napkin.

"Hawk's so happy you've come to see him, Nanna. It means so much to him having you, Dad, David..."

"Hawk feels bad that Turner can't get down here," Nanna was reflecting, "but maybe it's just as well."

Annie looked surprised. "What do you mean?"

"Turner never could cope with harsh realities, Annie. You know that. I love the boy deeply, but I won't make excuses for him."

"Turner's devastated by what happened to Hawk, Nanna. When I spoke to him last night he was so choked up he could hardly speak. He wants to be with Hawk. It's only that he can't get away right now. He calls Hawk every single day. And he's sent him all sorts of funny care packages... to cheer him up."

Lilli reached out and patted Annie's hand. "You always have come to Turner's defense. And Hawk's and David's. Those boys never could do any wrong in your eyes. And they all see you the same way."

"Nonsense. They still see me as a kid."

"They adore you, Annie. I imagine there isn't a thing any one of them wouldn't do for you. Or you for them."

"I'm worried about David," Annie said, following up on Nanna's observation.

Lilli smiled. "He said the same about you. He stopped by your father's house the other night and we talked."

"David told Dad he was worried about me?"

"No, of course he'd never say that to Ian. Your father's worried enough about his young, fragile daughter living on her own nearly thirty miles from home." Lilli smiled. "But you've managed quite nicely, Annie. You've grown up some."

"Some?"

Lilli clasped her hands together. "David thinks you've something on your mind that's troubling you. Something you don't want to talk about."

"How strange. I've been thinking the same thing about him. It's funny. Sometimes I think David's so open, so comfortable about expressing his feelings. He's been terrific with Hawk. Not doing what so many people do...you know, no pussyfooting around the patient, trying to minimize the injury, the suffering, the problems that will have to be faced. I don't mean he allows Hawk to get morbid. He's just showing Hawk that he still feels exactly the same about him."

"You're quite fond of David, aren't you?"

"Of course," Annie said without hesitation, misreading the knowing look in Lilli's eyes. "But I don't really understand him. Even after all these years. That's what I mean about being strange. Sometimes he's so open and other times...he's frustratingly, infuriatingly closed. Here I am, practically finished with my nursing degree, dealing with plenty of harsh reality, and there's David and Hawk, still calling me kiddo. Really Nanna..."

"Perhaps that's part of what's bothering David."

"I don't understand."

"That you aren't a kid anymore. That you don't come rushing to him with your problems...that you don't look up to him with those adoring blue eyes of yours. He is certain something is on your mind and he's hurt that you aren't talking to him about it."

Annie pushed aside her plate, the hamburger gone cold and hardly touched. She leveled her gaze on Nanna. "I'm planning to enlist in the Army Nursing Corps as soon as I graduate." She hesitated. "I have a guarantee to go to Vietnam."

To Annie's surprise Nanna took the news quite calmly.

"Yes, I thought you might. It is in the blood, after all. The Almont tradition. First me, then your mother, now you."

"I'm not doing it to carry on a tradition," Annie said in a low voice. "I have to go. Nurses are needed so desperately over there. And you should hear Hawk talk about how much they helped him, how he might not have pulled through without—I have to do whatever I can, Nanna."

Nanna studied her granddaughter thoughtfully. "They say that this war is far different, more brutal than World War I or II. Perhaps that's true. But I'll tell you something, Annie, all war is brutal and ugly. It scars the land, the heart and soul."

Nanna slumped a little, her age suddenly showing. "Oh Annie, you are still a child in so many ways."

Annie was truly hurt. "No, you're wrong. I'm older, wiser and tougher than I look."

Nanna nodded slowly. "Yes, you are much tougher than you look. Looks are deceiving. It's Turner who bears the stronger resemblance to your mother, but it's you, Annie, who has her Almont nature and spirit." Nanna smiled. "And stubbornness."

"Will you help me break the news to Dad? It's not going to be easy."

"No, no it isn't. Nothing's going to be easy from here on, Annie."

Annie got the message. If she was going to be grown-up she'd have to tackle her own grown-up confrontations.

Nanna reached across the table and gripped Annie's hand with surprising strength. There were tears in her eyes. "I'm proud of you, Annie. But I'm frightened for you. And for David, too."

"David? You don't mean he's thinking of enlisting when he finishes law school this year?"

"He dropped out of school. He's already enlisted."

Annie stared at Nanna for a moment in disbelief. "No, no he can't go, too."

Chapter Two

A time to seek, and a time to lose...

"You can't go," David told Annie sharply, pacing back and forth in the corridor outside Hawk's hospital room.

"You're going," Annie said with equal vehemence.

David's expression was a mix of anger and distress. "Annie, listen to me." He stopped talking as a nurse wheeled a patient past them. "Isn't there someplace more private where we can talk?"

Annie led David down the hall to an empty lounge. They ignored the Army-issue gray plastic chairs. David walked over to the window. Annie came and stood beside him. They were both quiet for several minutes.

"God, I hate this war. I hate everything about it," Annie said in a low, hard voice.

David turned and gripped her arm. "Then why are you going there? You, of all people? All those antiwar sit-ins and marches you were into..." His grip on her arm tightened. "You're just upset about Hawk, Annie. You think you owe it to him. That's it, isn't it? A rash decision..."

Annie pulled her arm away. "It isn't a rash decision. But Hawk is the point, David. Hawk and all the boys like him. And all the ones who didn't make it...they're the point."

"But you're helping them here," David argued. "You're doing your part."

"You mean I'm safe here." She shook her head. "But don't you see, by the time they get here . . ." She stopped, unable to finish the sentence. Most of what could be done for a lot of these vets had been done long before they got to a Stateside V.A. hospital.

After a minute she pulled herself together. "There are plenty of nurses willing to work in V.A. hospitals. But nurses aren't lining up to enlist for duty in Vietnam. An Army Nursing Corps recruiter came here a month ago. She talked about how desperate medical units in Vietnam were for nurses.

"Maybe like Nanna told me, it's in my blood. My mom was over in England during World War II, Nanna in France during World War I . . ."

"That's different. Those times were different."

"Okay, maybe this war is different. But just about every one of the boys here has a story of a special nurse who saw them through some of their roughest times, who not only helped save their lives but their spirits. I want to be one of those nurses, David. I need to be."

Annie saw that David's intense, worried expression was mixed with a new measure of respect as he looked at her. But she understood that no matter what she said, he would still try to talk her out of it. He was scared for her. Just like she was scared for him. He could come back like Hawk . . . or worse, he could never come back at all.

David broke through her tortured thoughts. "Hawk has been talking to me, too. He told me plenty about his hospital time in Vietnam, Annie. Rockets exploding inside the compound, Viet Cong infiltrating right into nurses' quarters—"

"And I suppose you'll be immune to rockets and enemy infiltration," Annie broke in defiantly.

"You don't understand, Annie."

"Then make me understand," she pleaded.

David's tone was stoic. "I have to go, Annie."

Annie's eyes narrowed as she looked up at him. "Because of Hawk? A minute ago you accused me of making a rash decision. Maybe you're the one doing that. You think you owe it to Hawk to get a junkyard full of shrapnel in your gut like he got?"

"Annie," David said with sharp surprise. He turned away, but not before Annie could see him struggling to hold his emotions in check. He stared out of the window at the flat, gray landscape with a sprinkling of leafless winter trees. She doubted he was really seeing anything out there.

"Your going to fight in Vietnam won't make Hawk walk again, David," Annie said softly. "And it won't bring back the youth or health of any of the other boys who've come through it."

His blank, distant expression made her angry and she grabbed his arm. "Don't you see, David, my feelings about this hideous war haven't changed one bit. I'm more convinced than ever that it's wrong, immoral, futile." She bit down hard on her lower lip as she saw a familiar stubborn glint in David's dark eyes. Not only was the war futile; so, she realized, was this discussion with David. He'd already enlisted and she knew him well enough to know he'd never let the Judge pull any strings to get him off the hook. David was going to Vietnam. The war would gobble him up like all the rest. Even if he made it back alive, his body unscathed, he would never be the same.

David gazed at her hand gripping his arm, then his eyes traveled to her face. Still, there was little expression in his voice as he said, "It's not just because of Hawk, Annie."

Annie felt that was no real answer. Damn him. Why did he have to be so closed, so self-contained? She'd tried to make him understand her motives for going. She'd tried to be open and honest with him. She'd reached out to him.

Frustration ripped through her and now she wasn't just clasping his arm, she was gripping it with all her might.

"Then why, David? Rebellion against your father? That old yearning of yours to live on the edge, see some action, have a hot adventure? Boredom? Does going to law school just seem too dull by comparison?"

She could see from his expression that he was truly shocked by her accusations.

"This isn't you, Annie."

She thumped her chest. "It is me, David. Damn it. I don't want you going off to war with some John Wayne notion in your head...like Hawk had."

David shut his eyes tightly. For the first time that afternoon, Annie could see a play of emotions on his face. The blankness, the stoicism was gone.

There was a desperate, ragged edge to his voice as he spoke. "Annie. Annie." He slowly opened his eyes, meeting her gaze clearly, earnestly. "I don't know if I can explain it, Annie. It's hard for me."

"I know," Annie said softly, her tender smile encouraging. This was her Nickel.

"Maybe part of it is that I think it stinks that I could have stayed out of it just because I happen to have an influential father who can pull strings for me. Why should I be one of the privileged few who gets to sit around a local law school bar sipping beers, take in a hit movie on a Saturday night, pop off to Bermuda for Easter vacation, sit around my safe, secure dorm watching the war on a thirteen-inch TV screen? My friends are dying out there, or coming home...crippled, broken."

Annie released her hold on David's arm and he began pacing.

"I've been here with Hawk some nights," David said in a low voice etched in pain. "Nights when he couldn't sleep and he'd beg me to stay around. We'd talk and talk until finally he'd drop off. Only I'd be afraid to leave in case he woke up. Sometimes he would and he'd reach out to me like he was...drowning. What right do I have to sleep the sleep of the innocent when Hawk and all these other guys are lying here tormented by nightmares night after night?''

Annie could only nod. Nights were the worst time at the hospital. During the daylight hours the boys would horse around, come on to the nurses, joke, tease. But when the blackness struck so did the memories.

David took a shaky breath. "Does it make any sense, Annie? I'm lousy when it comes to expressing my feelings." He hesitated. "All I know is I couldn't live with myself if I wasn't willing to take the same risk Hawk and thousands of others have taken, are taking every single day.''

Annie didn't even know she was crying until David gently brushed a tear off her cheek with his thumb. Her eyes were shining as she looked up at him. Her voice was charged with emotion when she spoke. "I understand. I feel the same way. I hurt for all of them, especially Hawk. It's just...David, I don't want to hurt for you, too. I don't want to...lose you.'' Annie felt her cheeks warm as she spoke, but her gaze didn't waver.

Neither did David's. "I don't want to lose you either, Annie. That's why I want you to change your mind. You still have time.''

Annie held up a hand in weary protest and managed a weak smile. "Time's up, David. Believe me. I won't change my mind. Right now, I've just put in a long shift and I want to go home.''

"Okay, I'll drive you.''

Annie hesitated to accept. "Only if you promise not to argue with me anymore about my enlisting. I've heard it all already from my father. Poor Dad. He never dreamed, once Turner was safe, that he'd have any more worries about a child of his going to war. He's beside himself.''

"I don't blame him. Have you thought what it would do to him if—''

Annie pressed her finger to his lips. "Life is full of risks, David. My mother survived the Blitz only to die young of something else. There are no guarantees."

"Annie..."

"Maybe I'd better catch a bus."

"No," David relented. "I want to take you. I won't say another word about your decision."

So they went back in together to say good-night to Hawk. Hawk gave his pal a broad wink when he heard David was taking Annie home. "Some of us have all the luck, man. Wait till you meet Annie's two gorgeous roommates."

Annie grinned. "They're on duty here tonight. So maybe you'll be the lucky one, Hawk."

Instead of coming back with a fast crack, Hawk gave Annie a thoughtful gaze. "Maybe David's lucky, anyway."

She felt her cheeks warm even as she gave Hawk a don't-be-ridiculous scowl.

David laughed, but it wasn't, Annie noted, an altogether easy laugh.

Once outside, David led Annie to his brand-new, red '68 Corvette.

"An early graduation present from the Judge," David commented offhandedly, opening the door for her.

She gave him a curious look as she slid into the low front seat. "Then he doesn't know that you...?"

"I thought we'd finished talking about that topic."

Actually, David had put no such stipulation on Annie, but she didn't argue the point. In two more weeks, he'd be leaving for boot camp. Annie wondered how the Judge would react when David finally did tell him. Knowing David, he'd wait until the last minute, to prevent the Judge from taking any action.

Annie and David not only avoided the topic of going to Vietnam, they avoided talking altogether for the fifteen-minute drive to Annie's apartment. Annie hated the tension between them. She wished she could somehow break through it. When David turned onto her street she was about to tell him where to stop when he braked right at the front door to her three-story brick building.

Annie donned a cheery smile. "Would you like to come up for a cup of coffee? Chris, Paula and I have done a pretty good job with the place." There was a touch of seduction in her voice, in her smile.

"I know. I gave Chris a lift home the other morning. We...uh...met outside Hawk's room and got to talking. It was snowing badly and she was worried about whether the buses would be running." He wasn't sure why he felt the need to explain.

"And you...came upstairs?"

David smiled awkwardly. "For coffee."

"Oh." She smiled thinly.

"I wouldn't mind another cup now," he said in a slightly strained voice.

Annie didn't seem to hear him. "She's nice, Chris. And gorgeous. You should have seen Hawk...when I introduced them."

"She's very nice," David agreed.

Not, Annie noted, a nice "kid." No, David didn't see the voluptuous brunette with the big brown bedroom eyes as a kid. Even though Chris was only four months older than Annie was.

She gave David a hard stare.

He laughed. Again, not his usual easy laugh. "Don't tell me you're jealous, kiddo?"

Annie felt a wave of fury wash over her. She wanted to slug David. Not a playful slug as she'd been known to unleash on occasion when his teasing went too far. No, this time she felt truly angry. Inexplicably so. She moved toward him in the snug confines of the sports car; not sure what she meant to do, but knowing she had to do something.

David's dark eyes locked with hers, his expression tense, uncertain.

Neither of them had planned to kiss, and when their lips met, the intimate contact startled them both. Startled and excited them.

Annie didn't pull back, but she expected David to. She thought he'd pull away and give her a joking, let's-forget-about-it look, or scold her playfully, or...

But he pulled her closer to him, wrapping his arms around her. After the briefest instant, his probing tongue slipped through her parted lips, gentle and caressing. Annie responded eagerly and their kiss deepened.

It was their first real kiss. Oh, they'd exchanged countless kisses on holidays, birthdays and such. Quick, friendly, chaste pecks on the lips or on the cheek, a hit-or-miss affair as far as that went.

There was nothing hit-or-miss about this kiss. Nothing brotherly. Nor chaste. This kiss was deliberate, urgent, passionate. It was a lovers' kiss.

They finally parted when the gearshift caught Annie in the ribs and she let out a sharp cry. And when the kiss was over, David, looking pale and shaken, leaned his head back heavily against the white leather seat.

He didn't say anything. He was too busy silently berating himself. This was his buddy's sister. She was young, innocent...and far too desirable. Suddenly boot camp couldn't come fast enough.

It took a few moments for Annie's labored breathing to steady a bit.

"I'll make a fresh pot."

"What?"

She managed a smile despite David's clearly troubled expression.

"Coffee. You said...before...you wouldn't mind a cup of coffee."

"Annie..."

"I make pretty terrific coffee, David. Believe me, you don't want to pass it up." Annie was shocked by her flirtatious manner, never having behaved this way with David before.

She felt a quickening of her pulse, a mixture of anticipation and puzzlement about what she was feeling, what David was feeling. All she knew was that she and David had crossed over an invisible line.

When David finally turned to face her his touch on her cheek was light, gentle . . . all too brotherly. She could see the decision in his eyes, a kind of internal battening down of the hatches.

"You've changed your mind about the coffee." Her voice held a questioning note.

"I don't think coffee is too good an idea."

"Oh."

He managed a ragged smile. "I'm sure it would be terrific, Annie. Maybe another time."

He pressed his palm lightly against the side of her face, his touch warming her whole body. "I think you're pretty terrific, Annie."

Not, I think you're a pretty terrific "kid." Well, Annie thought, that was progress anyway.

He dropped his hand into his lap and she reached for the door handle.

"Annie."

She quickly let go of the handle and swung around to face him with obvious expectation. Maybe he'd changed his mind about the coffee after all.

"Please do me one favor."

"What?" she asked.

"Please give it some more thought."

Her cornflower-blue eyes sparkled. "Oh, I will, David. You can be sure I will."

He smiled awkwardly. "Not . . . the kiss, Annie. I meant about joining the Army Nursing Corps."

There was no hiding the disappointment in her face even as she smiled back. "Okay, I'll think about that in between these other thoughts, but I won't change my mind about either."

Chapter Three

A time to keep, and a time to cast away...

Long Binh, September, 1968

Dear Hawk,

Well, I'm in-country all right. We landed in Tan Son Nhut on a Wednesday night. And what a landing. It was pitch black and we literally just dropped to the ground. Forget gradual descent. No lights on the plane or the landing field. All this to protect us from getting shot out of the sky. So, I get off the plane, trip on the bottom step in the dark and nearly kill myself falling over the suitcase of the nurse in front of me....

I got to spend a day in Saigon before being shipped to the 24th Evac. Hospital here at Long Binh. I wasted most of it trying to track David down only to discover he'd been shipped out of Saigon two weeks ago over to USAEV in—guess where of all places—you got it, kiddo. Long Binh. Still haven't seen him. He's off on maneuvers.

So here I am at Long Binh. I couldn't believe the size of the base when I first got here. It takes up the whole village. There are two hospitals, a fully stocked base store, excuse me, PX, a large rec center. Please, please tell my dad next time he visits you that things aren't so bad here for the nurses. I know he's worried sick about me, and still furious that I enlisted against his wishes. I tried to make him understand. Maybe you'll have more luck. And next

*time you speak to Turner, tell him he'd better write me,
even if it is just a few words scribbled on a postcard. I
know he isn't much of a letter writer, but I want to hear
how he's doing, how many home runs he's hitting. Baseball and apple pie. Those are two big topics of conversation out here as you well know.*

*Oh, one favor. Send me an occasional Beaumont pa-
per if you can. I know Dad brings one along to you every
now and then. I'd ask him to send me one directly, but
he'd probably write back and tell me if I'm so interested
in what's happening back home, I should just come back.*

*But I'm settling in, despite it all. I know I don't have to
tell you what it's like in-country, Hawk. I feel like I've
lived a lifetime and it hasn't even been two weeks.*

*Give my love to Wheeler and big kisses to Chris and
Paula for me. That shouldn't be too much of a hardship
for you!*

*As ever,
Annie*

Pelted by blinding rain, Annie made her way through
incoming mortar explosions, from the Quonset hut dormitory everyone called a hooch, and ducked into the
bunker a short distance away. In the three weeks she'd
been in Long Binh she must have made this trek at least a
dozen times.

Annie hurried in, wiped the rain from her face, took off
her helmet, nodded to two dozen others already inside,
and sat down holding on to her gas mask and canteen.

A minute later Sue Ellen Salvatore, a Red Cross worker,
came in and sat down beside her. They'd met down here
on Annie's first run. Sue Ellen, an old hand of three
months by then, had known exactly how terrified Annie
felt, and had taken her under her wing. They'd been pals
ever since.

Sue Ellen wasn't wearing her helmet and her long, dark, curly hair fell in glistening spirals down her face. With her wild hair, dark eyes, and rich olive skin she could have been a gypsy. After a warm smile in Annie's direction, she opened her canteen and took a long swig.

"Here, have some," Sue Ellen said, extending the canteen to Annie.

"That's okay. I have my own."

Sue Ellen winked. "Mine's got more punch."

Annie hesitated.

"Go on. You need some. You look awful."

"Thanks a lot." And then, with a sigh, Annie took Sue Ellen's canteen and took a swallow. She coughed. It tasted like brandy. She cleared her throat and smoothed a few strands of hair back into her French knot. "I thought you Red Cross girls were called Kool-Aid kids."

Sue Ellen grinned. "So, I'm a Kool-Aid kid with a little extra zing. Better?"

Annie smiled, then shrugged and fought back a yawn. "I don't know why the Army bothered to assign me a hooch. I'm living in surgery and in here."

Sue Ellen lit a cigarette, inhaled deeply, then let the smoke drift through her full, peach-tinted lips. Wry, effortlessly sexy, and yet warmly nurturing, Sue Ellen was only twenty years old, but she had a lot of street smarts. And she was diametrically opposite the cool, refined, stand-offish Southern belles Annie had known at home. Actually, Annie'd had few female friends at home and she still felt shy around other women.

But it was impossible to be shy around Sue Ellen. Sue Ellen demanded involvement. She nudged, cajoled, teased Annie into relating. And Annie was grateful. She needed a friend, although for the life of her she couldn't imagine why Sue Ellen had singled her out.

Sue Ellen gave Annie a little nudge. "Cheer up."

"Why? Does it get any easier?"

Sue Ellen shrugged. "No, but the tough get tougher."

Annie stared down at the gas mask in her lap. "Maybe I'm not as tough as I thought."

Sue Ellen offered Annie a drag of her cigarette. Annie hardly ever smoked, but she took a quick drag, hoping it would calm her nerves.

"So, have you tracked down loverboy yet?" Sue Ellen spoke with a thick New York accent that bore traces of her Italian ancestry.

"I told you, David's just a friend. A close friend. He's as far from being my lover as . . . Steve McQueen is." Annie had talked about David a lot, but she hadn't told Sue Ellen about that one brief moment when she and David had been more than friends. That was private. Sometimes, Annie found herself wondering if that fiery kiss had really ever happened. Certainly David hadn't followed up on it.

In the two weeks before he went off to boot camp, Annie had only seen David at the V.A. hospital. Because he'd dropped out of law school, he had no constraints on his time, so he spent long hours with Hawk every day. And he'd always made sure to leave before Annie's shift was up. Hawk had picked up on the tension between his two close friends. When he'd asked first Annie, then David, about what was up, they'd both said the same thing. Nerves about going to Vietnam.

"Okay, okay," Sue Ellen went on between the ear-shattering explosions. "Your close friend. So, have you seen him yet?"

"No," Annie said, her disappointment obvious. "I've made such a pest of myself over at the Army Engineers' offices that they run for cover when they see me coming. All I know is he's out on some hush-hush mission."

Sue Ellen studied the smoke rising from her cigarette. "He's back."

"What?"

"Your pal Nichols. He's back. I got to chatting with a first lieutenant in his platoon, over a game of gin rummy up at the rec center."

"When?" Annie's voice was a low whisper. "When did David get back?"

"Two days ago. But it was a real heavy mission from what I gathered. Of course, the lieutenant couldn't really say much, but I got the impression they scored big on their little outing. Nichols is probably holed up in some top brass's office being debriefed."

"Right," Annie said sullenly.

"Hey, buck up. He'll come round."

Annie managed a weak smile. "I can't believe it. I don't think I will ever understand that man. But if he thinks he can dodge me, he's got another think coming."

Sue Ellen detected a spark of fire in Annie's blue eyes and gave a perceptive smile. "So, uh, you two *have* been more than friends?"

Annie had to laugh.

NEARLY A WEEK went by and Annie still hadn't seen David, although she *had* gotten a note from him. The day after Sue Ellen had told her David was back, he'd stopped by the hospital asking for her, but she was in surgery. By the time she'd finished, three hours later, David had gone. His note was brief but friendly, mentioning that he was sorry he'd missed her, that he had to leave again that day on maneuvers, but he looked forward to touching base with her soon. After signing his name he'd added as a postscript that he longed to see a friendly home-town face almost as much as he longed for home itself.

That postscript had made Annie feel a little better, if a little more wistful. And at least he'd made some contact with her. It felt good to know that they were friends again.

But still, Annie worried about him. She knew he was in an especially dangerous and secret Army engineering unit. Their primary job was to check power lines and bridges, making sure the ones vital to the American unit were safe, and destroying lines and bridges vital to the enemy. That job made David a key enemy target as well.

Annie was endlessly grateful to Sue Ellen who had deliberately gotten more chummy with the first lieutenant in David's platoon, plying him for more information about David. Sue Ellen was able to confirm via the lieutenant that David really had been tied up in a grueling, three-day debriefing session, not just avoiding her. It buoyed Annie's spirits to realize David had sought her out as soon as he'd been free. Unfortunately his free time had only amounted to a few hours before he and his platoon had to go off on maneuvers again.

THERE WAS A PARTY scheduled at the rec center on Saturday night. There were parties most Saturday nights. Every week, Sue Ellen and her cohorts met to plan the next week's social agenda and figure out what they could do for the soldiers at the base.

This party was supposed to include the patients from the hospital who were mobile. So Sue Ellen, who invariably headed the party committee, had lassoed Annie into helping her with the logistics of getting the wounded boys over there.

Annie had been reluctant to get involved, but she did feel it would be a good thing for her boys to get out and have a few hours of fun. So, even though she was bone-weary, she was doing her best to cooperate. And she was discovering that making plans for the party was lifting her own spirits, too.

"Okay," Annie said, surveying her list, "I've got a small group on crutches who want to come. And a few from the psych ward. I lined up some medics who've agreed to help with transport. I am worried about a few of the boys though. A noisy party might be too much for them."

Sue Ellen gave Annie a reassuring pat on the shoulder. "We'll keep an eye on them. If anybody looks like they need some quiet time, they can go into the TV room. We may not get the latest shows, but I got my hands on films of several pennant games. Personally, I think the Mets are gonna pull themselves up by the bootstraps and walk off with a World Series win this year."

Annie smiled. "Hawk's with you."

"That's right." Affecting a Southern accent, Sue Ellen added, "I do believe, sugar, that sweet Southern boy is a rebel at heart."

Annie laughed. "He's that, all right."

Annie and Sue Ellen shared their letters and newspapers with each other. Like everyone in Nam, they were greedy for news from home, acutely aware of all the things they used to take for granted, like the aroma of an apple pie fresh from the oven, snowball fights on the front lawn, the laughter of children.

Although Annie had only been in-country a short time, she'd gotten two long, newsy letters from Hawk, a shorter letter filled with concern for her well-being from her dad, a care package from Nanna and one postcard from Turner.

Sue Ellen had seemed especially fond of reading Hawk's letters, laughing at his jokes and stories. She told Annie how impressed she was that, for all Hawk was going through, he could still hang on to his sense of humor and, even more to her liking, his sense of the ridiculous.

Annie loved the letters Sue Ellen got from her family and friends in Queens. Sue Ellen's mom wrote the best. They were colorful, lively, gossipy pages filled with the goings-on of the other members of Sue Ellen's family, assorted neighbors and relatives, who were rarely behaving the way Sue Ellen's mother thought they should behave. She also kept her daughter abreast of the latest shows on TV. *Marcus Welby, M.D.* was her favorite although she still thought Robert Young's best part was in *Father Knows Best*. Every now and then she'd even send Sue Ellen a recipe she had cut out from *Good Housekeeping* magazine, invariably an Italian dish.

Neither Annie nor Sue Ellen could figure out why Mrs. Salvatore sent the recipes. Surely she knew mozzarella, veal cutlets, fresh tomatoes and the like were not exactly easy commodities to come by in Nam, not even at the PX. And even if they were, Sue Ellen didn't exactly have time to cook intimate little meals for two out here in the boonies. Sue Ellen laughingly decided her mother just wanted to remind her that one day she'd be back home and she'd need a boxful of recipes so that she could cook some decent Italian dinners for the nice, Italian husband in her future. Vinnie Porcelli, who wrote Sue Ellen some hot and heavy letters, had seemed a likely candidate. But Sue Ellen had confided that Vinnie had been chasing her since grade school, and he was "never gonna" catch her even if he chased her all the way to the grave. Vinnie, Sue Ellen said firmly, was a dud.

After reading his letters, Annie had to agree.

"Oh, by the way," Annie said, folding her list and putting it back in her pocket, "I got a postcard from Turner yesterday. Just a few lines, typical of my brother, but he said to put my money on the Baltimore Orioles for a World Series win."

Sue Ellen made a thumbs down sign. "Well, you can join in on the sports talk in the TV room tonight if you get tired of dancing. Those fellows will love to meet a gal whose brother is a real, live baseball player. You'll have them eating out of your hand. You should write your brother to mail a stack of autographed pictures of himself in uniform for you to hand out." She hesitated, which was not like Sue Ellen at all. "You might tell Hawk, next time you write him, to send out a photo of himself, too."

"Oh?" Annie said with exaggerated innocence. She knew quite well that Sue Ellen looked forward to reading the letters Hawk sent almost as much as Annie enjoyed reading them herself.

Sue Ellen grinned. "Okay, so the guy interests me. He's got a good sense of humor, he roots for the home team, he . . . has a way about him."

"I don't know about the photo," Annie said. "He might feel a little uptight . . . because of the wheelchair."

"I've seen wheelchairs before," Sue Ellen replied in typical cavalier fashion. "I'd like to see what he looks like, that's all."

"I've shown you that photo of him in my room. The one with Turner and David."

"Yeah, but that was a few years ago and it wasn't in the greatest focus."

Annie grinned. "That was Hawk's fault. Just before I was about to snap it, he said something that made me laugh."

"See what I mean. He makes me laugh, too. I mean his letters. And some of the stories you've told me about him. You need a good laugh out here. And laughs are hard to come by."

"So," Annie said cautiously, "why not write him yourself. You could send a photo, ask him to send one back. . . ."

Sue Ellen scowled. "You think he wouldn't think it was weird?"

"I've written about you," Annie said with fabricated nonchalance.

Sue Ellen's scowl deepened. "You never told me that."

Annie grinned. "You are my best friend out here. You think I'd keep that from Hawk?"

"So, what did you write him about me?"

"What do you think? That you're terrific, gorgeous, smart, funny . . ."

Sue Ellen gave a throaty laugh. "So, if I did drop him a line, he'd pretty much know who I was."

Annie grinned. "I think he'd be pleased. I think you could make him laugh, too. He could use some laughs, himself."

Sue Ellen gave one of her street-wise shrugs. "Well, maybe I'll think about it." She must have caught the glint in Annie's eyes because she immediately switched back to the topic of the dance. "So, we've got everything set. Wait till you see what we're doing with the gym."

"I'll try to stop by for a few minutes before the dance."

Sue Ellen eyed her ruefully. "You're not copping out on me, Annie Magill. You've got to come to the dance."

Annie avoided Sue Ellen's dark-eyed stare. "I'm just not up for partying tonight, Sue Ellen."

"So, what are you up for? Some good old tossin' and turnin' all night?"

"I've got a few boys in post-op that I want to keep a close watch on."

"Annie, you will always have boys in post-op. You can't watch them round the clock." Sue Ellen placed her hands on Annie's shoulders. "Look, you're off duty. What you need is to let that gorgeous blond hair of yours down, put on a little makeup, throw on a sexy dress and high heels and dance the night away."

"No, not tonight. I can't...."

"If you don't want to have fun, think of the fellas. They need to see some pretty young faces around, Annie. They need to dance a little, feel a little...human...for an evening."

Annie smiled wryly. "You always know how to push the right buttons."

Sue Ellen grinned. "What can I say, honey? You wear your heart on your sleeve."

That observation didn't please Annie. She'd hoped that she had become a little less transparent. It seemed she still had some growing up left to do.

"It's a very good heart, Annie," Sue Ellen added softly.

Annie felt a surge of love for her friend, a sense of overwhelming gratitude that they had found each other in this godforsaken place. She gave Sue Ellen a winsome smile. "Okay, kiddo, I'll come."

Chapter Four

A time to mourn, and a time to dance...

Later that evening, as Annie got ready for the dance, she found herself thinking of David, remembering that Thanksgiving morning almost four years ago, when she'd gotten dressed with the intention of knocking his socks off. She could admit now, after all this time, that she'd been particularly focused on David that day even though she'd generally grouped her Three Musketeers together. Yes, she'd had a crush on David then. He was so mysterious, so intense, so sexy looking. He was made for schoolgirl crushes.

She could picture that whole day with vivid recall. She could almost smell the twenty-pound turkey which was roasting in the old-fashioned stove against the wall near the door. She remembered the plates of cranberry sauce, sweet-potato pie, and all the other trimmings for the Thanksgiving feast.

Annie sighed. She loved memories of home. Nothing, except for a new refrigerator, had been altered or moved since that fateful summer when her mother had died. Her father had wanted to keep the house unchanged, and Annie had always felt the same way. She hardly remembered her mother, but somehow keeping the house the same seemed to keep her mother's spirit alive.

Annie leaned against the wall of her hooch and closed her eyes to relive the scene in the kitchen that Thanksgiving afternoon. Dad was sneaking tastes of the gravy from the old cast-iron pot on the stove. Turner was tossing Hawk the silverware, Nanna giving the turkey its final basting, and David carefully handing Annie the special crystal goblets from the cabinet. She remembered how scared she'd been that she might drop one of the goblets, because David looked so good that day and her hands were trembling a little, her heart beating more rapidly than usual. And she was sure there must have been a rosy hue in her cheeks, a special sparkle in her eyes that gave away her secret crush on him.

Annie opened her eyes and pushed herself away from the wall. Slowly, she walked across the room toward the mirror over her bureau and stared long and hard at her reflection. It was not the same fresh, innocent, wide-eyed young face she'd stared at that Thanksgiving morning as she'd gotten ready for the boys' arrival home, not the same face that had snuck secret yearning schoolgirl glances at David that long-ago day. How different she looked today. There were dark rings under her eyes now. Her face was drawn, her complexion pale. With the endless monsoon rains, it seemed to Annie as if the sun had drowned, never to return. She focused on the reflection of her eyes. The bright luster had vanished from them, replaced by a haunted look. She forced a smile, but it immediately took on a sad, wistful twist.

She turned from the mirror and surveyed her room. As far as hooches went, Annie knew hers wasn't too bad. Some of the nurses who'd been at other bases and transferred to Long Binh had spent months in far more primitive quarters, often three or four nurses sharing one small space. Here, Annie had her own room. The bed was an Army cot with a mattress less than two inches thick, but for all the use Annie had given it, it wasn't too bad. Then she had her footlocker, a regular locker, and a wooden dresser with a small mirror above it. Thanks to the nurse who'd had the room before Annie, there was also an in-

tricately woven and brightly painted Vietnamese folding
screen that Annie used as a room divider.

A few of the nurses on her floor had small refrigera-
tors. Some had even brought back stereo sets and TVs
from their R&Rs in Hong Kong, but Annie had no crav-
ing for luxuries. She hadn't even had the energy or the
time to hang posters on her walls as so many of the other
nurses had done.

All she had displayed in her room were a few photos on
her dresser; the one out-of-focus shot she'd taken a few
years back of Turner, Hawk and David at the beach—
Turner in the middle with one arm slung over David's
shoulder, one arm over Hawk's; next to that a gold-
framed photo of her dad standing proudly beside Relay,
his champion racehorse; and finally there was an eight-by-
ten glossy of Nanna, a glamorous professional shot of her
taken when she'd been all of nineteen.

Annie lifted up the photo of Nanna and smiled at it.
Her grandmother, now a petite, silver-haired elderly lady
who always seemed to Annie to be full of breeding, beauty
and grace, was at the time of the photo the exquisitely
lovely, up-and-coming silent-film star, Lilli Almont. From
stories her dad had told her—stories, Annie guessed, once
told to her dad by her mom and by Nanna herself—her
grandmother could have become one of the immortal
greats of Hollywood. She'd had what it took. The camera loved her. Fans flocked to her films. But Lilli Almont
had given it all up for love. While doing a film she'd met
Tom Wilcox, who, shortly after the film was completed,
enlisted in the war. Nanna had given up her chance for
stardom and followed her heart. She'd run off to France
during World War I to find and finally marry Tom Wilcox. Tom had become a decorated flying ace. And together, Lilli and Tom had gone on to found their own
airplane company.

Lilli had told Annie about her trials and tribulations,
and ultimately her success in learning to run the com-

pany on her own after Tom's death. Annie thought her Nanna was one of the most remarkable women in the world, a feminist long before Betty Friedan had coined the word, long before women were demanding equal rights, burning their bras, avowing to "do their own thing." Nanna had done it. She'd been born with the courage of her convictions. Annie adored her grandmother and prayed that she herself would turn out to be even half the woman Nanna was.

Annie carefully set the photo back on the dresser, scanning the whole group. Her family and friends. Photos and memories were her only real tie with home. A reminder of simpler, happier times. She ached inside as she stared at the photos. For the first time since she'd arrived in Vietnam, she allowed herself to sink into the depths of homesickness. It was a rampant malady on the base. Annie had successfully fought against it, until now, and she was determined not to give in completely.

Brushing away the tears, she strode over to her locker, selecting a cream-colored jersey minidress. She slipped off her cotton robe and climbed into the dress, cinching a wide brown belt around her narrow waist. The dress had fit perfectly when she'd first worn it, a couple of months ago, but it was big on her now. She must have lost a good ten pounds since coming to Vietnam, ten pounds her lithe frame couldn't spare. Frowning, she silently vowed to herself she'd start taking better care of herself. Meanwhile she cinched the belt a little tighter and rummaged in her footlocker for a colorful scarf to help brighten her appearance.

Rock music was blasting when Annie arrived at the gym in the rec center. The Kool-Aid kids, as everyone called the Red Cross workers, had done themselves proud with the decorations. It was amazing what some crepe paper, poster paints and clever lighting could do. The gym had been transformed into a tropical paradise: painted palm trees swaying in the breeze, looking out over blue horizons. All the folding tables ringing the outer walls were covered with bright yellow paper cloths and the chairs were festooned with multicolored balloons. A huge strobe light flickered on the couples moving about on the dance floor, their bodies bending and turning in wild gyrations to the beat of the Rolling Stones.

Annie stood at the entrance surveying the scene, wondering what she was doing here. She simply wasn't in a party mood. The gaiety seemed eerie, and Annie found herself more homesick than ever. Still huddled in her wet Army-issue poncho, she almost did an about-face and left. Then she noticed David.

He was less than ten feet away, talking to the soldier playing the records, standing casually, his right foot propped up on a chair. He had a can of beer in his hand, and when he took a sip he threw his head back.

He looked the same and yet different. When he smiled, Annie noticed deeper grooves in the corners of his mouth and around his eyes.

He must have felt her eyes on him. He looked up, meeting her gaze. His smile instantly faded, a look of consternation replacing it.

Oh no, Annie thought, he can't still be uptight about that one dumb kiss. She felt like crying again, and she'd only just dried her eyes.

As if he were caught by a slow-motion camera, David dropped his foot to the floor, set the can of beer down on a table, said a few words to the Army D.J. and started across the crowded floor toward Annie.

She held her breath as he approached, unsure of what to say or do now that she'd finally found him in this wasteland.

And then, as he stood in front of her, Annie forgot all about her anxiety. She threw her arms around his neck, and David's arms went around her. Amidst the blaring music and the dancing, they clung to each other like soul mates. There was nothing sexual about the embrace. It was a far more basic feeling, like coming home.

Annie laughed breathlessly when they eased their hold on each other, neither letting go fully.

"God, it's good to see you, Annie."

"Ditto, Captain." Annie touched the bars on his shoulder.

He searched her face, the look of consternation back. "You look beat, kiddo."

More than beat, Annie knew.

As David was surveying her, he was thinking that she showed all the signs of the shock that was so common in newcomers. David had seen that look plenty in the months he'd been in Nam. He'd experienced it himself. The physical exhaustion and the grueling hours were only part of it. It was the stunning emotional impact of the unrelenting danger and horror of it all that really brought it on.

Annie couldn't read his mind but she clearly saw the sharp-edged worry on his face and she tried her best to don a spirited smile.

"I'm okay," she said, only to find herself unable to stifle a yawn and a shiver.

"Come on, let's get that wet poncho off you," he said, helping her lift it over her head and going off to find an empty hook on the wall to hang it on. When he returned, Annie felt his large, firm hand pressing against her back as he steered her over to a quieter corner of the gym. They found an empty table and sat down across from each other.

"You've been avoiding me," Annie said. "I've gone over to your headquarters . . ."

"And I've been over to your hospital," David said. "You did get my note?"

"I hoped it would be followed up by a visit one of these days."

"I just got back from maneuvers late this afternoon. Business, as they say, is booming, if you catch my drift." He winked.

"I catch it," she said solemnly, unable to enjoy David's familiar teasing.

He seemed to deliberately ignore her grim expression. "I've got to smile at the irony of it. The Judge pulls all kinds of strings to get me attached to some cushy unit in Saigon and I end up..." He stopped abruptly and grinned. "When I arrived, the commanding officer had a nice big desk ready and waiting for me. But as soon as I told him I wasn't in Nam to smoke stogies and push papers, his beady little eyes brightened and he said to me, 'Boy, I got just the job for you.' So I spent a month in some rigorous, mind-boggling training and here I am heading a special unit. Not that I'm bragging or anything, but my boys make up the best damn platoon in this man's Army." His grin broadened.

"And what does the Judge say about all this?" Annie asked.

"What I do out here is not for home consumption, Annie. As far as the Judge knows, I'm sitting safe and sound behind that desk."

"You never were the type to sit back and let everyone else have all the fun."

David's whole demeanor changed, a hardness etching every line of his face. "It's no fun, Annie."

Annie took his hand. "Believe me, I know that, David." Her grip tightened on his. "I guess this is one time I wish the Judge had gotten his way. I'm so scared for you, David. I know enough about that platoon of yours to know how dangerous—"

"It's dangerous for every grunt, every platoon leader." David gave her a long, hard look. "It's dangerous for every doctor and nurse. Especially stationed at this base. Long Binh's the biggest ammo dump in Nam and you're under constant incoming rocket attack. There are better places you could have put in for.''

"And worse," Annie countered.

"There are plenty of nurses who go Stateside before their due date, Annie. You could . . ."

"I'm not leaving." Her voice was firm.

David stared at her, but he didn't argue. Instead he said, "It sure is a baptism by fire."

Annie studied her hand entwined in David's. She squeezed a little tighter. "You don't know how good it is to see a face from home again."

David smiled softly. "Like hell I don't. You, kiddo, are a sight for sore eyes."

They shared a brief smile, then the corners of Annie's mouth drooped. "They tell you you'll get used to it in time, that it won't be so shocking." Her eyes lifted to David's face and he looked stunned by the raw anguish he saw in them.

David came around the table and drew Annie up from her seat. He pressed her against him. "Oh Annie," he whispered. "Poor Annie."

He rubbed her back gently.

She lifted her head, anguish burning in her eyes. "Do they really think we'll get used to it, David?"

"We never will, Annie. But . . . I guess that's the way it should be. I guess that's what we've got to cling to."

There was something so desperate in his voice that Annie not only forgot her own grief, but felt a terrible wave of guilt for sharing her burdens with David. He had more than enough burdens of his own to shoulder. Thanks to Sue Ellen's conversations with the lieutenant in David's platoon, Annie knew how much the men under his command looked up to him. They not only respected him as a leader, they were incredibly loyal to him and considered him to be a cunning and fearless soldier. They said he'd take all kinds of risks, but never let his men take any that weren't absolutely imperative. Annie wasn't surprised to hear it. David had always felt compelled to put himself on the line. Perhaps it was in his blood; perhaps he felt driven on some deep level to rebel against his father's constant efforts to control his life. Whatever the reasons, the price he paid for his fearlessness had never been so high.

"I'm sorry, David," she said softly.

"For what?"

"You don't need a damp shoulder on top of everything else."

He touched her cheek. "You can dampen my shoulder anytime, kiddo. Anytime."

She scrutinized him closely. He looked older, a bit haggard, but still so good, so strong, so tough. But she had the feeling that beneath his tough exterior, David was having as rough a time of it as everyone else. She started to say so, but he must have sensed she was about to tap on that shell of his because he quickly changed the subject.

"Hey, I got a letter from Hawk the other day. Typical Hawk. He sent me an ad he'd cut out of *Life* magazine. It was a swimsuit ad featuring this very buxom chick. And right across her chest was the copy, Some Girls Have Developed a Lot More than Just Their Minds. He wrote me not to tell you about it," David added with a sly smile. "He was sure you'd give me a lecture on women's lib."

Annie laughed. "He was right."

"Well, if it makes you feel any better I passed it on to one of my buddies. He's got it hanging over his bunk."

"And what do you have hanging over your bunk?" Annie asked with real curiosity.

He didn't answer immediately. "Nothing. I guess I just can't get into decorating out here."

They both felt the hovering gloom close in.

"Hey," David said, attempting to dispel the cloud, "Hawk also wrote that this physical therapy regime they've got him on at the V.A., especially the swimming, seems to be helping a little."

Annie smiled wanly. "It's too soon for there to be any real change, David. But what's important is that Hawk's spirits are up. He's optimistic. If he can just hold on . . ."

"Have you heard from home yet?" David asked.

Annie's face brightened. "I got a care package from Nanna the other day. She sent me a dozen bottles of perfume. Said she remembered from when she was in France how the injured soldiers had loved the scent of perfume on the nurses. And she sent ribbons for me to wear in my hair. To cheer the boys up, too. She was right. They all like to see a big bright ribbon in my hair and they are always saying how good I smell, how much it reminds them of home."

David smiled, noting the bright red ribbon she was wearing in her hair this evening, breathing in the flowery scent of her perfume. "I like it, too."

Annie smiled back, a soft, inviting smile.

"And Turner?" David hurried on. "How's our famous first-base man?"

A faint scowl clouded Annie's features. "He's sent a couple of postcards. Scribbled a few words. He was upset about my coming here. No, not upset exactly. Dad was upset. Man, was he ever upset. But Turner, Turner was baffled. Truly baffled. He couldn't imagine why I'd want to volunteer for anything so grisly." She smiled crookedly. "And something so unbecoming to a proper Southern belle."

"That's being pretty harsh, Annie. If you were my sister . . ."

Annie grinned. "But I'm not your sister, David."

He looked uncomfortable. "No, no you're not." And then a sparkle lightened his dark blue eyes. "But if I'd had a sister, I'd have wanted one just like you, Annie. All those years, growing up, I always thought of you as almost like a sister, Annie. Yes I did."

Annie stared at those still-mesmerizing eyes of his. "Not always, David Nichols. Not quite always."

For a brief moment David looked taken aback by Annie's provocative reply. But then he laughed. "You got me there, kiddo. But even a good man, with all the best intentions, can have a momentary lapse." His expression turned serious. "Do you forgive me, Annie?"

"I kissed you right back, Nickel. It was a mighty good kiss, too, if you want my opinion. Anyway, what's a little lapse between good friends? You are my friend, David. Always that, whatever else."

"Ditto, Lieutenant," he replied sincerely.

A pretty, dark-haired woman danced by with a soldier and gave Annie a broad wink.

"Who's that?" David asked.

Annie raised a brow. "A good friend of mine. Sue Ellen. She's a knockout, isn't she?"

David didn't argue.

"Want to meet her?"

He grinned down at Annie. "And risk making you jealous again? Uh-uh. Remember what happened last time, kiddo."

"Okay, then dance with me, Captain Nichols."

"Last time we danced..."

"I remember. My senior prom. I'll never forget the sight of you, Hawk and Turner strutting across that gym, lookin' like proud peacocks—all those senior girls swooning over you-all."

"And their fellas fit to kill till they realized we just came to have a dance with our favorite gal."

Annie laughed. "You did a wild twist that night, Nickel. I'll...never forget that dance. Neither will my date, Pete Gerard. He wasn't exactly pleased as punch when I went whirling off to the dance floor with each of you in turn."

"But we brought you back to him good as new."

Annie sighed as David took her in his arms and they began to sway to a nice slow tune by Diana Ross and the Supremes. "Oh David, those days seem so far away."

He pulled her a little closer, his lips finding their way to her soft, scented hair drawn back from her face by the bright red ribbon. "Don't give up hope, Annie. It's all we've got."

They never got to finish the dance. Annie was called back to the hospital to assist in surgery. David went with her despite her telling him there was no point. He insisted he was going to wait for her to finish up, then they'd go over to one of the cafés on the base and have a nightcap together.

It was morning by the time Annie was able to leave. David, as he'd promised, was sitting outside post-op waiting for her.

She started toward him only to discover she was walking with an unsteady gait. Her knees were rocking. She blinked several times as colored spots started swimming in front of her eyes so that she couldn't get David in sharp focus. She flung a hand out, as if to brace herself, only it hit nothing but thin air. She could barely make out David coming toward her. Her head was swimming, her vision increasingly blurred.

"Just give me a minute..." she started to say, but couldn't finish the sentence. Her voice gave out along with her whole body as blackness engulfed her.

She came to slowly, felt herself being lifted up, cradled in strong arms. She still couldn't get David's face in focus, but she could hear his warm, soothing, tender voice against her ear. "It's okay, kiddo. You're going to be okay."

Annie wanted to tell him it was about time he finally stopped calling her kiddo...but she found she didn't have the strength even to speak. She let her head fall heavily against his shoulder as he carried her off. She had no idea where he was taking her, but she didn't really care. It was enough that he was there.

The last thing Annie remembered before she slept was David's hand undoing the ribbon in her hair so that her pale golden locks fell free. For a moment, then, her vision cleared and she saw him tuck the strip of red satin ribbon into his breast pocket.

Chapter Five

A time to cast away stones...

Annie slept for hours and then drifted in and out of sleep for a while. Once, when she half woke, she saw David peering down at her anxiously. Her mind drifted back to the last time she'd seen that drawn, worried expression on David's face.

It had been in Beaumont when she was fourteen years old, lying in a hospital bed with double pneumonia. For the first few days she'd been put under an oxygen tent. Only her father, Nanna and Turner had been allowed in to see her, and then only for short spells. Once she was out of the woods, and the restrictions were lifted, Hawk and David were there for her. Hawk was his regular joking self, pretending to be a doctor, imitating Groucho Marx, trying to stick a bedpan on David's head. But David was incredibly grim and solemn. Hawk tried to tease him out of his gloomy mood, telling him this wasn't a wake.

That afternoon in the hospital was the only time Annie had ever seen David come close to striking Hawk. He was practically shaking with a rage that neither she nor Hawk could comprehend. Of all of them, David had always been the most self-contained, the most on guard about expressing anger. When he was mad or upset, he'd go off on his own, often as not trying some daredevil stunt like racing his motorbike up and down back-country canyons or hopping a freight train for a few stops and then hitching home. When David stormed out of the hospital room that afternoon, Hawk and Annie were bewildered.

David didn't come back to see her at the hospital. But one day, about a week after she'd gone home, David was over at the house shooting the breeze with Turner, and he dropped into her room to say hi. Annie wasn't about to mention his near outburst at the hospital, and at first she thought David wasn't going to, either. But after a few minutes of awkward chitchat, he apologized.

Timidly she asked him whether she or Hawk had done or said something that had set him off.

"No. No way. It had nothing to do with you guys," David was quick to say.

"Then, what got you so fired up?"

He walked over to the window in her sunny, floral-papered room and stared out at the rolling Beaumont hills.

"My mother once had pneumonia. Double pneumonia." He hesitated. "She was in the same hospital as you. She...looked awful." He cast her a brief glance over his shoulder. "Just like you." He gave her a sad, faint smile.

Annie didn't remember David's mother. His parents had gotten divorced years back. Annie must have been about four and a half at the time, which meant David had been almost eight.

Before that day, David had never spoken to her about his mother. All she had known for a fact was that Joyce Nichols had left Beaumont right after the divorce, and that she'd died about two years later. Rumor had it that she'd been an emotionally unstable, alcoholic woman who drank herself to death.

David once again stared out the window. When he continued speaking his voice sounded far-off. "She was pretty like you, too. Fair and blond. Delicate."

David had never told her she was pretty and delicate before. Fourteen-year-old Annie felt a little charge of electricity shoot through her.

After a few silent minutes, David sat down on the window seat, facing Annie but gazing down at his hands clasped between his knees. Having mentioned his mother at all seemed to lift some invisible barrier and he began to talk more openly about her and that whole painful period of his childhood.

David's picture of his mother was far different from the negative image of her Annie had created out of rumor. He described her to Annie as beautiful, but quite frail and reserved. With a distinct edge in his voice, he added that his mother had always been easily intimidated by his father.

That afternoon, up in Annie's bedroom, David shared his bittersweet memories of the treasured moments he and his mother had shared together. To him, she was loving, nurturing and tender. He recalled how much she'd adored taking him into Baltimore to the art museums and concerts. And even though he'd been very young at the time, he'd loved going with her. Away from the Judge she was quite gay and carefree and they'd had festive, wonderful outings.

When his mother had taken ill and been admitted to the hospital, David's father had decided it would be best for David not to visit her. David had been mad as hell, but no matter how much he pleaded, his father would not be swayed in his decision.

"I was desperate to see her," David said. "I was sure she was going to die. I guess I thought maybe I could somehow magically revive her. So I snuck up to her hospital room one day. She was barely conscious, didn't even recognize me at first."

Annie saw David's knuckles whiten, and a wave of sorrow washed over her. For herself as well as him. They were both motherless children.

He stared pensively down at his hands. "That was the last time I ever cried. I fell right on top of my poor, weak momma, sobbing, begging her not to die. I remember," he said softly, "how she somehow managed to put her bone-thin arms around me, trying to comfort me."

Tears welled up in Annie's eyes. "Oh, David, how sad."

"I was bawling so loud one of the nurses heard me and came charging in. She had to pry me and Momma apart. Man, was that nurse mad. Children under sixteen were not allowed to visit patients, except with a parent. My unforgivable infraction was reported to the Judge, who chewed me out when I got home, not only for sneaking into the hospital, but for making a spectacle of myself, blubbering so loud I could be heard clear down to the nurses' station."

Annie had never much cared for David's father. The Judge was grim, authoritarian and always put on superior airs. But that afternoon, listening to David, she hated the Judge.

Annie was touched by the irony of David's mother pulling through her illness only to end up, quite soon afterward, facing divorce proceedings.

"She wasn't home six months," David told Annie, "when my father filed for divorce. I don't think the Judge ever forgave her for getting so sick. He was always thinking about his career, his rise to power. He felt she held him back. Even when she got home from the hospital, she was weak, tired all the time, and thin as a rail. How could she eat or sleep with the Judge always harping on her, telling her she was deliberately malingering to avoid accompanying him to very important functions that would further his advancement in the court system?"

Annie could see David visibly fighting the anger rising in him. "Could anyone blame her for wanting an escape? I never did," he said in a very low voice. "Even when the drinking started getting bad..." His voice trailed off.

The only time he'd almost lost control of his emotions, David admitted with difficulty to Annie, was the day he had sat beside his father in the courtroom after his father had been awarded full custody.

"I saw my momma go white with shock as she heard the court's decision and the declaration that she was an unfit mother. I watched her just slip off her chair, like she'd turned to rubber, and sink to the floor of the court. Her sobs echoed through the whole room. I tried to run to her, but my father held me back, telling me to behave myself, ridiculing Momma for being drunk and making a public spectacle of herself."

David clenched and unclenched his hands. "She wasn't drunk at all. She was stone cold sober that day, Annie." His eyes looked sad and grim.

Annie kept wishing there was some way she could cheer him up. "Don't be sad, David," Annie whispered. "Don't be sad. Please, David...."

She felt herself being gently shaken.

"Annie, it's okay. You've been dreaming. Some sad dream. It's over now."

Her eyelids fluttered open slowly, and she stared up at David. My, oh, my, but he was all grown-up. She gave him a weak smile—it was the best she could muster—and she reached out unsteadily for his hand. His grip was warm, comforting, solid and familiar.

"What hit me?" she muttered.

"What didn't?" was David's wry response. Some of the worry had lifted now that she was awake and he could see some color back in her face.

Annie kept blinking as she looked around the small unfamiliar room. "Where am I?"

"In the doctor's lounge. A couple of med-techs set you up in here. It was one of the few private spots in the hospital."

"Hospital? Med-techs?" And then she remembered. Nam. She was in Vietnam...with David. Both of them all grown-up... still together just like when she was four-teen. Gradually, Annie became aware that she was hooked up to an IV. She gave David a frightened, baffled look. "Was it a rocket attack?"

"No, but a rocket was just about the only thing that didn't attack you. You're wiped out, kiddo, running on empty..."

"Me and every other nurse."

"Yeah, but they don't all take their work home with them when they're off duty. According to your pal Sue Ellen—oh, she dropped in a couple of times to see how you were doing—you hardly ever sleep, and I didn't need her to tell me you obviously haven't been eating much."

He sat down on the edge of her bed, his grip on her hand tightening. "I don't see how you're going to make it here, Annie. There's no shame in it, believe me. Give me an out and I'd grab it for all it's worth. Go back to the V.A. hospital in Oakdale, Annie. Or any damn V.A. hospital. Just tell your superior you need a transfer. One look at you and she'll reissue your orders."

"I'm tougher than you think, Captain." Annie wished she felt stronger so her voice would radiate more conviction. But the conviction was there. It was in her eyes, bloodshot as they were. She met David's gaze with stubborn defiance.

His features hardened. "What are you going to do, Annie? Play this Florence Nightingale bit to the bitter end? Just like Hawk played John Wayne? Look where it got him. You're not immune, Annie. No one in this nightmare we're living in is immune."

"I just want to do my job. And get through each day," she retorted, some of her strength returning. One thing she could be grateful to David for, he was getting her adrenaline flowing again. "Just like you."

"You're not like me, Annie. You can't turn it off. And you can't survive this nightmare unless you learn how."

"I'll . . . learn," she said, distressed by the fierce cast in David's dark eyes, the bite in his voice, the deep, grooved lines etched into the corners of his mouth. He suddenly looked alarmingly like a younger version of his father.

"No, you won't. You've got too much heart."

Instead of arguing, Annie said, "I don't think cutting off all your feelings is the way to survive. All that you end up saving is an empty shell. And shells crack, Nickel. If they're hard and there's no give."

David merely shook his head. He looked tired. Annie guessed he'd been watching over her the whole time she slept.

"You've always got an answer, kiddo."

"If I had all the answers, Nickel, I wouldn't be lying here flat on my back. How long was I out, anyway?"

"About eighteen hours, give or take a few minutes. You slept like a log. The doc said you didn't even budge during his exam."

"Well, I feel a whole lot better now. How about getting someone in here to unhook me. I've got a shift starting . . ."

"Whoa, forget the shift. You've been given a three-day reprieve from duty, Lieutenant."

Annie glanced wanly at her IV hookup. "Some reprieve!"

"Relax. You get unhooked in a couple of hours. And you get to go back to quarters tomorrow morning. Your head nurse told me she doesn't want to see hide nor hair of you in this hospital again until your shift on Wednesday morning."

"You mean I have Monday and Tuesday off? How much time before you have to head back to the boonies?"

David's old easy smile returned. "A few days. Maybe we can spend some time together and catch each other up." For just a moment he looked like the boy she used to know, not the hardened, tough fighting man who gave calculated speeches on survival.

"Hey," Annie brightened. "I know. Let's thumb a copter ride into Saigon on Tuesday."

"Saigon?"

"Well, I'd prefer Hong Kong or Bangkok. But beggars with only a couple of days off can't be choosy."

"Saigon isn't exactly the kind of place to go for soothing relaxation."

Annie laughed dryly. "Is that so, Nickel? Gee, now I've been hearing from a lot of the guys on base that Saigon's just the place to go for some soothing relaxation."

David actually blushed. "Come on, Annie."

"Well, it's true, isn't it?" she asked, a bright glitter in her blue eyes.

"Is that a general question, Miss Magill? Or do you want an answer from my own personal experience?"

Annie raised a finely shaped eyebrow and turned her soft Southern lilt up a notch or two. "I always believe people speak best from personal experience."

David grinned. "I tell you what. You get an okay from the doc and I'll take you to Saigon on Tuesday. We'll check out a couple of my favorite haunts." Annie's cheeks reddened at that offer and David broke into a wide, amused smile.

Despite her blush, however, she gave him a game smile in return, and a saucy little salute. "It's a date, Captain Nichols."

He bent closer and brushed her lips with his. "A date."

"If you're going to seal a date with a kiss, Captain, then do it like you mean it."

"Are you using your weakened condition to take advantage of me, Lieutenant?"

"If that's what it takes, sir," she replied with a challenging smile. A little of Sue Ellen's boldness was definitely rubbing off on her, Annie decided. A little of the war, too. One thing she'd learned about survival even in the short period she'd been in-country was that time was a precious commodity and you didn't waste it. You couldn't afford to.

Instead of meeting her challenge, David released her hand and rose abruptly from her bed. "Annie..." His teasing expression gave way to discomfort.

Annie's brief flirtatiousness vanished and she felt a tightening of her throat, suddenly struggling with emotions she was reluctant to name. "I'm sorry, David. I didn't mean to put you on the spot. I was just joking." She paused, slowly shaking her head. "No, that's a lie. I wasn't joking. Maybe donning a hard shell is what you need to survive. What I need to survive is...to experience a moment or two of passion...to feel feminine again. I think what keeps us going in spite of all the unspeakable horrors, is to feel love, friendship, compassion." She knew she was getting heavy so she deliberately donned a playful smile. "And I guess I wanted to feel a little better than I must look right now."

He stared down at her, the hard cast gone from his eyes, a poignancy there instead. "Oh Annie, don't you know you always look beautiful to me? I thought you were beautiful when you were five years old and you'll still be beautiful to me when you're sixty-four. Right now, kiddo, you're the most beautiful sight I could ever hope to see in this barbaric corner of the world."

"So what makes me so...unkissable?" she asked, feeling deflated.

"It's got nothing to do with you, Annie. It's me. It's this war. It's...a lot of things. But it's not you. You are very special to me, Annie."

"Forget it, David. You don't have to explain." She gave a little shrug and a crooked smile. "Maybe they've put some kind of aphrodisiac in my IV solution. You wouldn't believe some of the wild stunts the nurses and med-techs pull around here. Even a few of the docs. Anything for a laugh."

Her light, teasing tone didn't win so much as a smile from David. He looked restless, brooding.

Annie fully expected him to turn on his heels and run out. Probably now he'd find some excuse to weasel out of their "date."

But she should have known by now that David wouldn't act according to her expectations. He stayed put, almost as if he were frozen to the spot. Their eyes met and held. She watched in fascination as his whole expression turned dark and compelling. He muttered something under his breath that she couldn't make out. Then he leaned forward, took her face between his hands, a low groan escaping his lips as his mouth moved over hers. His kiss was fierce, greedy, explosive. His arms moved around her so that her breasts were crushed against his chest.

This time it wasn't a gearshift digging into Annie's ribs that interrupted their heated kiss, but the amused "Ahem" of the doctor standing at the open door.

Annie and David quickly broke apart at the sound, and it was a toss-up who looked more embarrassed.

At first the doctor's expression was stern. "I came in to take you off IV. But I see that it hasn't greatly impeded your maneuverability, Lieutenant."

Annie, whose heart was still racing, who was still thrilling to the exultation of her all-too-brief, passionate exchange with David, turned scarlet at the doctor's wry remark. "No, Captain. I mean..." What did she mean? While David had been kissing her she hadn't even been aware she was in the hospital, much less hooked up to an IV. When she was kissing David, she wasn't even in Nam.

"Relax, Lieutenant." The doctor's eyes twinkled and he grinned. "You must be feeling a lot better than you were eighteen hours ago."

Annie laughed. "I haven't felt this good in months," she admitted.

David laughed too. "Ditto for me, Doc."

It felt so good to laugh again with David. She thought about how long it had been. And with a flicker of fear, she wondered how long it would be before they laughed together like this again.

ON TUESDAY AFTERNOON, Annie and David were walking hand in hand down Tu Do Street, Saigon's garish, neon-lit main drag; a honky-tonk parade of open-fronted cafés, bars, massage parlors, run-down shops and tawdry souvenir stands. It was a hodgepodge of a street—teeming with military convoys, cars, motorbikes, throngs of off-duty GIs in camouflage jungle fatigues, ARVNs in their red berets, saffron-robed monks, farmers in black pants, black shirts and sandals. Then there were the hustlers, the money changers, the mascaraed, miniskirted bar girls, the black marketeers and the throngs of homeless refugees.

Weaving in and out of the crowds were endless numbers of eager street urchins with their sad, serious almond-shaped eyes. In mangled U.S. Army lingo they begged from any passing "round eye" for food and money, or offered sundry "services" for pay.

In sharp contrast to this ragtag troupe of small-fry wheeler-dealers, were the delicate, fine-boned local women smelling of Chinese soap, gracefully walking along the crowded sidewalks in traditional *ao dais,* long, silk, fitted dresses, high collared, slit to the waist and worn over white satin loose-fitting pants. These dainty, entrancing women reminded Annie of swans unknowingly plucked out of a tranquil lake, as yet unaware that they had been displaced.

For the first time in weeks the sky was cloudless. Annie took it as a good omen. Before Nam, she'd never believed much in good or bad omens. But she'd quickly discovered that being in-country made everyone desperate to ward off bad luck. Most of the GIs wore an assortment of talismans to protect them from death and mutilation. They wrote their girls' names in magic markers on their boonie hats, wore green towels as headbands, hung beads and lucky necklaces around their necks. Superstition ran high in Nam and it was contagious. Annie remembered Sue Ellen telling her about one soldier who never ate canned fruit because his best buddy had just finished eating some canned peaches before stepping on a land mine. Now Annie couldn't eat them either, just because it reminded her of the story.

But during their short stay in Saigon, Annie was determined to see only good omens. She gave David a cheerful smile. "Not a cloud in sight. I knew coming to Saigon would be a great idea. This is the first day it hasn't rained in over a week."

David edged Annie around a cluster of GIs, all of whom gave her appreciative stares. One GI gave out with a long, low wolf whistle. Annie smiled, but David was clearly irritated and cast the soldier a threatening gaze.

"Maybe this outing wasn't such a good idea," he muttered gloomily.

Annie gave David's sleeve a little tug. "Yes it is. Come on, Nickel. We're on an exotic adventure, just the two of us."

"Yeah, the two of us and a million other people."

Annie grinned. "Tune them out."

He laughed.

The sound of his laughter lifted her spirits higher. "So which are your favorite hangouts, Captain?"

"Be patient, kiddo."

"Only if you promise not to call me kiddo today," Annie countered.

He gave her a quick, enigmatic look. "It's a term of endearment."

"There are plenty of others to choose from," she said so earnestly that David smiled.

"Okay, how about babe, sweet thing, honeychild, beautiful . . . ?"

"Any or all of the above will do, darlin'," Annie drawled.

David grinned, but Annie noticed that he didn't fully relax until they were off crowded Tu Do. They slowed to a more leisurely pace, strolling down Cong Ly, a quiet street studded with palms and old French Colonial villas behind intricate wrought iron fences. The villas were run-down and the gardens overgrown, but instead of breathing in gasoline fumes, here the wafting scent of poinciana blossoms pervaded the air.

They came to an open parkland that had once been part of a private estate. The grounds, originally laid out by French Colonial landscape gardeners, had long gone untended, but Annie found the setting quite beautiful in its wild state. Here among the trees and tropical flowering shrubs, a small breeze managed to break through the heat. The park was nearly deserted, holding none of the attractions or excitement of the main thoroughfares of the city.

David led Annie over to a bench under one of the palm trees and, with a Southern gentleman's flourish, gestured for her to have a seat. Then he sat down beside her, his arm casually resting across her shoulders.

They sat quietly for a while, enjoying the soft breeze, the delicious scent of grass and flowers, the tranquility, the pleasurable ease they felt in each other's presence.

Annie broke the silence. "I love it here," she said quietly. "It's as close to feeling like I'm back home as I think I'm ever going to feel till I get back."

"Yeah, I feel the same way. That's why I used to come here sometimes when I was stationed in Saigon."

He reached behind Annie and plucked a bright pink flower from a bush, toying with it for a moment before sticking it festively in her soft, silky hair.

She noticed a faraway look in his eye. "What are you thinking about?"

"It's funny. When I first got to Saigon, I was so homesick I'd come to this park as often as I could. But in the past couple of months, I've rarely thought about home. I guess it seems so far away. Now, being here with you ..." He stopped, obviously unsure whether to go on.

"Tell me, David," she prompted gently.

David looked at her indecisively for a moment and then said in a low voice, "You bring out ... a kind of yearning in me, Annie, for everything clean and fresh and sweet..."

"And pure?" There was no way to hide the disappointment in her voice.

David tenderly touched her cheek. "Yes, doll. And pure." He tried to sound flippant, but there was a distinct emotional edge to his voice as his gaze fell on her.

Annie looked rested again, almost radiant. She wore a soft lavender sundress, her creamy shoulders smooth as velvet, her shiny blond hair falling in soft waves to her shoulders. Her beauty had such a touchingly vulnerable quality, it tugged at David's heart.

"David, did you know that I had a mad crush on you that Thanksgiving before you graduated from Yale?"

The corners of his mouth slowly curved upward. "I had an inkling."

She laughed softly. "I wanted you to think I was the coolest, hippest woman you'd ever laid eyes on. Instead, you looked shocked and distressed, and made some snide remark about my appearance."

David sighed. "You caught me off guard. You've been doing it ever since."

"Is that bad?"

"It can be...dangerous." He spoke slowly, as if thinking aloud.

"Sitting on this bench is dangerous, David. Saigon could be overrun at any time just like during the Tet offensive. Every moment we spend in-country is dangerous."

"There are dangers and there are dangers," David said stubbornly.

"I've outgrown my crush on you, Nickel," Annie said breezily.

David's dark eyes widened and he shot her a look of unmasked amazement.

His shock was so genuine that Annie laughed airily. "I'm too old for crushes, David." Her laughter faded, but a soft smile remained, lighting up her face. "And I guess I'm too young and too inexperienced to know what real love is all about." She gave a wistful little shrug. "I suppose I'm caught somewhere between the devil and those deep blue eyes of yours, Captain Nichols."

"Move over and make some room there for me."

She pressed her palm against his cheek. "You bring out yearnings in me, too, David. And when we kissed the other day, I felt . . ." She didn't know how to put her feelings into words.

"I felt it, too," he whispered.

Her eyes searched his face. "So, what do we call it?"

A surprisingly sad expression took hold of his features. "Precious moments," he murmured solemnly.

Annie nodded slowly. Yes, they were precious, every moment she and David could steal together here. She rested her head on his shoulder. In the solitude of the park grounds, they could temporarily put aside the casualties, the rocket attacks, the boonies, and find a measure of solace. Annie hadn't felt this good, this content in a long time. David had a magical healing effect on her, and perhaps she, to some extent, had the same effect on him. For it all, Annie thought she was pretty lucky.

"Come on," David said finally, rising and bringing Annie to her feet. "I've got another favorite haunt I want to show you."

David's next "haunt" turned out to be just half a block down from the park on Cong Ly. Annie hesitated as David swung open a creaky wrought iron gate that led to a private villa.

"What is this place?"

"A kind of home away from home for some friends I met when I was based in Saigon."

"But, shouldn't we call first . . . or something."

He smiled. "They're expecting us. Aren't you hungry?"

It was close to dinnertime and now that David mentioned it, Annie realized she was ravenous. "Who are these friends?" she asked cautiously as he guided her down a worn brick path. Not military. They certainly didn't get housed in private quarters like this.

"Bao chis."

"Huh?"

David grinned. "That's what the Vietnamese call journalists, newshounds, correspondents."

"Oh."

"There's one in particular I want you to meet. A real classy lady. Her name's Jessie Morgan. She's a free-lance foreign correspondent. Writes for *Atlantic Monthly, The New York Times Sunday Magazine, New Republic, Life.* You've got to get her to show you some of her stuff. It's fantastic. She really writes about this war. Been covering it for nearly two years now. You name a trouble spot and she's been there. When the Tet offensive hit last January, she was caught in the cross fire at Hue. Somehow, she got through it in one piece which is more than I can say for the city. Hue is nothing but rubble now. But Jessie's a tough cookie. She's a survivor, all right," he said, his voice laced with admiration.

Annie cast David a rueful glance. "And I thought we'd both outgrown crushes."

He chuckled. "This isn't a crush, Annie. I love her." He gave Annie a sly wink. "Like a sister. In this case, a much older sister."

JESSIE RENTED Hondas for all three of them.

"Why do we need motorbikes?" Annie asked.

"I have to go to a meeting with a group I'm doing a piece on, and I thought you guys might enjoy tagging along," Jessie said with a touch of mystery in her voice.

"Which piece?" David asked.

Jessie shrugged. "I'm not sure yet. Sometimes my pieces run together and overlap. Sometimes I start out at one point, get lost along the way, and come out with something completely different in the end." She gracefully swung a leg over her bike. "I'll lead. It's just on the outskirts of Saigon."

Annie edged her Honda up beside Jessie's. "What is 'it'?"

"You'll see." She chuckled. "Your generation is so impatient."

David shot Annie a sly wink. "And impulsive."

Jessie caught the little exchange and grinned, tapping the button pinned to the collar of her blouse. David had told her that Jessie had a box full of buttons, many of them gifts from GIs. She always wore at least one. The sayings printed on them were all outrageous, which was Jessie's way of making a personal statement about where she was at. Today's button read, Make Love, Not War.

Annie thought that Jessie, like Sue Ellen, probably believed there was something sexual going on between her and David. Why was it so hard for people to imagine a platonic friendship between a man and a woman, Annie mused? Then she laughed to herself. Well, it was hard for her to live it, too. Damn hard.

Jessie pulled into the crowded inner-city district, Annie and then David following behind, single file. Once they maneuvered their way through the crowded city streets, they were able to pick up a little speed, even though the roads were narrow and winding.

Twenty minutes later, Jessie drew up in front of a thick iron gate. She switched off the ignition and motioned to Annie and David to do the same.

Jessie was banging on the gate as Annie and David came up beside her. Annie peered through the metal bars. She saw nothing but a flat expanse of sodden reddish brown mud. "What is this place?"

Jessie didn't answer. She was too busy banging on the gate.

Annie looked over at David and he looked back at her, both of them bewildered.

"Pitch in," Jessie barked.

When Jessie barked, she got action. Annie and David joined in, shaking and banging the gate.

Just as Annie was about to say this was crazy, she saw a figure slowly, cautiously approaching from a distance on the other side of the gate. As the figure advanced, Annie realized it was a young boy. He looked as if he was carrying a large bundle. It must have been heavy, because he kept having to stop and hoist the bundle up every few steps.

When he drew closer, she realized the sack was actually a small child. She shot Jessie a puzzled look.

"Who are they?"

"Luong and Tai."

Jessie wasn't very enlightening.

David grinned. "Which is which?"

Jessie smiled wryly. "Luong is the one walking."

Luong moved more quickly now. Shifting the smaller boy onto his hip, he freed one hand and waved, his somber young face brightening. "Hey, Jessie," he called out cheerfully. "Whatta ya say, babe."

Jessie chuckled. "Whatta ya know, Joe."

Annie grinned. "He probably knows more than me," she muttered to David, guessing Luong was probably no more than eleven or twelve.

David winked. "Me too."

As Luong got to the gate, he once again shifted the little boy onto his hip so that he could free one hand to grapple with the lock on the heavy iron gate. As he worked at it, Luong chattered away with Jessie.

Annie was only half listening, her eyes drawn to the small child in Luong's arms. It was difficult to guess his age. Annie thought he must be three or four, but she knew that he could be older. Many of the Vietnamese children looked younger than they were. Trauma and lack of food and care often stunted their growth. Tai's little body did look bone thin, but his face was round and full, his features surprisingly serene. He had a beautiful, delicate face.

Annie gave Tai a smile when their eyes made contact. He smiled back. Or at least, there was a little upward quirk of his mouth. The rest of his expression didn't change.

Annie's heart went out to him. She guessed Tai was crippled, because for all Luong's difficulties unlocking the gate, he didn't put the child down.

David helped Luong with the task, slipping his large hand through an opening in the bars. Together they managed to get the lock undone, then Luong stepped back to swing the gate open.

"Where is everybody?" Jessie asked Luong as they stepped inside.

"Up at the house. A truck come with cartons. Everybody excited. Lots of good stuff."

Jessie clapped her hands as she trudged through the mud beside the boy. "Sister Marie must be jumping for joy."

Luong laughed. "Sister Marie don't jump, Jessie."

Annie was glad they were all wearing high rubber boots as they made their way toward the house. Once or twice Luong slipped in the mud and almost lost his balance. Jessie took hold of the boy's sleeve to right him, but she never offered to carry Tai for him.

David did offer, but Luong just flashed him a bright smile and said, "Tai let nobody carry him but me. Tai my buddy, right pal?"

Again the small child made the slightest attempt at a smile.

"Does he understand English?" Annie asked Luong.

"Sure. He understand all right." He gave Tai another hoist so that the small child's waist was practically at Luong's shoulder. It would have eased his load a little if Tai had let himself be carried fireman fashion, but he held his tiny frame so stiffly, he didn't bend at all. Nor did he make any effort to hold on to the older boy. His hands hung limply at his sides. Annie wondered at the extent of poor Tai's paralysis. Had he been thoroughly checked out by a doctor? Could she arrange something . . . ?

After walking a few more yards, a large, white, ramshackle, two-story house came into view.

"This place used to be a monastery," Jessie offered without waiting for any questions. "Now a small group of nuns from a Catholic order in Buffalo, New York, has taken it over for an orphanage. I better warn you before we go any further," Jessie added smiling, "be prepared for a surprise attack once we get inside. They're gonna jump at you from all sides."

"I thought nuns didn't jump," David said with a wry smile.

Luong found David's remark very funny and he laughed so hard Annie was sure he'd drop poor little Tai in the mud. But it was as if Tai were invisibly attached to the older boy. No matter how much he slipped and slid, how hard he was jostled, Tai stuck on.

As Jessie and David continued walking on either side of Luong, Annie deliberately hung back a little, so that she could see Tai's face. She found herself inexplicably fascinated by the solemn little boy. Even though she knew she shouldn't stare, she couldn't seem to take her eyes off him. She looked into his almond-shaped dark brown eyes, a child's eyes and yet so ancient, and she saw the war.

Tai seemed undisturbed and generally disinterested in Annie's close scrutiny. He didn't intentionally make eye contact with her, nor did he seem to try to avoid it. His whole demeanor was strangely unchildlike... inscrutable. Paralysis, trauma, what other horrors had this poor child suffered through? Annie wondered, her heart going out to him with a stunning intensity.

"So, you gonna play five-card stud with me today, Jessie?" Luong asked as they tromped up the crumbling concrete steps to the house.

"Are you kiddin'? You cheat something awful."

Luong grinned. "Everybody cheat."

David gave Luong's shoulder a squeeze. "Everybody don't cheat," he countered, mimicking the boy's phrasing. He gave Tai's thick black hair a little tousle. "Right squirt?"

Tai made no response. But Annie noticed the slight compression of his lips. David's friendly touch had disturbed Tai. She wondered if the child ever let anyone but Luong have physical contact with him. Were the nuns able to touch him without him cringing? Could they ever hold him, comfort him, show love for him in any way?

As they all stepped onto the porch, Jessie motioned for Annie and David to wait. "I better warn the Sisters we've got company, or all hundred and ten kids will pounce on you at once. They love American visitors. Oh wait, before I forget." She dug into her pouch bag and started pulling out chocolate bars. She gave the first two to Luong. He immediately handed one to Tai who took it in his little fist but made no attempt to eat it. Luong, on the other hand, instantly unwrapped his treat with his one free hand and some help from David, and proceeded to down it while Jessie passed out a few handfuls more to Annie and David.

Just then, the door flew open, and as Jessie had warned, a gleeful, noisy swarm of children surrounded them, their eyes all fixed on the chocolate bars in Annie's and David's hands. Jessie smiled at her companions, sympathetic to their dilemma. "Just give them out to the closest ones. And tell the rest you'll bring more next time. They'll understand."

Chapter Six

A time to rend, and a time to sew...

Long Binh, October 28, 1968

It was far from the first mass casualty push at the hospital, but it was one of the worst Annie had been involved in. Gurneys were squeezed tighter than sardines in the ER, spilling out into the hallways. And the medevacs were still coming in with more wounded.

Annie and her team were working triage, deciding which boys had to be treated first, which were likely to make it and which weren't. Chest wounds, belly wounds, burn cases...they could barely maneuver around the close-packed gurneys to examine the victims. It was a mess, but they worked with cool, calm precision, their training and instincts carrying them along.

Annie was passing a stretcher when a hand weakly tugged the skirt of her uniform. "Nurse, nurse, I can't feel my leg."

Annie pressed a comforting hand to the soldier's shoulder. "You're going to be okay."

"Is it...gone?" The grunt couldn't have been more than eighteen. He looked even younger. He was wet, mud caked, terrified and slipping into shock.

Annie threw another blanket over him and glanced at his dog tag. Lieutenant Jackson Bennett. "You're going to be okay, Jackson. Or is it Jack? We're going to prepare you for surgery now.'' She smiled down at him as she motioned to one of the ER nurses to get an IV going.

What she didn't tell eighteen-year-old Lieutenant Jackson Bennett was that when he woke up from surgery later that night, his leg would be gone, just as he now feared. But if she told him what he was in for right now they might lose him. Sometimes the belief that you'd be right as rain again, was all that kept the badly wounded fighting to pull through. Annie made a mental note to stop in to see the lieutenant in the next day or two, before he was shipped off to Guam for long-term medical care. After that he'd be going home. One of the lucky ones....

Annie gave the boy a tender, reassuring smile, checking her own emotions to keep them in tight control. But as she left him—as she left each one of her boys—a piece of her heart stayed behind. There were times she wondered how much of her heart she'd still have by the time she left.

Annie didn't leave the ER until after the last medevac copter—or dust-off, as they were tagged—had unloaded its wounded. It was close to 10:00 p.m. when she headed for the nurses' lockers. She took off her blood-soaked white uniform and slipped into the shower. A month or so ago, she would have had to fight back nausea as the blood of so many poor young men washed off her and went down the drain. Now, she hardly noticed the blood. Tomorrow there'd be more. And the day after that. But the faces of the boys she treated, day in and day out, were imprinted on her mind. Those faces would never leave her.

After changing into Army fatigues, Annie slipped her aching feet into her thick-soled boots, then threw on her rain poncho and helmet. The monsoons were in full swing, and with them had come a stepped-up series of rocket attacks near the compound. Several times, while she'd been on duty in the ER, Annie'd heard the rounds going off. They had sounded closer than usual. But by the time she left the hospital they had stopped...for the night anyway. That was Charlie's usual pattern, strike for a couple of hours straight after nightfall and then take off before they could be tracked down.

Stepping outside, Annie pulled her hood over her head, but didn't bother with the helmet as she made a running dash through the raging downpour for the Quonset hut about thirty yards away.

Sue Ellen was in Annie's room, kneeling on the floor picking up shards of glass. One of the rocket attacks had come close enough to shake the walls and knock down Annie's mirror.

"Hi," Sue Ellen said breezily. "Welcome home."

Annie gave her friend a weary grunt and bent down to help her pick up the broken pieces of glass. "That's my fourth mirror in two months. How much bad luck does that add up to?" Annie asked with a sigh.

Sue Ellen grinned. "I was always lousy at addition. I knew that would come in handy sometime."

Annie yawned. "I'm beat."

"You forgot, didn't you?"

"Huh?" Annie sank onto her cot.

"Jessie Morgan. The ace reporter you're always yakking about."

A gasp escaped Annie's lips as she jumped up. She'd forgotten all about Jessie's visit.

Sue Ellen popped a piece of bubble gum into her mouth as she dumped the last of the broken mirror into Annie's trash basket. She was wearing a pair of snug-fitting jeans, a black turtleneck and multiple silver chains and bead necklaces around her neck. She jingled like sleigh bells every time she moved. "You think she'll still show up tonight? It's pretty late."

Annie yawned. "Not for Jessie. She could drop in at midnight, the crack of dawn, anytime. And start popping questions, telling war stories. She doesn't live by any clock." She walked over to her bureau and started tidying up the top of it, putting her comb and brush and makeup in neat order.

"She's certainly made quite an impression on you," Sue Ellen commented. "And on Captain Loverboy. You haven't stopped talking about that reporter since you met her in Saigon last month and she took you to that orphanage."

Annie had given up telling Sue Ellen to stop calling David loverboy. No matter how often Annie protested that nothing "hot" was happening between the two of them and that they were just good friends, Sue Ellen wouldn't buy it.

"You're going to love Jessie, too," Annie said, some of her energy returning at the prospect of seeing the correspondent again. "Jessie's ... incredible. There's just no other way to describe her."

Jessie Morgan, like Annie, had been born in Maryland, but she'd been raised in Washington, D.C. Her father had been an adviser to Eisenhower while he was president and her grandfather had been the ambassador to Great Britain for many years. Indeed, Jessie's ancestry read like a who's who in Republican politics and international diplomacy. But Jessie Morgan, an outspoken individualist, had strayed from the fold, politically, physically and psychologically.

"What takes you back at first," Annie reflected, straightening the photos on her bureau, "is that Jessie looks so classy. She's got to be nearly fifty or so, but she has a sort of ageless patrician quality about her. Kind of like my Nanna. Boy, would those two get on." Annie stared at the photo of her grandmother, her voice fading as a wave of homesickness washed over her.

Sue Ellen, so good at reading Annie, brought her back to the here and now. "You were saying?"

Annie gave a little laugh and met Sue Ellen's inquisitive gaze. "Right. Well, anyway, here's this woman who looks like she could have just stepped off the society pages, hopping choppers out to the DMZ, mingling with troops at fire support bases, crawling on her belly through the jungle to interview grunts. She's absolutely fearless. I read a few of her articles. They're unbelievable. She tells it like it is. Not like a lot of the news people here who gather official military press releases to wire back to their home offices." Annie's voice was thick with admiration.

"She sounds like quite a woman. Larger than life." There was an edge of dryness in Sue Ellen's voice.

Annie knew that Sue Ellen was a little nervous about meeting Jessie. "You'll be crazy about her. She's completely down to earth and doesn't take any bows for what she's doing here. Not by a long shot."

"I still don't understand why she asked to meet me?"

"I told her about you and she said she'd love to include you in a piece she's putting together."

Sue Ellen stretched out on the cot as she watched Annie fold some of her clothes and put them away. "What kind of a piece?"

Annie shrugged. "Jessie didn't really say too much about it. Something about women in war." She stuck a still-damp shirt into her drawer. "Anyway, she's bringing along a photographer..."

Sue Ellen jerked up from the bed and scooted over to the bureau, bumped Annie out of the way, and grabbed up her hairbrush. "Groovy. Why didn't you say so in the first place? So she wants to take pictures...." No hairbrush could ever tame Sue Ellen's wild locks, and she gave it up after a few strokes.

"Relax. You look great," Annie said sincerely.

"What a time for your mirror to break." Sue Ellen sucked in her cheeks and puckered her lips. "What do you think? The next Marilyn Monroe?"

Annie laughed. "Somehow I can't see you as a blond bombshell."

"Okay, okay. How about the new Raquel Welch?" she asked, puffing out her chest.

Annie smiled distractedly at the pose, but gazed thoughtfully at Sue Ellen. "Is that what you want to do when you get back to the world? Head out to Hollywood and become a sexy movie queen?"

Sue Ellen blew a large bubble with her gum, removed the wad from her mouth and stabbed the bubble with a long, pink-painted fingernail. "I'll tell you one thing I don't want to do. Go back to Queens, stand in front of a hot stove cooking all those recipes Momma sent me, listening to the patter of little feet mixed in with Vinnie's clodhopper work boots. No sirree, honey chil', that's not my scene."

She popped the gum back into her mouth. "What about you, Annie? You wanna settle down with loverboy and raise a houseful of kids, cook the whole brood some Southern-fried chicken, sit on your porch in the evenings sipping...what is it you-all drink again down in Tara land?"

Annie grinned. "Why, mint juleps, of course. Scarlett would roll over in her grave otherwise."

"Well, I have to admit, you and that Rhett Butler of yours would look just right on the porch of Tara." Sue Ellen started to giggle as she sauntered back to the cot and stretched out.

"What's so funny?"

"I was just picturing you playing Scarlett O'Hara..."

Annie's eyes narrowed. "Oh, and that tickles your funny bone?"

Sue Ellen grinned. "Actually, you've got some of Scarlett's fire in you. But you're a lot nicer, thank heavens."

"Too nice," Annie said with a short, exaggerated sigh. "As David once said I remind him of everything clean and sweet and pure."

Sue Ellen got up and came over to give Annie a sympathetic pat on the back. "Nothin' wrong with that. What's the rush?"

Annie walked over to the cot and tucked in a corner of her blanket. "What about you and Vinnie? Did the two of you ever...?"

"Porcelli? Are you kidding? Have you gone and lost that sweet Southern mind of yours, Scarlett?"

Annie laughed dryly. "I don't get it. We're supposed to be part of the sexual revolution. So what are we doing back in the Civil War?"

"Nothing civil about this war, gal."

Sue Ellen's remark brought Annie up short. "That's for sure."

"Hey...guess what?"

"What?" Annie asked with a curious glance, observing that her cool friend looked as if she'd just swallowed a cat.

"I...uh...got a letter...from your old buddy...Hawk."

Annie eyed Sue Ellen with surprise. "Just like that? Out of the blue?"

"Well...no. I...uh...wrote to him..." Sue Ellen strolled over to the cot.

"When? You never told me."

"I wasn't sure he'd write back."

"Of course he'd write back. You don't know Hawk."

Sue Ellen sat down on the cot, feigning intense interest in adjusting the novelty rings decorating each of her fingers. "I'm getting to know him...a bit better."

Annie raised an eyebrow and stared harder at Sue Ellen. "Wait a sec. Was this letter from Hawk the first one he's sent you?"

To Annie's downright amazement, Sue Ellen actually blushed.

"Well, I'll be damned," Annie exclaimed. "You two have become pen pals. Out with it, girl. Just how many letters have the two of you exchanged so far?"

"A...few." Sue Ellen gave Annie a sly look and laughed. "Okay, maybe more than a few. I guess we both...kinda got into the habit...of writing...pretty often." She sat down on the cot.

Annie's eyes narrowed. "How pretty often?"

Sue Ellen glanced at her watch. "When did you say that reporter was gonna get here?"

"Quit stalling. I want the straight dope." Annie sat down beside Sue Ellen. "So?" she nodded.

"So? Sew buttons," Sue Ellen mumbled.

Annie smiled. "You really like him."

"What's not to like?" Sue Ellen's New York accent thickened for lighthearted effect.

"And he likes you?"

Sue Ellen shrugged.

Annie answered her own question. "Of course he does. I knew he would. Anyway, why else would he be writing you every day?"

"Did I say every day?"

"Every other day?"

Sue Ellen didn't answer.

Annie frowned. "That bum. And he never once wrote a word about it in his letters to me. Wait until my next letter..."

"I made him promise not to. Don't take it out on Hawk."

Annie looked puzzled and hurt. "Why wouldn't you want me to know?"

Sue Ellen hesitated. "I guess at first I didn't want you to rib me about it. And then..." She scratched an imaginary itch on the bridge of her nose. "I started...getting scared."

"Scared?"

"I've never known anyone like Hawk, Annie. I think he's terrific. If you wanna know the truth, I...live for his letters."

Annie was stunned. She didn't know what to say.

"You never really thought it would get...serious between me and Hawk, did you, Annie? You thought we'd just get a few laughs out of writing to each other now and then.''

"Is it serious?'' Annie asked quietly.

Sue Ellen fiddled with her rings again. Then finally she looked sideways and met Annie's gaze directly. "I've never felt this way before, Annie. When I write Hawk, it's...wild. I can really open up to him. I've never been straight with a guy before. I mean...you know...I always did the sexy flirt routine, did my little number. But I didn't wanna end up like some of my friends and some of my cousins for that matter. I didn't wanna get pregnant by the time I was eighteen and...all that. I was a tease. But I was careful.''

"Well, one thing about letter writing. You don't have to worry about being careful.''

"I'm thinking...maybe when I leave here next summer, I might go...visit Hawk.''

Tears started to trickle down Annie's cheeks.

Sue Ellen gripped Annie's arm. "You're upset. You're angry that...''

"No. No, I'm not upset. And I'm not the least bit angry.''

"Then why are you blubbering?''

"Because...I'm happy for you. And for Hawk.'' Annie sniffed, swiping her tear-stained cheeks with the back of her hand. "And jealous.''

"Hey, don't get too carried away. We aren't walking down the aisle yet.''

A troubled look shadowed Annie's happiness for her friend. "Hawk may never 'walk' down the aisle, Sue Ellen.''

"It was just a figure of speech.'' Sue Ellen looked hurt. "Is that what's bothering you? You think once I meet Hawk in person, see him in that ol' wheelchair I'll turn on my heels and scram? I thought you'd give me a little more credit.''

"I'm sorry, Sue Ellen. It's just...well, if things do end up being real serious between the two of you..."

"We've talked about that." Sue Ellen stopped and let out a little laugh. "See what I mean about figures of speech. When I read his letters I always feel like he's talking to me. You know what I said before about being able to be open with Hawk?"

Annie nodded.

"I haven't pulled any punches and neither has he. We've talked...written each other...all about the hassles...about his limitations...about how we feel about it. Even if he ends up in that wheelchair for the rest of his life, even with two bum legs he's got more on the ball than any man I ever came across. And he's got a great attitude. Like the other day he wrote me how this volunteer was getting on his case, hounding him about not trying hard enough, not pushing himself to get better. You know what he told her?"

Annie grinned. "No, but I can imagine, knowing Hawk, it was a zinger."

"He told her, 'Yeah, isn't it great how everybody knows how to be a paraplegic.'"

Annie and Sue Ellen were both laughing when a very wet, bedraggled pair of civilians appeared at the front door of Annie's room.

It was Jessie Morgan and Phil Evans, Jessie's sidekick and cameraman whom Annie had also met back in the villa on Cong Ly in Saigon.

"Hold it just like that, ladies. Evans, snap it," Jessie barked.

Phil grappled with the waterproof camera case and finally managed to extract the camera. Unfortunately Annie and Sue Ellen had stopped laughing by then. No sweat. Jessie told them an off-color joke that cracked them up again and Evans got his shot.

Jessie grinned. "Terrific. Fun and laughs in the midst of blood and guts."

Sue Ellen was taken aback by such a cold-blooded comment, but Annie merely grinned. "That's Jessie for you."

Sue Ellen relaxed. "You wanna see fun and games, Miss Morgan, you oughta come hang out at the rec center on Halloween. We're throwing the bash of the season."

"Sounds like a blast. I might do that if I'm still around." She pointed a long finger at Sue Ellen. "But only if you drop the Miss Morgan bit and call me Jessie. Being around all of you beautiful young things makes me feel old enough," the reporter said, unzipping her wet rubber parka and shaking her short, straight hair so that little sprays of water shot out around the room. Then she turned her focus on Annie. "What do you hear from your buddy, Nichols?"

"Hear?" Annie asked dryly. "Last I heard, the V.C. disconnected all the pay phones out in the boonies."

The others all laughed, but a line of worry broke across Annie's forehead. David was off on a mission. When he was gone, Annie felt like a part of her was out there with him. She didn't breathe fully and she didn't feel complete until he returned. And each time he took off, she feared, with good reason, that it would be the last time she'd ever see him.

Jessie and Phil hung their wet parkas on wall hooks and stuck their mud-caked boots close to the door. Jessie was dressed in a pair of gray wool slacks and a snowy white pullover decorated with a large button that read Save Water. Shower With a Friend. Phil, a small, ruddy man with thinning red hair, absently tucked his blue work shirt into his jeans and took a spot on the floor, adjusting a couple of cameras that were dangling from his neck. Jessie sat on the one chair.

"How about something to warm up the old creaky bones?" Phil asked, rubbing his hands together.

Annie had started to say she didn't have any booze when Jessie dug out a flask from her overstuffed safari pouch bag. She took the first swig and then passed it around.

"So, David's still out in the boonies," Jessie said as the flask made a second pass.

Annie nodded, not bothering to mask her anxiety. "I thought he'd be back by now."

"I don't know why you miss that character so much, Annie," Jessie said, reaching in her pouch for a pack of Marlboros and a gold embossed lighter. She offered the cigarettes around. Only Sue Ellen took one.

Jessie gave Sue Ellen a light. "What's so great about that buddy of yours, anyway?" she asked Annie. "Just because he's got a dynamite build, the face of a heart-throb, the cunning of a jackal and the mind of a young Socrates? What's the big deal?"

Sue Ellen chuckled. "Are you kiddin'? Scarlett here just about pines away when ol' Rhett is diddy-bopping out there in the jungle."

Annie gave her friend a sharp look. "It's nothing to joke about. Every time a dust-off lands and starts unloading the casualties..."

A familiar head appeared in the doorway. "That's why I never hitch rides with dust-offs if I can help it, kiddo."

Annie leaped up from her cot, her eyes wide with surprise and delight. "David."

Jessie winked at Sue Ellen. "We bummed the same ride from Saigon."

Without thinking about the cozy little gathering in her hooch, Annie ran across the narrow room and threw her arms around David, kissing him full on the mouth.

The envious onlookers applauded and then Jessie barked at Phil, "Get a shot of those two, Evans. We'll sell it to the Army. Make an outstanding nurse recruitment poster."

Everyone laughed. And for a brief time, they all felt a rush of exhilaration. Somehow, in the midst of the insanity that was Nam, they had pulled together to create their own little haven of sanity. For as long as it lasted, they felt safe again, rejuvenated.

The little group all ended up sitting in a cozy circle on the floor, sharing anecdotes from their pasts, telling jokes, and discussing the upcoming presidential election. Evans was pro-Nixon while the rest of the group was for Humphrey although, all of them agreed, had Bobby Kennedy lived he'd have won all their votes.

As they finished off Jessie's flask and started in on her "spare" survival kit, their moods lightened and they got into taking turns coming up with the silly things they missed most from the real world, things they longed to have again.

Phil went first. "Popcorn. The kind you get in movie theaters," he said without hesitation. "Drenched in butter." He smacked his lips.

"Give me a sirloin steak and I'd give you anything you wanted," Jessie said emphatically. "I swear, when I leave this hellhole I'm never even going to say the word, buffalo, much less eat it again." The others had also had their fill of buffalo meat. No matter how it was disguised, as steaks, chops, or hamburger, the tough, chewy meat would never come close to good old U.S. of A. prime steer beef.

Sue Ellen popped a fresh piece of gum into her mouth and chewed until it made a cracking sound between her teeth. "Okay, you wanna know what I miss the most? Cracker Jacks. Well, not so much the Cracker Jacks as the prize in the box."

Everyone giggled. Annie confessed to never having eaten Cracker Jacks and Sue Ellen promised, once they were back home, they'd get together and change all that.

"So what about you, Annie?" Jessie, ever the inquisitive reporter, asked.

Sue Ellen chuckled and said, "Why, Southern-fried chicken and mint juleps. Right, Scarlett?"

David grinned. "Is that so, Scarlett?"

Annie gave both Sue Ellen and David rueful smirks. "I detest mint juleps. And I'd take a nice roast turkey over Southern-fried chicken any day. But what I miss most of all isn't food or booze of any variety. What I miss is dry linens, dry blankets, dry clothes, dry walls. I feel like I've been swimming in rain and mildew ever since I got in-country."

"And don't forget the mud," Phil piped in.

"The monsoons will end," Jessie said philosophically. "Of course, they'll be back next spring. What a paradise!"

"Yeah," David muttered, his voice thick with irony and disgust. "What a paradise."

Annie, seated beside David, felt his harsh tone wrenching her from their temporary little haven. When she reached a hand out to him, he pulled away. He gave her a half smile, but Annie could see behind that smile to a hard, bitter hurt. A hurt that refused comfort. At least hers.

The others took in the brief exchange. They, too, felt the shift back into the real world. Jessie and Sue Ellen smoked, Phil fiddled with his cameras, David sat stiff and silent, determined to bury his personal pain a little deeper, and Annie fought back that all-too-familiar dry, bitter taste that rose up in her throat at the thought of the war.

Finally, out of the silence punctuated only by the steady beat of the hard rain outside and the ticking of a wind-up alarm clock on the floor beside Annie's cot, David said quietly, somberly, "What I miss most from the world...is the me I left behind." He smiled a humorless smile as he eyed the others in the circle. "What do you think my chances are of finding that again, when I get home?"

Chapter Seven

A time to keep silence...

Long Binh, November 1, 1968

Annie grabbed up her two letters at mail call and hurried back to her hooch to read them in private. Letters from home had become her most treasured possessions and it had been several days since she'd received any. Both of the letters were postmarked Beaumont, Maryland. One was from her dad, the other from Turner. Annie opened Turner's letter first.

Hi kid,
Well, here I am back at the old homestead. Got a break and figured I'd pay the old man a visit before heading south to Florida where I plan to spend the rest of my time off lying on the sands of Miami Beach, soaking up some sun, swimming in the blue-green sea, and checking out the... well, you probably get the picture.
It's been a hectic few months for me, but I've loved every minute of it. You just might get to see me hitting a slam-bam home run up in Boston next fall when you get back. Depending on how well I do down at training camp in Tampa, the sky's the limit.
Oh, by the way, I spoke to Hawk the other day. I had every intention of going over to Oakdale to see him, but I guess he's got a pretty tight schedule, what with his ther-

*apy programs and all. He sounded great, though. Really
great. Told me he's waiting for my picture to show up on
a baseball card so he can pass it around and make his
buddies jealous. He figures he'll be leaving the V.A. in a
few months. Soon as he's up and about. Great news, huh?*

*As for Dad, he's got some fine new horses and he's real
busy. Of course, the minute I walked in the door he put
me to work. Doesn't the old man realize I'm a rising star?*

*Only kidding, kid. My head hasn't grown any, I swear.
Still the same old Turner. With maybe some new muscle.*

*Hey, Nanna told me to send you something nice. I told
her I'd love to send you anything your sweet little heart
desires. She said you like bath powder. So, I've sent you
a case. When it shows up, if it's not what you want, maybe
you can sell it to the other nurses and buy yourself something with the cash. Hawk said when you get leave and go
over to Hong Kong or wherever for your R&R you can
pick up some neat stuff.*

*I miss you, kid. Dad's got the flag hung out every day.
He figured Nixon's a shoo-in and that he'll put a quick
end to the war. I know you're not a Nixon fan, neither am
I, but after the circus the Yippies made out of the convention in Chicago back in August, you can't blame a lot
of Democrats for making a switch. Well, if Dad's right—
and I sure hope he is—maybe you and David will be
coming home earlier than you expected. When you're
back we're all going to have ourselves one heck of a celebration. It'll be just like old times.*

*Love,
Turner*

Annie read the letter through a couple of times. She was
tucking it back in its envelope when David showed up at
the door of her hooch.

"Hi."

She gave him a distracted nod.

"How's your head?"

"My head?"

He leaned against the doorjamb. "Mine's not great. I'm sorry about last night, Annie."

Annie's mind was still focused on Turner's letter and she didn't respond to David's apology.

David smiled sheepishly. "I guess I had one glass of punch too many at that crazy Halloween party. Your pal Sue Ellen and her cronies sure know how to program a wild bash. And then, after I cut out of the rec center, I hung out with Jessie and Phil for awhile. Jessie had her trusty flask." He grinned, closing his eyes for a minute. "I don't drink that much too often. And boy did I regret it when I woke up this morning."

Annie shrugged. "You looked like you were having fun. Whatever gets you through the night."

David was thrown by Annie's cavalier response. "You cut out early. I lost you somewhere between the Supremes and Country Joe and the Fish." He hesitated. "Were you pissed off at me?"

She paid full attention to David for the first time. "No. Of course not. I just wasn't in a partying mood."

He studied her more closely. "What is it, Annie? I almost never see you so down."

She stared at the envelope containing Turner's letter. "I just got this from big brother."

"Is anything wrong? Turner didn't get himself booted out of the majors or anything, did he?"

She laughed dryly. "No."

David smiled. "Didn't think so."

Annie extracted Turner's letter from the envelope, crossed the room and handed it over to David.

He stayed in the open doorway, leaning against the jamb as he read the letter through and then glanced over at Annie, who was busying herself fixing the blanket on her cot with smooth, neat hospital corners.

David tapped the letter against the palm of his hand. "I bet Turner has himself a ball in Miami Beach. I envy the bastard."

"Do you?"

David frowned. "What's bugging you, Annie?" He gave the letter a second glance. "I don't know. Maybe I'm dense, but I don't see anything here that would bum you out like this." He broke into a smile. "I get it. You hate the powder he's sending you."

"He might as well have been writing me at summer camp," Annie said, an unusual vehemence in her voice. "It's such a breezy, superficial letter, full of good cheer."

"Come on, Annie. What do you want Turner to write about? Back in the world they can't begin to understand what's happening here. Turner can't imagine what it's like for you . . . or any of us."

"But in my last letter, I sent Turner a copy of one of Jessie's articles . . . so he would understand . . . just a little. It was the one she wrote for the *Nation* based on her interviews with that platoon out in a Pleiku fire-base."

David nodded. He'd read the article. It was weird in a way, given that it didn't contain anything he hadn't already experienced himself, that it still affected him. The fear, the loneliness, the deprivation, the whole tragedy of it—indeed, he could have said the same words those soldiers had spilled out. Maybe that was it. Despite all the individual differences among them, it was as if they had one universal voice.

Annie sighed. "I don't think Turner even read that article. He prefers the fantasy that it isn't all that bad here, or that we're on the road to victory, or at least to a fast pull-out if Nixon gets in. How can he be so naive?"

"You know what Jessie says. The people back home aren't being told the truth, Annie. Especially now that the political tune has changed. Nixon's running on an 'end the war' platform and a lot of people want to believe he can do what Johnson couldn't."

Annie sat down on her freshly made bed, propped her elbows on her knees and rested her chin in her cupped palms.

"I don't believe it," she said. "The only way he'd end the war is to win it. And you and I and every grunt out in the boonies knows that short of nuking them we can't win. And as for the folks back home not getting the real message, that's not entirely true. Jessie's sending back the truth. And so are some of the other correspondents. Why do you think the Doves are gaining so much ground? I think plenty of people just want out. Plenty of them think we shouldn't have been here in the first place. It's people like Turner...who go about their ordinary lives with blind complacency—"

"Annie, that's a pretty heavy...."

"Nanna once told me Turner had never come to grips with life's harsh realities. I looked at her with the same shocked expression that you're looking at me with, right now."

"It's not that he doesn't care, Annie."

"You're right," she said softly. "It's that he's so good at avoiding or escaping anything that he might find upsetting. Can he honestly believe we're both going to come back home and celebrate and act just like nothing much has happened? Doesn't he know that none of us will ever be the same again?"

"Turner is Turner, Annie."

"He didn't even go to see Hawk," Annie said sadly. "And we both know it has nothing to do with Hawk's so-called busy therapy schedule like Turner wrote." She gave a sharp, dry laugh. "Hawk just let Turner off the hook, because he knew how upsetting it would be for Turner to see him in a wheelchair. Everyone lets Turner off the hook." She paused. "Nanna's the only one who doesn't make excuses for him. She keeps confronting him, trying to make him see that he can't be a part of real life if he stays adrift in a cloud all the time. Well, now I'm trying to confront him, too. Because I want him to…grow up."

"Turner means well, Annie. He'd give any one of us the shirt off his back."

"Meaning well won't cut it, David. Giving me the shirt off his back, sending me a caseload of bath powder, wanting me to have whatever my little heart desires, isn't where it's at. I want him to reach out a little, feel some of those harsh realities."

"He's scared."

"We're all scared." She looked sharply over at David. "What if he hadn't gotten that 4F?"

"He'd have gone to Canada. He'd have gone to the moon if he'd had to. If your dad could have arranged it."

Annie looked down at the still-unopened letter from her father. "That's one thing your father and mine have in common. They both like to arrange things."

David gave Turner's letter back to Annie. "Look, I'm the last one to sing the Judge's praises, but all either of our fathers ever wanted to do was try to keep us alive, keep us out of this bloody war. You can't really blame them for that." He smiled faintly. "I can't believe it. Me having some understanding for the Judge? I guess I must be growing up."

Annie scowled. "Most of us are growing up—you, me, Hawk…. But Turner isn't, David. He's still living in his own little dreamworld. Baseball, women, days of sun and fun. Leaving it to others to sweep up the debris. And if they don't sweep fast enough, he just closes his eyes and pretends it isn't there."

"Maybe he's better off." David stared her straight in the eye, his tone flat.

Annie leapt to her feet and stared right back at him. "You don't really believe that, David. No matter how much you try to fight it, you're really compassionate. You face life, you don't run away from it. That's why you showed up the minute Hawk called you from the V.A.

That's why you camped out in his hospital room all those weeks. That's why you've always been there for Turner and for me. That's why you're here in Nam.''

David laughed sharply. ''Well, I'm glad one of us knows why I'm here. I sure as hell don't know anymore.''

''You're here for the same reason I'm here, David. Because we had no other choice.'' Her voice was soft and her eyes were sad for both of them.

There was a somber silence which they both understood.

He stood there looking at her, running his hand through his hair as he slowly shook his head. ''And here, all this time, I've been worrying that you weren't tough enough to make it.'' There was a slight edge to his voice. It seemed to bother him just a bit that she wasn't the helpless little kid he'd thought she was.

''I'm not that tough,'' she whispered, wanting to give him a realistic picture of what made her tick. It wasn't so black and white. It wasn't strong versus weak. ''Sometimes I'm so scared I can't think straight. I question my judgment, my motives, my faith. Nanna warned me that would happen. She warned me that I'd end up with more questions than answers.''

''Did she tell you what to do when that happened?''

Annie sighed and sat back down on the edge of her cot. ''No.'' She stared around her hooch...her world. ''Sometimes these walls feel like they're closing in on me.''

David crossed the room and knelt in front of her, resting his hands lightly on the bed at either side of her. ''I think we're both suffering from cabin fever, kiddo. What do ya say we get outta here? Jessie's got a ride into Saigon and she invited us along. I told her I'd ask you.''

''I thought she was going to stay in Long Binh for a while, doing her piece about women in Nam. She hasn't done much interviewing.''

"That's not how Jessie operates. She hangs out, listens, takes a lot of mental notes. Anyway, she's coming back here tonight. Actually I think she wants to make you the star of her piece, Annie."

She gave him a wary look. "The star? What are you talking about?"

David sat down beside her on the cot and grinned. "What's the matter, kiddo? Don't you want to be famous?"

"Famous for what?" Annie asked incredulously.

He placed a hand lightly on her knee. His touch sent a warm glow through her. "Word's out that you are one of the best damn nurses in Nam. Don't you know that, Annie? Ask any of the other nurses, any of the med-techs, the docs. Jessie has. She's talked to some of your patients, too. The ones whose hands you hold in the dark of night when you should be tucked up in bed. The ones you pay special calls on, even though they've long left your unit. You bring them ribbons and picture frames for their snapshots. You talk to them about how to tell their girls or their moms that they're not coming back looking the same as when they left home. You make them laugh, you cry with them, you make them feel whole again, Annie."

She smiled faintly, knowing that her cheeks were red. It wasn't only hearing her praises sung, it was hearing it from David. "You're in the wrong line, Nickel. You should be in public relations."

"Jessie's been doing her homework on you. The truth's out. You're a real Florence Nightingale, kiddo."

"You're exaggerating, Nickel. Anyway, it isn't so selfless," she insisted, her smile vanishing. "I need the contact as much as they do. Otherwise . . . I couldn't survive. I have to keep on feeling what I'm doing out here has some meaning, some true value. Or else it really would all feel utterly pointless."

He gave her blond hair a gentle tug and then smoothed it back from her face. "You're wonderful, Annie."

There was a pregnant pause. One of his hands was still on her knee, the other on her hair. Their gazes met and held. She felt that old magnetic pull and she knew David was feeling it too, but something made her stand up abruptly and put a little distance between them. She could tell from David's expression that he was both surprised and disappointed. Here he was, finally making the first move, and she was the one calling time out.

She gave a little nervous laugh. "Cabin fever can make people do crazy things, Nickel." Her voice had a breathy quality. It wasn't as if she didn't have an overwhelming urge to do those crazy things. But however much she yearned for David in a physical way, she simply couldn't risk doing damage to their emotional connectedness. She'd seen David withdraw from her before when he felt he'd overstepped whatever invisible line he'd drawn between them. She knew he still had a long way to go in sorting out his feelings about her. And for the first time, she realized that she, too, had some sorting out to do.

"Come on," she said with a forced airiness. "Let's find Jessie and go to Saigon for some...soothing relaxation." She smiled mischievously.

David raised a thick, dark eyebrow and eyed her pensively, appraisingly. Then he smiled back at her, almost boyishly. "Yeah, you're right. Cabin fever can be...dangerous." He rose from the cot and brushed off the dusty knees of his trousers.

Annie grabbed her pocketbook and tucked the unopened letter inside.

"Who's that one from?" David asked.

"My dad."

"What did he have to say?"

"I don't know. I didn't read it yet."

"We have time."

Annie hesitated. "I'll read it later."

"He still giving you grief about your being here?"

"He doesn't mean to. He tries so hard in his letters not to be disapproving." She sighed. "I guess I'd feel better if he didn't try so hard; if he'd just let me have it. Instead he sends me these dutiful missives, asking all the appropriate questions: How am I? Am I eating and sleeping all right? Did I get the care packages he and Nanna sent? He never says he's worried or scared or boiling mad, but I don't have to read between the lines to know what he's going through. He'll probably never forgive me for putting him through this hell . . ."

Something hardened instantly in David's eyes. "You've got it cockeyed, kiddo. He's not the one going through hell."

Annie hated to hear that fierce, cynical tone in David's voice. She hated to see him turn to granite right before her eyes. Not that she was any different. In Vietnam, her moods swung back and forth like a perpetual metronome. When she was down, David pulled her up, and when David was in the pits, she did her best to drag him out. So she strode over to him now, with purpose and determination in her walk, and looped her arm through his. "We can go to hell tomorrow, Nickel. Today we're going to Saigon."

An irresistible sparkle lit up David's dark eyes. "Did I ever tell you that, once upon a time, I had a crush on you?"

Annie blushed and laughed at the same time. "When?" she asked, challenging him.

He blushed and laughed, too. "Back when it was uncool to be wild about your best friend's little sister."

She flashed David a dazzling smile and gave his arm a little squeeze. "Isn't it nice that we're both all grown-up?"

David didn't answer, but he returned the smile as they headed, arm in arm, out the door.

Chapter Eight

A time to laugh, a time to weep...

Thanksgiving, Saigon, November, 1968

In her wildest imaginings Annie would never have been able to dream up a Thanksgiving celebration like this one. But here she was, newly promoted First Lieutenant Annie Magill, breaking bread and giving thanks along with foreign correspondent Jessie Morgan, photographer Phil Evans, Sue Ellen Salvatore, Captain David Nichols, nine nuns, and one hundred and ten children, in an orphanage on the outskirts of Saigon.

By borrowing, begging and a little black-market negotiating, Annie and her cohorts had managed to scrounge up six real turkeys and a caseload of canned cranberry sauce. They filled in with good old buffalo meat, sliced as thin as they could make it, a varied assortment of canned vegetables and a mountain of freeze-dried mashed potatoes. The visitors, the nuns and the older children all helped cook and serve the food. While only a few of the children had even an inkling about what the American holiday was about, they all joyfully, boisterously, enthusiastically took part in the celebration. There'd been so little to celebrate in their short, war-torn lives.

Only Tai had seemed removed from the festivities. He remained seated at the long T-shaped table well after most of the other children had downed the feast and gone scurrying off to the front room to play. A few of the older children hung back, including Luong who sat in a chair beside Tai, coaxing his little "shadow" to eat some more of the food on his plate. Tai made a halfhearted effort, but only when Luong prodded him.

Tai, as Annie had learned during her first visit to the orphanage, turned out not to be suffering from any physical paralysis at all. Sister Mary Catherine, the nun in charge of the smaller children, explained that emotional trauma manifested itself in different ways among the children. For Tai, it meant a severe physical and emotional withdrawal. Only Luong seemed able to relate to him, to reach him on any but the most minimal level.

When Annie had asked the nun if she knew anything about Tai's family, Sister Mary Catherine told her that he'd lost them all during a napalm attack on his village. Fortunately Tai had been rescued by Luong, a neighbor's child, who had carried him for many days and nights through difficult and dangerous terrain all the way to Saigon. One of the other Sisters from the orphanage had happened to be shopping in Saigon one day and spotted the two boys, cold, dirty, starving, huddled together in a dank alley. She brought them back with her to the orphanage. That had been fourteen months ago. Tai and Luong had been there ever since.

"That turkey was delicious," Sue Ellen exclaimed, pushing aside her empty plate and giving Annie a little poke. "You think I oughta send my mom the recipe?"

Annie laughed. "It's good, but Nanna's turkey is still better."

David agreed, smacking his lips. "Especially her chestnut and sausage stuffing. We used to have great times around the old Magill dining table on Thanksgiving." He gave Annie a nostalgic smile. "Didn't we?"

Jessie, ever the curious reporter, asked David to tell her about those happy holiday memories with the Magill family. But he turned reticent. Thinking back to happier times made his time here harder. Hard time. That's what he was doing all right. And it was still nearly two months till his hump date—the halfway point of his tour of duty. Then it was countdown. Six months after hump and he'd be making the big swoop, catching the Big Bird to Paradise, as they all called it, back to the world. But even if that day came for him, which he knew better than to bank on, he would have to face leaving so many others behind . . . his buddies, his friends . . . Annie. She would still have two months left of her tour.

Annie might not have been able to read his mind, but she was an ace at reading his moods. She saw him retreat and shot him a wiseacre grin. "Come on, Nickel. Tell Jessie about that first Thanksgiving morning when you showed up on our doorstep with a suitcase in your hand."

David scowled. "Tell Jessie anything and we'll have ten million people back home reading about it," David shot back, a faint smile curving his lips. "And my dad doesn't know the true story to this day."

"Your father wouldn't read my stuff even if it made front-page headlines, Nichols," Jessie teased. She didn't know the Judge personally, but she knew of him. "Anyway, this is strictly off the record, guys. I swear."

David laughed dryly.

"I'm just naturally nosy," Jessie went on. "Can I help it?"

Sue Ellen tapped her own nose. "Me, too. Give with the story, Nichols."

Luong, sitting a few chairs away from David, waved his fork at his nose. "Yeah Joe, I got a natural nose, too. Give."

Everyone laughed, including the nuns and the few other children still sitting at the table. Even little Tai's lips bore a trace of a smile.

"Okay, kid, you win," David relented, addressing Luong, but letting his eyes linger for a few moments on

Tai. He, like Annie, could feel this sad, quiet, beautiful child pulling on his heartstrings.

Settling back in his chair, David rested his arms across his chest and stretched out his legs, crossing them at the ankles. "Well, now...once upon a time..." He gave Luong a wink. "All good stories start that way."

"Gotcha, Joe." Luong called every soldier Joe. He was wild for the GI Joe dolls that were a big craze over in the States. Last Christmas a few of them had been donated to the orphanage. But all the children had to share them. Then, a few months ago, when Jessie'd started making periodic visits to the orphanage, she'd won Luong's heart forever by bringing him a GI Joe doll of his very own.

"Okay, so once upon a time when I was ten..."

"Nine," Annie cut in.

"How would you remember? You were in kindergarten."

"Exactly. Which meant you were in the fourth grade. Mrs. Campbell's class, remember? Which also means you were nine. Anyway, Nanna's told me the story a dozen or more times."

"You want to tell it then?"

"No, I'll just keep you honest, Captain."

David grinned at Sue Ellen. "Man, ever since she traded her 'butter bar' for her silver First Lieutenant's, she thinks she's hot stuff."

"Go on, go on, Nickel. Tell your story," Annie said with a smirk tinged with pride. She knew David was proud of her promotion, too. He'd been at the ceremony. And when the silver bar had been pinned on her shoulder she'd spotted a tear or two in David's eyes.

David gave her a little salute. "Okay, so there I am, ten years old, give or take a year, and my father tells me he's planning for us to drive down to some hick town in Georgia to spend Thanksgiving with his two sisters. My two maiden aunts. I don't think either of them has smiled since FDR got elected to office. Not to mention that they hate kids. Especially boys.''

Annie chuckled. "They weren't crazy about girls, either. Remember that time they were in Beaumont visiting and I had the misfortune to stop over at your house to return a football you'd lent Turner?''

David started to laugh. "Oh, you mean the time I shouted down from the top of the stairs telling you to throw me a pass and Auntie Evelyn accidentally intercepted it?''

"She just darted out from nowhere," Annie said amidst the laughter. "It was a great pass, too. Turner'd given me some pointers.''

"What did Auntie Evelyn do?" Sue Ellen asked, still giggling.

David's eyes sparkled. "Before or after we hoisted all two hundred and fifty pounds of her up from the floor?''

Everyone cracked up, even the nuns, although they tried not to. Tears ran down Annie's face, she was laughing so hard, and when she caught sight of Tai, wearing the biggest smile she'd ever seen on his face, her heart lurched with a kind of happiness she'd never felt before.

Luong urged David to continue and he and Annie told the group at the table how they'd had to sit in the drawing room for over an hour being lectured to by the Judge, Aunt Margaret and, once she got her wind back, Aunt Evelyn. Annie was sent home with a note to her father suggesting that he take a firmer hand with his wild and wayward football-throwing daughter.

"What did you do with the note?" Phil asked.

Annie gave the photographer an incredulous look. "What do you think I did? I ripped it into tiny bits and threw it away.''

David grinned. "Yeah, and lived in terror for nearly a month, afraid the Judge might call her dad and bring up the letter.''

"I did not," Annie said, affronted.

"Did too. Turner told me."

"I knew I shouldn't have confided in that brother of mine."

"You should have known there were never any secrets between the Three Musketeers."

"Hawk knew, too?"

"Turner wouldn't tell me something and not tell Hawk." He looked at Annie as if she had absolutely lost her mind.

"What else did Turner blab about?"

David's eyes sparkled. "What didn't he tell us?"

"Oh, you think you're so smart, Nichols."

"Speaking of smart," David teased, "I seem to recall Turner telling me about a time when you were eleven or twelve and cribbed one of big brother's old book reports."

"I never..."

"You got an A on it, too. That's what ticked Turner off. When he'd handed it in, back in the same grade, he'd only gotten a C-plus."

"That is an absolute lie, David Nichols. I have never cheated in my entire life..."

"I'm just telling you what Turner told me..."

"Well, if you're so smart, how come you..."

"Children, children," Jessie broke in.

Annie blushed. "Sorry."

"Yeah, sorry," David said, grinning. "We used to go at each other like this when we were kids. But we're not kids anymore. We should be more mature."

Annie glared at him, but David went right on grinning.

"So anyway, Nichols," Sue Ellen said, lighting up an after-dinner cigarette, "get back to the Thanksgiving day you showed up at the Magill doorstep with a suitcase."

David cocked his head, eyeing Annie, waiting for her okay.

"Go on," she said airily.

His smile softened. "So, maybe I was nine at the time. Anyway, there was no way I was going to spend my Thanksgiving break with the cheery Nichols clan down in Peachtree, Georgia. So I told the Judge that the Magills had invited me to spend the holiday with them."

"And your father agreed?" Jessie asked.

"Agreed? The Judge was thrilled. He didn't cotton to the idea of having me along anyway. He knew his sisters would spend all their time fretting over me, being terrified, with good reason, that I'd break something, spill something, say something.... They believed children should be seen and not heard. And if they didn't have to be seen too much, all the better. Problem solved."

"Only," Annie said, "the Magills hadn't extended the invitation. In fact," she went on, a note of sadness in her voice, "we weren't planning on much of a celebration that year. My mother had...died the summer before and no one in the house was in a very festive mood. Nanna came down to visit and we were just going to have a small, quiet family dinner."

David's hand slipped over Annie's. "Of course, I didn't think about that when I told my dad the lie. And since he sprung the news of the trip to Georgia on me the very morning of Thanksgiving, I didn't exactly have time to make arrangements. So I packed my bag, got into the car with the Judge, and he dropped me in front of the Magill house and took off."

Annie smiled. As David continued, she drifted off a little, remembering Nanna's rich, full voice recounting the story, filling in the missing pieces.

"You were so young, Annie," she could hear Nanna saying. "You really hadn't taken your mother's sudden death all in. You kept thinking somehow, magically, your sweet, beautiful momma would come back. Turner was struggling, too, but in a different way. He refused to mourn. He didn't even cry at Joanie's funeral. He simply dug his hands deep into his pockets and his lips kept moving although no sound came out. He didn't think I knew, but he had a handful of his favorite baseball cards in each of his jacket pockets. Later, at the cemetery, after the service, he wouldn't leave the grave site. Your father wanted to go get him, but I told him to leave Turner be for a few minutes. I guessed what was in your brother's mind. He took those favorite cards of his and buried them in the ground next to your momma's grave. He never spoke of it to anyone. To this day he doesn't know that I know."

Annie's eyes always filled with tears whenever Nanna told that part. It was so much like Turner. He always did bury his feelings away, refusing to acknowledge pain or fear or sorrow. He was so single-minded, so unwilling to be hampered by his emotions. And yet, burying those favorite baseball cards by his mother's grave revealed how deeply he felt.

"When Thanksgiving morning rolled around," Nanna used to say, "your father was too depressed to even help cook up the turkey. He kept saying that it wouldn't be a holiday without your momma. I'd insisted, though, that you and Turner should not be deprived of celebrations. Granted it would be modest and subdued under the circumstances, but I went about preparing for a traditional dinner with turkey and all the trimmings. And then the doorbell rang. It was quite early, maybe ten o'clock and I couldn't imagine who it could be."

This had always been Annie's favorite point in the story. David's arrival.

"To this day," Nanna would say, almost word for word, each time she told Annie about that morning, "I can picture David's face as he stood at the door. Such a beautiful child, his dark eyes with those long, thick lashes, intense and magnetic even as a little boy. And he wore a smile of such heartfelt earnestness that it quite won my heart for all time."

Nanna had always paused at that point, and Annie'd urged her on. "And then you spotted the suitcase."

Nanna would laugh. "Yes. There it was, a small plaid overnight case, resting on the porch right beside David. I gave him a puzzled look and asked what he had there. And he answered quite matter-of-factly, 'My things. I've come to visit. If you don't mind, that is?' I asked if he was expected. Well, he stood there on that porch and quietly, endearingly explained his perplexing situation. That boy always had a most persuasive quality. He'd have made a fine actor. I told him so that morning."

"And he persuaded you to invite him," Annie'd always say with satisfaction.

"Well, actually Turner did the persuading. He'd heard the bell ring and was on the stairs listening to David's tale of woe. And before I could say a word, Turner charged for the door and begged me to let David stay. I hadn't so much as nodded my head when they immediately decided it would only be right for them to invite Hawk, too."

"Which they did."

"Yes, Annie, and of course Hawk was thrilled. His family was poor and there were problems at home. It wasn't a very happy place."

Then Nanna would get teary-eyed and say, "The start of a tradition." And it had been tradition. From that day on, though nothing formal was ever set, it had always been Nanna, Ian, Annie and the boys who'd gathered round the huge mahogany dining room table for the Thanksgiving holiday.

Until Nam.

Annie closed her eyes, tears rolling down her cheeks. Lost in her thoughts, she was unaware that David had finished talking and that everyone was quietly watching her.

David squeezed her hand. "Reminiscing is for the birds," he said with a soft smile. "And speaking of birds, let's clean up fast so we can go play with the kids for a while before we have to get back to base."

Annie blinked several times and sniffed. Everyone at the table busied themselves with the clean-up, giving Annie a few minutes to compose herself. Everyone but Tai. He sat in his seat watching Annie with quiet but intense concentration. As she wiped her tear-stained cheeks with the back of her hand, she shifted position to sit beside Tai.

She made no attempt to touch him or even address him directly. She lifted an empty cup from the table and idly toyed with it. "I get sad when I think of my family. I get sad when I remember how happy we all were together."

She had no real idea if Tai comprehended what she was saying. Luong had said Tai understood everything, but there was no way to be sure since Tai only spoke in Vietnamese, and then only to Luong.

Yet, when Annie glanced sideways at Tai, there was something in his captivating eyes that made her believe he not only understood, but that he was silently sharing in that sorrow with her.

Finally Annie rose and gathered up the dishes in front of her. But she left Tai's plate where it was. There were still a few bites of meat and some cranberry sauce on his plate. Although she thought he probably wouldn't eat any more, especially without Luong coaxing him, she simply couldn't bring herself to remove it. The very thought of taking anything more away from this child who had lost so much—everything—made her feel ill.

Luong reappeared within moments. He gave Annie a bright smile. "Great kid," he said, giving Tai's back a gentle pat. Tai looked up at Luong and smiled sweetly.

Annie felt a wave of envy. She suddenly longed to gather Tai in her arms, hold him, comfort him, nurture him. She'd never even known she had maternal instincts, and suddenly they were threatening to overwhelm her.

"You okay, Annie?" Luong asked. "You gonna cry again?"

Annie pulled herself together, and gave both children a broad grin. "No. Crying time is over. Time for fun."

"Okay, babe," Luong said enthusiastically. "How 'bout poker?"

Annie quirked a brow. "Five-card stud?"

Luong grinned impishly. "I won't cheat."

Annie gave Tai a quick glance. "Tell you what. I'll take you both on."

Luong shot Tai a questioning look. As far as Annie could tell, Tai made absolutely no response. But he must have communicated in some way to Luong, because the next thing the older boy said was, "Okay. Tai won't cheat, too."

For two hours straight, right up to the minute she had to leave to catch her ride back to the base, Annie played poker with Luong and Tai. At first she was amazed that Tai would actually play. Then she was awestruck to find that he not only played, but he played well. He gave the game absolute concentration. Not only did he have the poker face of a pro—he cheated. He cheated better than Luong. The child hadn't even turned five and he could have beat out half the card sharks in Saigon.

"He okay," Luong said with a wink, when Tai won the final hand. "I teach him. Now he win me."

Annie smiled at Tai, who during the entire two hours had not spoken a word or hardly moved from his yoga-style position on the floor. "You're very smart, Tai. Very clever." Her smile deepened. "You're okay." She glanced at Luong. "Do either of you know how to read English?"

"Pretty good. Sisters teach," Luong replied, then looked at Tai and shrugged. "Maybe little bit, Tai too."

"Next time I come, I'll bring you some books," Annie promised.

"And chocolate bars?" Luong asked immediately.

"Do you both like chocolate bars?" Annie's eyes rested on Tai, desperately wanting him to make just the minutest response to her. But Tai continued to wear his solemn, stoic expression.

"Tai crazy about chocolate bars. Me, too."

David came over. "Hey, who's giving out chocolate bars?"

Annie smiled up at him. "I was telling Luong and Tai that next time I came I'd bring books."

"And chocolate bars," Luong piped in.

"And chocolate bars," Annie agreed.

"Hey, Joe," Luong addressed David. "You teach Annie better poker for next time, okay?"

Annie laughed as she looked up at David. "Yeah, Joe. You teach me how to cheat like these two and I'll take 'em both to the cleaners."

Luong protested, "No cheat."

David grinned, addressing the poker trio. "I tell you what. If I can, I'll come too and teach you all a few tricks."

Annie saw that David's eyes lingered on Tai. She thought she saw a tiny hint of a smile on the child's lips, but maybe she was simply seeing what she wanted to see. Maybe it was enough for now to share with Tai in whatever way he could accept. There was certainly no way to rush it. Anyhow, she had nine more months of her tour to go. Plenty of time for working at the relationship. She'd already decided there was no better way to spend her off days than visiting the orphanage.

Later that night, after they got back to the base, Annie and David stopped off for a nightcap at one of the officers' clubs. They sat at a quiet little table sipping luke-warm beers, listening to the melodic strains of Herb Alpert drifting out from the jukebox speaker.

For a couple of minutes, David seemed to be concentrating on the music, so it took her by surprise when he said, "You better be careful, Annie. I think you're falling in love."

She took in a sharp breath, immediately thinking David was referring to her growing feelings for him. "That's...ridiculous."

David ignored her denial. "It's too risky, Annie. There are too many unknowns. It can't bring you anything but heartbreak in the end."

"Always the optimist," Annie muttered, unable to look him straight in the eye.

He gazed at her with a rueful smile. "You've got too much heart, Annie. It's going to wind up getting you in trouble. You could get in over your head."

"I'm a strong swimmer. I've even beaten you on a few occasions, Nickel."

"But you're swimming against the current now."

"I told you a while back that I'm not the least bit sure what love is all about. Don't worry about it, friend."

He took her hand. "Look Annie, Jessie was telling me that she's been pulling some strings back home for... Luong."

Luong? Where did Luong fit in? What did Luong, or Jessie pulling strings, have to do with her feelings for David? Annie wondered.

She decided David was easing off the awkward topic of their personal relationship, which was a relief to her as well. "What kind of strings?"

"Luong's very bright. Jessie took a shine to him the first time she met him. He's got no one left here in Nam— his whole family was wiped out by Charlie."

"He's got Tai," Annie said. "Those two are closer than many real siblings."

He sandwiched her hand between both of his. "Jessie thinks she can get Luong into a very good private boarding school in Virginia. She's gotten a politically influential family to sponsor him."

Annie's heart felt like lead. "What about Tai? What will happen to him? Jessie can't mean to separate the two of them."

"It wouldn't be right to keep Luong bound to a life without possibilities—staying here in Nam. And Tai's much too young to go to an American boarding school,

Annie. You know that. Anyway, the kid has serious emotional hang-ups. One of the Sisters was telling me that she's seen quite a few kids like Tai and . . . well . . . you've got to be realistic about their chances."

"What do they know about Tai? He's an extraordinary child who's suffered unimaginable sorrow. Given . . . enough love and understanding . . ."

David squeezed her hand between his. "See. I was right. You are in love."

Annie was momentarily stunned. "With . . . Tai?"

David laughed good-naturedly. "Who did you think?"

Annie blushed to the roots of her hair. "I thought . . . I didn't think . . ." She shrugged her shoulders. "I'm nuts about Luong, too," she said lamely.

There was an awkward silence, as the humor faded. David stared across the room, his thoughts obviously far away. "It's a weird feeling, Annie. We're in limbo. We can't go back—can't ever go back to what it was. And we can't go forward, either." He made a fist with one hand. "I hate this place. Hate the misery, the brutality, the death all around me. I keep wondering how long I can make it . . ."

"Oh David," Annie said, desperation ringing in her voice. "Don't talk like that. You'll make it. You'll go home, go back to law school, probably find yourself a beautiful female lawyer-to-be and live happily ever after."

"Always the optimist," he said with a wry smile.

She threw her damp cocktail napkin at him. "And, for your information, Captain, it was Turner who stole one of *my* book reports and got that C-plus, not the other way around."

David laughed, throwing the napkin back at her. She ducked and it hit a passing WAC. The WAC picked the napkin up, rolled it into a tight wad, walked over to David and dropped the wad right into his half-finished beer.

Annie bit back her laughter until the WAC walked off. After she got her giggles under control, she leaned closer to David. "I think she digs you, Nickel. Probably scribbled her phone number on that napkin before she gave it back to you."

David reached over and finished the rest of Annie's beer in one long swallow. "She's not my type." There was a challenging look in his eye. He knew the question on the tip of her tongue.

But Annie decided not to ask it.

Chapter Nine

A time for war...

Long Binh and My Tho, early December, 1968

Sue Ellen, dressed in her crisp, pale blue Red Cross uniform, slid into a chair across from Annie's in the cafeteria.

"You finished up your shift?" Sue Ellen took a French fry off Annie's plate and nibbled.

Annie nodded.

Sue Ellen smiled brightly. "Great."

Annie gave her friend a cautious look. "Whatta ya want?" She did a comical imitation of Sue Ellen's New York accent.

Sue Ellen pretended not to hear the question and answered with one of her own. "Hard shift?"

Annie shrugged. "Actually the casualties have slowed."

Sue Ellen nodded. "The V.C. are taking a break. Unfortunately, they don't seem to require long breaks."

"I keep worrying about how it's going to be when Tet rolls around. If it's anything like last February, the V.C. are going to ring in their New Year with more than fireworks." A little shiver crept up Annie's spine.

"I don't think it's going to be bad this year," Sue Ellen said philosophically. "With Nixon coming in, it's a whole new ball game."

"Don't tell me you think Nixon's going to win us the World Series out here?" Annie asked facetiously. "Kennedy wanted to end the war and couldn't. Neither could Johnson. And of all people, Nixon's not going to want to be remembered in history for being the president that lost us the war."

Sue Ellen eyed the rest of Annie's hamburger. "You gonna finish that?"

Annie pushed the plate across the table. "Doesn't the Red Cross feed you?"

"I'm nervous. I always eat when I'm nervous." She gave Annie a broad grin. "Good thing I don't get nervous too often or I'd be busting the seams of my uniform."

"You going into the field?" Annie knew that Sue Ellen wasn't crazy about her Red Cross uniform and only wore it when absolutely necessary. Which boiled down to field missions. Being in uniform was not only the rule when the Red Cross girls visited field units, but like so many things in Nam, there was also the superstitious aspect. Sue Ellen had told Annie that shortly after she had arrived in Nam, word traveled around that a small group of Kool-Aid kids had been sent out into the field to a unit at a fire-base. They were dropped off at an LZ—a landing zone—in a helicopter, only to discover that the unit they were supposed to be visiting had moved out. The helicopter pilot had taken off, thinking that the girls were going to be picked up by Jeep. So there they were, stranded in the middle of a field with no means of communication. Only luck and those recognizable blue uniforms had saved them. An Air Force plane flying overhead spotted them, immediately recognized the light blue uniforms and called in for a pick-up.

Sue Ellen finished Annie's hamburger before answering. "Me and Janice are heading out to My Tho. Show time at thirteen hundred. Wanna come on the run? We're gonna play some games and sing a few songs for the boys in the boonies. We'll be back by nightfall. Plenty of time for you to get your beauty sleep.''

"Uh-uh. And stop looking at me like that.''

"Like what, Scarlett?''

"No way.''

"No sweat,'' Sue Ellen said with airy nonchalance.

"Fine,'' Annie said firmly.

"Hey, I got a letter from Hawk yesterday. Wanna read it?''

Annie gave Sue Ellen a cautious look. "The whole letter?'' Sometimes Sue Ellen read her little excerpts from Hawk's letters, but she always kept certain parts—the best parts—private.

"Why not?''

Annie remained suspicious. "Okay. Sure, I'd like to read it.''

Sue Ellen grinned. "It's kinda . . . sexy, Scarlett. Think you can handle it?''

Annie stuck out her tongue.

"Okay, okay. I tell you what. I've got the letter packed in with my gear. Walk me over to the landing field and I'll show it to you.''

Annie smiled ruefully. "I knew there'd be a catch.''

"A catch? What catch?''

"You're not high-jacking me to My Tho for some of your fun and games, Sue Ellen. Anyway, it's against the rules for me to go off with you guys.''

"Give me a break, Annie. Everyone bends the rules a little now and then. Anyway, think of all the happiness you'll bring to those poor, lonely boys out in the field.''

"Oh no. You can't pull that one again. You take care of the poor, lonely boys out there. I'll take care of the ones here.''

Sue Ellen stuck the last of Annie's French fries in her mouth and rose from the table. "Okay, have it your own way. Actually, I probably should let Captain Loverboy have a look at that letter from Hawk, first. There's some stuff about him in it and he might feel a little funny about you reading it."

Annie narrowed her gaze at Sue Ellen. "What stuff?"

Sue Ellen smiled. "Wouldn't you like to know?"

Annie crossed her arms over her chest. "Well, David's on maneuvers so you won't be able to show the letter to him for a while."

Sue Ellen's smile deepened. "Well now, Scarlett, didn't I mention that Captain Loverboy and his merry band of outlaws happen to be in My Tho paying a call on the same unit we're going out to program? Of course, they're not putting on the same kind of show, but . . ."

"You're lying, Sue Ellen. You couldn't possibly know for certain where David and his unit were sent. All of their operations are top secret."

Sue Ellen batted her eyes. "Well now, that's true. But you know that sweet kid from David's platoon who I've gotten chummy with, the one who's a real whiz at gin rummy?"

"He told you?"

"No, of course he didn't outright tell me. He could be court-martialed for that." Sue Ellen slid back into her seat and leaned across the table. "He just happened to be around the rec center last week when I was working on the songs for this unit, and he kinda smiled and asked if I were planning to do any tunes by Simon and Garfunkel for the show; that he'd sure like to hear a medley of their hits."

Annie wasn't convinced. "If David's unit has been sent to My Tho, it means that LZ could get hot. Your people wouldn't risk sending you out to a potential hot spot."

Sue Ellen shrugged. "No, of course not. So, the unit at My Tho is probably going to be pulled out soon. And David and his boys are probably out there to make sure the move goes well. And we're being sent out to give them all a walloping send-off." She dipped her pinky finger in the dollop of ketchup, which was all that remained on

Annie's plate, and made a question mark with it. Then, slowly, slyly, she lifted her dark eyes from the plate and met Annie's gaze. "Of course, I'm only puttin' two and two together, and, like I always say, I'm lousy at addition. Whatta ya think?"

Annie laughed. "I think I'll read that letter of Hawk's on the flight over."

Sue Ellen smiled sweetly. "And go over some sheet music. I already assigned you that Simon and Garfunkel medley. You've got such a pretty voice, Scarlett. Those boys are gonna be tickled pink."

11 November
Dear Sue Ellen,

Crazy as it sounds, if I had two good legs I'd re-up to-morrow and hightail it right back to that hellhole we so fondly call Nam just so I could grab hold of you and never let you go. Tell me, can a guy say he misses a gal he's never laid eyes on? I miss you, sugar pie. I feel like we've gone through a lifetime together. A no-account Rebel and his Yankee lady. My beautiful, sexy, funny Yankee lady.

I'm real sorry if I bummed you out in my last letter, sugar. I know you're right about my having to fight even harder now than I did in Nam. I do feel like there's more at stake now. Maybe that's why I get down. I want it all now, sugar. I want a future. Before you came riding into my life on a postage stamp, all I ever thought about was the here and now. Live for the day. That was my golden rule. No ties, no plans, no big hopes and dreams. Just go with the flow.

Not anymore. You changed all that. And I've got to tell you, sugar, I've never been so scared. I sure wish your momma would stop sending you those recipes and that you'd stop getting love letters from that bozo, Vinnie. I know you don't encourage him, sugar, but I'm as jealous as a momma hen. And speaking of mommas, I keep fret-ting over how your momma and poppa are going to feel about their Italian Yankee princess having the hots for a poor, crippled Southern boy? And, worse still, hearing that that busted-up Rebel's got the hots for their little girl?

Speaking of family, my dad showed up the other day. He was reeking of cheap booze (do you think maybe I'm a snob and wouldn't feel so disgusted if he could afford to down good whiskey instead of the rot-gut stuff he guzzles?) Anyway, I pretended I didn't even notice. He was telling me how he's got this chance of a job down in Atlanta and he and my mom might be pulling up stakes. He shuffled his feet, wondering if, when I did get released from the V.A., was I planning to move back home with them. I told him no way and gave him my blessing. Even if I'd come back from Nam paralyzed from the neck down—hell, from the brain down—I wouldn't have gone home.

I know sometimes I sing the blues about never getting my act together, but you'll be pleased to know, sugar, I just enrolled myself in a special program at the V.A. that teaches us wheelies to do everything from cooking to car repair right from the comfort of our chairs. Okay, okay, what would your Hawk be without a touch of cynicism?

So, what else is happening, sugar? You've got to update me on the David and Annie saga. What's with those two? What do you think is holding up the works? Okay, I admit, I didn't buy this little love story at first. I mean, I've known them both practically all my life. Sure, there was a time I was damn sure David had a crush on Annie. I teased him mercilessly but he never admitted it. And Turner wouldn't buy it. He couldn't imagine his good buddy, David, having any interest in his pesky little sister. As for Annie, there were times when her crush on Davie boy was so obvious I'd lay odds everyone in Beaumont felt the vibes she was sending out. Everyone but David. From what you say, he's feeling the vibes now and so is she. But I tell you what I think. Annie's too inexperienced to make the push, and Davie-boy's had too much experience to make it. I believe what David's gone and done is put our favorite Southern belle on a pedestal. You've only got to read his letters to know he worships her.

Well, to my way of thinking, sugar, worship's all well and good between a man and his God. But when it comes to relations between a man and his woman, I say you've got to unclasp your hands from prayer and get down to the meat and potatoes of the matter! Romantic as all get-out, ain't I?

I confess, I really am a romantic, sugar. I've even taken to waxing poetic about my feelings for you. I even keep a little journal and every now and then I find myself composing honest to goodness love sonnets to my exquisite, sexy Yankee lady. I have even more mysteries about myself to reveal. And if real life doesn't get in our way, I will reveal them all to you. So good night, sugar pie, and whatever you do, don't let the bed bugs bite.

Crazy over you.
Hawk

The chopper kicked up whirlpools of dust as it landed in My Tho. A jeep took Annie, Sue Ellen, her co-worker, Janice, and their supplies to the fire-base three miles inland. The first thing the women did when they arrived was to hand out comfort kits to the men in the unit. There was a comb, a razor, a toothbrush, toothpaste and soap in each box. Then they got one of the grunts, an eighteen-year-old kid with love beads and wire-rimmed glasses whose name was William, to help them lug the five-gallon carton of chocolate ice cream they'd brought along.

Annie didn't see any familiar faces as they were led into the mess tent. About twenty-five men followed them inside. The long tables had been moved against the walls, and the benches were lined up in rows. Moving in single-file order, the men moved into their seats.

"I don't see David. And I don't see anyone from his unit," Annie muttered as Sue Ellen tuned her guitar.

"Relax. They'll be here."

Janice, a small plump Californian, gave Sue Ellen a nervous look. She'd only been in-country for a few weeks and this was her first field run. "You sure we're not going to be attacked or anything?"

Sue Ellen grinned. "By these sweet young boys?"

Janice flushed. "By rockets, mortars. By the enemy."

"Nah. Relax. That only happens at the perimeter. We're close, but not that close. Anyway, they usually don't hit until after dark."

Janice didn't look reassured by Sue Ellen's cavalier response. She sidled over to Annie. "Aren't you nervous?"

Annie smiled. "Of course I'm nervous. I've never sung in front of an audience before. Simon and Garfunkel yet."

"No. No, I mean, well, you hear all kinds of stories about...attacks. Enemy attacks," she hastened to add, not wanting Annie to misinterpret her concerns.

Annie's eyes registered sympathy. "This is a quiet time. Casualty count is way down in general. And My Tho isn't considered a hot LZ. We don't have to worry about any strikes. We'll play a few games to loosen the boys up, eat some ice cream, sing a few songs and be on our way. Don't be scared."

Janice relaxed a little as Sue Ellen sent her out into the audience with rubber bands, paper and magic markers. The men were enthusiastic. They'd do almost anything for the chance to spend a couple of hours with attractive young women. It felt a little like home; made the men feel connected again to their sweethearts, their wives, their sisters, even their moms. And for a while they could forget their troubles, forget about the next big push, laugh, play games and get a bit of relief from the war.

Soon, the men were laughing and teasing each other while Annie, Sue Ellen and Janice cheered them all on.

David and three men from his unit walked into the mess tent just as one guy was leaping up from the bench shouting out, "I won. I did it."

Annie was a couple of feet away from the victorious GI who swooped her up in his arms and gave her an enthusiastic twirl.

Flushed and laughing, Annie's eyes made contact with David's. His complexion was rather ruddy, but he wasn't smiling. Nor did he maintain eye contact with her for more than a few seconds, after which he spun around and walked out of the tent.

Annie rushed out after him. He was waiting for her.

She grinned. "Don't tell me you're jealous, Nickel."

He flashed her a look of angry impatience. "What are you doing out here?"

"Having a little fun," Annie retorted irritably. "Cheering up the boys."

"The fun's over, Annie. You ladies are sitting on a land mine."

Annie tensed. "My Tho's expecting company?"

David didn't have to answer. His dark expression did it for him.

"But...then why would the Red Cross send Sue Ellen and Janice out here?" Annie frowned.

He took her arm and led her farther away from the mess tent. "The right hand never knows what the left hand's doing. I wasn't sent to My Tho for fun and games."

"We figured the unit was moving out and you were here to..."

"You knew I was here?"

"No. No, not for a fact." She closed her eyes. "Sue Ellen just...fit a few pieces of information together.... She wasn't sure."

"But if you guys were smart enough to guess I was here you had to be smart enough to figure out this LZ was going to get hot."

"No. No, I told you. We figured they were preparing for a push to some region you guys had already mapped out."

His scowl registered frustration and fury. "You figured wrong. And another thing—I could get that silver bar ripped off you for being out here with those two."

Annie stared at David in disbelief. "You're going to report me? Why don't you just court-martial me on the spot, Captain. Throw me in the brig..."

"I'll tell you where I'll throw you. On the first chopper I can commandeer to get you back to Long Binh."

She glanced over her shoulder toward the mess tent as she heard the muted sound of music from Sue Ellen's guitar. Turning back to face David, she gave him a pleading look. "We can be done in thirty minutes tops. If it's going to get hot, it won't be till tonight...."

"No."

"Come on, David. We might be the last breath of fresh air these boys see in a long time." A cold shiver shot through her. "For some, it could be their last breath...altogether."

"Look Annie, there's a V.C. infrastructure—a cadre— in the area. We've got a helicopter team standing by at the airstrip. The minute the mortar hits, they take off and fly around until they spot the next mortar flash. Then they dive in and blow the..."

"I get the picture. What happens to the others? To...you?"

"We do our best not to get caught in the cross fire."

Annie began to tremble.

He took pity on her and smiled. "We've got a well-fortified TOC here."

"TOC?"

"Tactical Operations Center," David decoded. "The bunker is dug deep into the hill. Sandbags, rafter, the works. The rest of the unit will sit it out there."

"And you?" Annie persisted, knowing David was not the type to sit anything out, for all his hatred of the war, for all the confusion and doubt flowing through him. Even now, she could almost feel the rise of adrenaline in him. His anticipation was palpable.

Immediately David's expression hardened. "My activities are top secret, Annie. I've already told you more than I should."

She shoved him in the chest, hard. "You haven't told me anything. You haven't told me anything at all."

"What I'm telling you is that you're packing up your fun and games and I'm having you flown out. Now, Annie."

She glared at him as he stormed past her and headed for the mess tent to round up Sue Ellen and Janice. Two minutes later, he came back out with the women in tow. Janice was white with panic, but Sue Ellen was her usual cool, take-it-all-in-stride self. As she approached Annie, she gave her an apologetic smile. "Looks like we didn't add right, after all," she muttered.

"I'm not going," Annie said defiantly.

David merely shrugged off her remark, grabbing her arm. "I've got a man calling for a chopper. We'll have you on it within ten minutes."

Annie broke free of his grasp, motioning with her head toward Sue Ellen and Janice. "Put them on it. I'm on swing shift. I don't go back on duty until eight tomorrow morning. I'll stay here for the night."

David looked at her as if she'd gone crazy. "Haven't you heard a word I've told you?"

"I've heard every word. There could be casualties here."

"We've got medics..."

"Medics aren't immune to mortar fire. I'll set up a temporary ER in the...the TOC...and fly back in a medevac copter with the injured in the morning."

"No. No way," David said as one of the men from his unit came running up to them.

The soldier saluted quickly. "I've got a chopper ready to go, Captain. You want me to escort the ladies?"

"Yes. All three of them," David said firmly, giving Annie an ominous look.

She matched the glaring intensity of his stare, but when he turned to go, panic and worry for him overrode her anger. She ran after him and touched his arm.

He stopped. She could see his back heave as he took a deep breath.

"Please," she whispered. "Be careful." She saw a flash of tenderness in his eyes.

"Okay, Ross," David barked at the soldier. "Get moving."

Annie swallowed hard as David started walking off. Sue Ellen put a comforting arm around her shoulder. "Come on, Annie. David will be okay. He's an ace specialist. He's made it through the toughest spots without a scratch."

Annie let herself be coaxed along. As she walked toward the heliport she kept thinking that her last moments with David could have been that angry exchange, her last sight of him his ramrod-stiff back. She had no right to argue with him right before he had to face combat. And the last thing he needed was to be worrying about her, on top of everything else. At least she'd been able to prevent that. Meanwhile all she could do was pray.

Yea, though I walk through the Valley of the shadow of Death, I shall fear no evil...

ANNIE, STILL DRESSED in her fatigues, was lying on her cot in her dark hooch when Jessie came in. It was close to 11 p.m.

"Are you awake?" Jessie asked softly.

Annie didn't answer.

"Can I put on a light?"

"No."

"Are you okay?" Jessie asked, threading her way in the dark to Annie's cot.

"I'm tired," Annie said in a flattened voice.

Jessie hesitated. "I saw Sue Ellen. I heard about what happened this afternoon at My Tho."

Annie glanced over at the illuminated dial of her alarm clock. "Well, it's prime time. The V.C. will start hitting them soon. Probably go on right till dawn. A nonstop barrage of incoming. When I close my eyes I can see the choppers in the air scouting out the mortar flashes. I can smell the cordite stench of war...."

Jessie sat cross-legged on the floor beside the cot.

"It's going to be a long night, Annie. Why don't we get through it together?"

There was such tenderness and compassion in the older woman's voice that Annie turned and threw her arms around Jessie's neck and broke down, agonizing sobs erupting from her.

Jessie hugged Annie, rocking her gently, patting her back, smoothing her hair away from her face. "That's it, baby. Cry it out. Just cry it out."

"Oh Jessie...I'm so...scared," Annie gasped between sobs.

"I know. That's the worst part."

"He...he was so...angry. So...cold. Sometimes I think...I don't know David...at all."

Jessie unwrapped Annie's arms from her neck and clasped her hands firmly. "You know him better than you think."

Annie stopped crying. "What do you mean?"

"He knew, and you knew, that if you'd seen the slightest sign of his weakening, you'd never have gotten on that chopper. He was trying to save your life, Annie. As long as you're okay, he believes he can make it. You must know that. He had to get you out of there, not only for your safety but for his."

"Do you really believe that?" Annie asked.

Jessie cupped Annie's chin. "Certainly, but what's more important, right now, is that you believe it."

Annie let her head rest against Jessie's shoulder. "I believe it."

"Good girl."

"Did you mean what you said? About staying with me tonight?"

"If you want me," Jessie answered, a hint of a question in her voice.

Annie lifted her head. "I was very angry at you, Jessie. Because you're sending Luong away."

The reporter smiled. "I know."

"I thought it was wrong of you to separate Luong and Tai. I guess I…identify with Tai. Luong's his lifeline just like…David's mine."

"Tai's stronger than you think, Annie. And so are you."

"David's a part of me. I love him. I don't know if that means I'm in love with him. I can't sort that part of it out. And David isn't much help in that department." She hesitated, then went on. "Our relationship is…strictly platonic. We've never slept together. We've never even really fooled around."

Jessie was smiling. "I know."

"Is it that obvious?"

Jessie gave Annie a little hug. "Only to an ace reporter."

"Jessie?"

"Yeah?"

"You're experienced. And smart. So tell me, how does a gal get off a pedestal?"

ANNIE WAS SHAKEN from a deep sleep by Carol, one of the other nurses from her section. "A call just came in from the hospital. They want us to hustle to the pad, Annie. A dust-off's in with a dozen casualties."

"What time is it?" Annie mumbled.

"It's 5:00 a.m."

Annie groaned, but rolled over and threw off her covers. She'd only been asleep for about two hours. It had been good to talk with Jessie, and it had eventually helped her to get tired enough to drift off.

Carol made sure Annie was on her feet before heading for the door. "There's a jeep waiting outside for us."

"I'll be there in two minutes," Annie said, pulling off her nightgown. Carol was halfway out the door before Annie asked groggily, "Where are the casualties from?"

"My Tho. There was a big ground attack."

My Tho. The words cut through Annie like daggers. And she felt a terror so profound she had to fight to keep from sinking to her knees right there on the spot.

Chapter Ten

A time to kill, and a time to heal...

Long Binh, late December, 1968

Annie and the rest of the triage team got to the heliport just as the medevac copter crew was unloading the casualties. Annie rushed over to the first stretcher and let out a little gasp.

It was William, the boy with the love beads and wire-rimmed glasses, the one who'd helped them with the ice cream at My Tho less than twenty-four hours ago.

His eyes were closed, the glasses gone, the love beads still around his neck. It didn't look like he was breathing and Annie moved into action. Within a few seconds, a barely audible sound escaped his lips. Annie quickly motioned to two corpsmen. "Belly wound. Move him. Fast."

Each time Annie approached a stretcher, she was terrified she would see David lying there. Each time it wasn't him she breathed a guilty sigh of relief.

She was almost through the line of stretchers, working hard to revive a young boy with strawberry-blond hair and the face of a cherub, when she saw David out of the corner of her eye. He was lying on the last stretcher in the line. One of the other triage nurses was working on him.

Annie felt her whole body quake, but she forced her attention back to trying to save the life of her patient. Only after she got a pulse from the boy and the medics came over to take him in, was she able to race over to David. Two corpsmen were just about to lift his stretcher into the ambulance. David was as still as death. "How is he?" Annie asked, unable to mask the panic in her voice.

"Not too bad. Head wound. We're taking him to X-ray."

Annie breathed a little easier. The worst cases didn't go to X-ray. They were so acute they had to go straight to OR for surgery.

"I'll ride in with him," Annie said, hopping into the ambulance. The corpsmen shrugged.

Annie rested her hand lightly on David's arm as the ambulance made its way to the hospital. She stared down at him, crying inside, whispering her prayers and her thanks to God that David was alive.

Once they reached the hospital, Annie had to head straight for the OR to assist in surgery. She hated leaving David, but she had no choice. Her orders were to go where she was most needed, and there was nothing she could do to help David.

Four hours later Annie finally got her first breather. Still in her scrub gear, she made a beeline over to X-ray to check on David's condition and find out where they'd sent him.

One of the corpsmen glanced over David's chart. "Oh yeah, Captain Nichols. Saw him a few hours ago. He came to, just before we started snapping pictures. A possible concussion, a couple of fractured ribs and a busted wrist. Piece of cake. You a friend of his?"

"Why?"

"Just thought I'd warn you that he's in a pretty foul mood. Demanded an instant update on every single one of his men. Wanted a body count then and there. Wanted to go see the survivors himself. We ended up having to restrain him to keep him down enough to tape him up."

Annie smiled sadly. "That sounds like David."

The corpsman grinned. "He's on Ward C—head injuries." Maybe he's calmed down enough by now that he won't bite your head off for visiting."

"Thanks."

When Annie found David, he was staring up at the ceiling, his right arm in a plaster cast from his hand up past his elbow. He didn't shift his gaze until she came up beside him and took hold of his uninjured hand.

"How do you feel?" she asked softly.

"I guess I feel lucky." His eyes were a little glazed, probably from shock. "Shouldn't I feel lucky, Annie? I mean...I'm alive and kicking. More than I can say for some of my boys. We lost a couple. Did you know that?" He didn't even register her nod. "And I can't get much in the way of a status report on the others in my unit. Nobody around here will tell me anything."

"We're hoping all the others will pull through," Annie said, trying to ease David's sorrow.

"Thank you, Nurse," he said with a patronizing drawl, extracting his hand from her grasp. "You've memorized that so nicely."

"David..."

"Don't play nurse with me, Annie. Give it to me straight," he demanded sharply.

"I am giving it to you straight, David. Even the worst hit made it through surgery. Some of them are bad, but they're still alive. We're doing everything we can to keep them that way."

He flinched as she smoothed his hair from his brow.

"Can I get you anything?"

His mouth twitched. "Save it for the ones who need it, Annie."

"Come off it, David..."

A humorless smile curved his face. "Watch it, Nurse. You're losing your professional edge."

She was glad David couldn't see just how much of a professional edge she had at this point. In the past few months she'd been forced to cope with plenty of men who were tormented by rage, helplessness, fear and, with the lucky ones, guilt. Guilt just for being alive. Guilt, for not suffering any life-threatening or permanent injury like their unlucky buddies. The irony was the lucky ones got patched up so they could be sent back out to the field to put their lives on the line once again. It was hard for Annie to see them as lucky. Luck lasted only so long.

"I won't stay long. We both need rest, David," Annie said firmly. "But before I go, I'm going to fix you a shot..."

"No."

"I wasn't asking, Captain. Your doctor ordered antibiotics, and I told the nurse on duty I'd see you got it." She strode off to prepare the medication and was back a minute later.

David gazed hostilely at her. "Why don't you just leave me alone and look after the guys who need your TLC?"

"The quicker you cooperate, the quicker I'll be able to do just that. Now do you want this shot in your arm or..."

He extended his good arm, giving Annie a resigned but unhappy scowl.

She grinned. "Too bad, Nickel. You could use a good, swift shot in the butt right about now."

David's scowl deepened. "Quick with the quips even under fire."

"It's not as easy to do as you think." There was no joking in her eyes or her tone, now. "I'll see you." She hesitated. "You can give me hell for it later, Nickel, but I've never been so glad in my life to be arguing with you as I am right now."

She had turned to leave when, suddenly, David made a grab for her hand.

They met each other's gaze as his grip on her hand tightened. They were only a foot apart, but Annie knew it was going to be a hard distance for either of them to cross.

Finally, still clutching her hand, he smiled ruefully and shook his head. "I'm sorry, Annie, for giving you a hard time. None of it's your fault." His voice was tinged with regret, sorrow and exhaustion.

Annie leaned closer, brushing her lips against his cheek. "Goes with the territory, soldier."

Slowly, slowly, she saw him smile, a faint semblance of his old, familiar smile. He threaded his fingers through hers and closed his eyes.

"Let me hold on," he whispered, "just for a minute."

"Hold on for as long as you like," Annie whispered back, tears rolling down her cheeks.

DAVID WAS RELEASED from the hospital a week later, but he was remanded to the base until his cast came off, which meant that he'd be at Long Binh through Christmas and the New Year. He spent a good part of each day visiting the injured men from his unit. A couple of them were going to be shipped Stateside because of the severity of their wounds, but the others would be back in the field with him.

Annie was thrilled by how well David's physical recuperation was going, but she worried about his emotional health. Even though he was cheerful, supportive and upbeat when he visited his boys in the hospital, the rest of the time he was short-tempered, embittered and withdrawn. Sometimes Annie was able to pull him out of his bleak mood, but other times he was unreachable.

One morning, when she was coming off duty, she spotted David heading out of one of the wards.

"Hey, wait up," she called out. He slowed, but she still had to run to catch up with him.

"Where are you going?" she asked.

David shrugged. "Officers' Club for a beer." They headed out of the hospital together.

"Isn't it kind of early?"

"Savior, nursemaid and momma-san all rolled into one." His voice cracked with contempt.

Annie grinned, undaunted. "Your bark's worse than your bite, Nickel."

He smiled begrudgingly. "Don't be so sure. One of these days I might prove you wrong."

"Is that a threat or a promise, Captain?"

"You never let up, do you?"

"No," she admitted. "Never."

"Want a beer?"

"No. But I'll watch you drink one. Unless you'd rather..."

He gave her a quick glance. "Rather what?"

A little laugh escaped her lips. "Unless you'd rather go over to the rec center and help plan the Christmas party for the kids from the orphanage."

"Oh."

"What did you think I was going to suggest?"

"Nothing." His eyes narrowed and he came to an abrupt stop. He stared at her for several moments without speaking.

Annie met his dark gaze but she couldn't tell what was going through his mind. She knew Sue Ellen had shown him her letter from Hawk, but David had never said a word about the part of the letter concerning the two of them. Did David have her stuck on a pedestal as Hawk had written? Did she seem as untouchable to him as he was unreachable to her? Was he waiting for her to make the first move? Was David too experienced, as Hawk had put it, to make a move on her? Did he even want to?

David's gaze slipped away from Annie's. Relief played on his face.

"Hey look," he said, motioning behind her. "It's Jessie. She must have finished up her story down in the Mekong Delta."

Just as Annie turned round to wave, Jessie reached them. She hugged Annie affectionately and then gave David a bright smile. "Well, well, well, Nichols, when did you get sprung from the hospital?"

"A few days ago. How are things down south?"

"Ugly. Very ugly. But our boys in Washington are happy. We're cleaning out the front-held regions, bombing villages, defoliating crops, forcing the farmers and the peasants to evacuate. In a few months the generals and the politicians figure we'll be able to lay claim to a vast wasteland. Ain't that good news?"

David muttered a few obscenities under his breath.

"Where are you two off to?" Jessie asked.

They both answered at the same time, Annie saying "To the rec center" and David barking "For a beer."

Jessie sighed. "A beer sounds good, David, but I guess the rec center wins. I'm just about to send off my pieces on you and your cohorts, Annie, but I need to check a couple of points with you."

"I thought you'd put that article on hold," Annie said.

"No. I was just juggling it with a few other pieces. But it's looking good."

"Can I read it?" Annie asked with a mix of anxiety and anticipation. Jessie had been very secretive about the article. Annie had no idea about the content or even the focus of the piece.

"Sure," Jessie said breezily. "As soon as *Life* prints it."

David looked impressed. "*Life?* Wow. Annie really is going to be a national celebrity. Don't I get a sneak preview?"

"No way," Jessie said. "You know I don't play favorites." As soon as the words came out, she cast Annie an apologetic look. "I guess that's not always true."

Annie knew immediately that Jessie was referring to her special efforts on Luong's behalf. Jessie had lost her heart to the older boy in much the same way as Annie had lost hers to Tai.

Annie had been spending all of her free time with Tai. Not only had she visited him at the orphanage, but on a couple of occasions she'd taken him into Saigon for the day. The small boy remained withdrawn and uncommunicative for the most part, but a few times Annie had actually managed to get Tai to smile. And, miracle of miracles, the last time she'd been to see him he'd actually whispered her name.

"How are you coming along with that boarding school for Luong?" Annie asked, her tone sympathetic. She was no longer angry at Jessie about trying to help Luong. Because of the cramped quarters and the lack of funding, the nuns had been forced to set an age limit for the children they sheltered. The cut-off age was thirteen and Luong would turn thirteen in May. Not only would he have to leave the orphanage at that point, but he'd very likely be scooped up by the South Vietnamese draft and put in an ARVN uniform as soon as he hit the street. It was yet another of the hard, cruel facts of the Vietnam war. Childhood here in Nam was very brief. And, all too often, so was manhood.

Jessie dug her hands into her pockets. "Every time I think I have the whole deal set for Luong, I get a faceful of red tape thrown at me."

"Hey, better red tape than a grenade," David muttered.

Both Jessie and Annie gave him a sharp look of surprise.

David merely scowled and strode off for the Officers' Club.

"Is he always a bear this time of the morning?" Jessie quipped as she and Annie headed in the direction of the rec center. "Even I wait until noon to start gulping down the brew."

"He's worried about his boys. He's had it with the war. He feels helpless. He's angry, frustrated, bitter. . . ." Annie sighed.

"He's lucky he has you."

"I doubt he feels that way. Sometimes...I think I'm making it even harder on him. He resents me. Somehow, he's gotten it into his head that I've got it all together, even though I tell him I'm scared and angry all the time, too."

"David could use a good cry," Jessie said.

"Ha! David cry? No way. He has a thing about shedding tears." Annie picked up her pace. "He keeps telling me I'm tough, but he's the one with the iron will. He's getting so brittle, though. If he doesn't give a little, I'm afraid he's going to shatter into a million pieces."

Jessie put a maternal arm around Annie's shoulder. "You want some advice from an old lady?"

"You're not so old." Annie smiled affectionately.

"David's on hold here until that cast comes off, right?" Annie nodded.

"I think you could both use a little R&R. Why don't you wangle yourself a three-day pass and ask David to take you to Vung Tau? It's relatively safe, there are beautiful beaches, lush greenery. Think about sitting on the sand, watching the tide roll in, toasting the New Year...."

"I doubt David would go. With me, anyway."

"Ask him."

Annie hesitated. "You mean, I should make the first move."

Jessie grinned. "Gals are doing it all the time these days. You want to keep up with the times, don't you, Annie?"

Annie laughed dryly. "In-country you lose touch with the times pretty fast."

Sue Ellen spotted them as soon as they reached the rec center and came racing over, her face flushed with excitement.

"Guess who's coming to Long Binh for Christmas?"

Annie and Jessie both shrugged. "Who?"

"I'll tell you who. Bob Hope, that's who. Isn't that too much?"

"That's great," Annie said enthusiastically, thinking how wonderful it would be for the children from the orphanage as well as the boys on base to see a real professional show. Bob Hope traveled with a polished USO troupe and he always had special guest stars. Singers, dancers, magicians—a real holiday treat.

"What I thought we'd do," Sue Ellen went on, linking arms with both Annie and Jessie, "is plan a special Christmas party that morning for the kids who are coming over from the orphanage. I've spoken to Sister Marie and she says there'll be around forty kids in all. We'll get the boys on base to pitch in. They love getting involved with kids. Of course, we'll have to corral someone into being Santa Claus. We'll give out little gifts, play games, the works. Then lunch. We're gonna decorate the cakes with candy canes..."

"I'll bring Phil in to take pictures," Jessie said, her mind racing. "This is just what I need for my story on the orphanage. It'll be a perfect contrast for my other photos. It's the children who suffer the most in war. That's the message I've got to bring home."

"Yes," Annie reflected sadly. "War is not healthy for children and other living things."

Dear Nanna,

Thanks so much for the Christmas care package. Yes, it came through in good shape. Your fabulous homemade chocolate pecan cookies took a bit of a beating, but they went so fast no one noticed. I loved everything—the silver earrings, the blue silk blouse, the electric blanket. The pink sweater is my favorite and it fits perfectly. Don't pay attention to what David writes you. I am not skinny as a rail.

Speaking of David, I really am worried about him. I can't really talk to anyone here without seeming like I'm sneaking around behind his back. But I've got to talk to someone so you're elected. Every time I try to talk to him he jumps down my throat and tells me to leave him alone. I know he doesn't mean it. I know he needs me just like I need him. When we're together I can tell. But it's still hard to take it when he's angry.

He's not always like that, though. Last week I talked him into coming out to the orphanage with me to visit Tai. David has a terrific knack with kids. And there's something so endearing and poignant about Tai that David can't resist him anymore than I can. We had a wonderful afternoon, the three of us. The best part was that for the first time, Tai didn't put up a fuss about being separated from Luong for the day. He knows it's only a matter of time before Luong leaves and he's taking the fact with typical stoic acceptance. I keep telling him that I'll be around and so will David and Jessie and Sue Ellen. I try not to think of what will happen to him after we're gone. The nuns are doing their best to arrange adoptions for the children, but it's hard to get Stateside families to take in the older ones. And at four, Tai's already considered old. What a strange world we live in.

Nanna, I try to keep my spirits up. For the poor boys in the hospital, for Tai and the other orphans, for David. I keep telling myself they all have it so much worse than I do. I want them to know there's somebody here who cares about them. I wish more people back home knew what it was like here. Maybe if some of Washington's big brass spent a few weeks in-country they'd understand. It's like no war I ever read about in the history books.

I better sign off before my spirits wilt down to my shoes. My new shoes that you sent me. I love them. And I miss you more than ever. . . .Annie.

"No way." David eyed Sue Ellen with grim resolve.

Sue Ellen eyed Annie with a pleading look.

Annie didn't hold out much hope but she gave it her best shot. "Why not, David? You'd make a terrific Santa

Claus. And you know most of the children by name. You can relate to them, put them at ease..."

"What about Phil? He's been out to the orphanage with Jessie a half dozen times taking photos..."

"And that's what he's got to do tomorrow morning at the party," Annie told him.

"Whoever heard of a Santa wearing a cast..."

"Come on, David," Sue Ellen broke in. "Most of these kids have never seen Santa Claus. They're not going to know the difference. And Annie's right. You can rap with these kids. Some of them might get scared if a perfect stranger hauled them onto his lap and started giving them the 'Ho, ho, ho' bit."

David looked like a trapped tiger. "I'm not up for this."

"All the more reason," Annie said, knowing that she was laying herself open for one of David's sharp remarks about her compulsion to tell him what was best for him.

Surprisingly, this time he smiled at her and then at Sue Ellen. "Women," was all he muttered.

Sue Ellen winked at Annie as she gave David a hearty pat on the back and dumped the red and white Santa Claus suit in his arms. "All you need is a pillow and you're set."

"All I need is to have my head examined," David grumbled.

Sue Ellen hurried off before David could change his mind, but Annie lingered at the table in the Officers' Club.

David finished his beer and stared morosely at the costume. "I must be drunker than I feel." He shot her a wry glance. "Now you're supposed to say 'You're drunker than you should be.'"

Annie grinned. "I was going to say, 'How about buying me one, Captain?'"

He closed his eyes for a moment, then opened them and met Annie's gaze. "Why do you put up with me, Annie?"

"I sometimes wonder that, myself," she said in a philosophic tone.

"You really want that beer?"

"I'd really like to ask you something, David." There was a catch in her voice that made David focus on her more closely.

"Okay. Shoot," he said, laughing dryly. "Bad choice of words."

Annie toyed nervously with the ashtray on the table. "I put in for a three-day pass. Jessie was telling me about this quiet town... Vung Tau. It's right on the coast and the weather is pretty mild. Anyway, the pass came through. For New Year's weekend."

"Oh? Well, that's nice, Annie. You could use a little R&R."

Annie fixed her gaze on the ashtray. She didn't dare look at him. "So could you."

David didn't say anything.

Finally Annie continued, feeling awkward and hesitant, "Yeah, I really do want that beer." Slowly, she willed her eyes to meet his.

The guarded look was still there, but his features were less taut. Annie found herself reaching out to take his hand. "You know, David, we can both get through this war without tenderness and laughter, but it's the lonely way to go."

David ordered her beer and got another for himself. When the drinks arrived, he lifted his glass and gently tapped it against hers. Then he leaned closer to her. "I guess I like your way better," he whispered huskily.

Annie felt the tip of David's tongue graze her lips in a light caress. She parted her lips slightly and tasted the bitter piquancy of the beer.

Chapter Eleven

A time to be born, and a time to die . . .

Christmas, Long Binh, 1968

On Christmas Eve Annie and David sat alone in Annie's hooch watching a miracle. A panoramic shot of the lunar surface spread across Annie's TV screen, as the Apollo 8 astronauts William Anders, Frank Borman and James Lovell read from *Genesis*. After that Borman signed off saying, "God bless all of you, all of you on the good earth."

When it was over Annie switched off the TV and stretched out on her cot.

David lit a cigarette. He'd taken up the habit quite recently. "The good earth . . ." He took a long drag and let the smoke drift out of his mouth as he echoed the words.

"I remember when I was a kid, and still believed there was a man in the moon," Annie said dryly. "And now it's true."

David stared at the dark TV screen. "I keep thinking of everyone at home, watching and cheering the astronauts. The space program is something they're all caught up in, something they're all proud of. But what about us?"

Annie was feeling pretty depressed. "I keep thinking about everyone at home celebrating Christmas. Turner and I always decorated the tree together on Christmas Eve, Nanna directing us and Dad directing Nanna. When we were done we'd get our presents out from our hiding places and pile them under the tree and we'd all try to guess what everyone got us.'' She rolled over on her stomach as David shared his reminiscence.

"My favorite part of Christmas was coming over to your place with Hawk on Christmas Day."

Annie stared over at David who was sitting cross-legged on the floor. She said, "We had such good times."

"It seems unreal now," David admitted.

"My dad wrote me that he invited Hawk to come for this Christmas. I hope Hawk accepts. He needs to get out of the hospital for a while. And now that his folks have gone to Atlanta he has nowhere else to go."

"If Hawk had it his way, he'd be out here with Sue Ellen. At least that's what he wrote her."

Annie's breath caught. It was the first time David had mentioned that letter. An uneasy silence captured them both. Finally, Annie broke it. "I think Hawk means it," she said in a low voice. "I really think he's fallen in love with Sue Ellen."

"Pretty crazy way to fall in love, don't you think?"

"What's a sane way?"

He laughed. "I don't know."

"Have you ever been in love?" Annie asked, observing him through the shifting shadows. Whenever David truly felt on the spot his mouth gave him away. It was the only clue to his real feelings in a face otherwise impenetrably composed. It was giving his distress away now.

"I've had my moments," he said in an elusive drawl.

"Yes," Annie said in a whisper, "I suppose you've had plenty of moments."

A small frown cut across his brow. "I never wanted a life of celibacy, kiddo."

"I was talking about love, not sex, Nickel," she said evenly.

"Touché. It's quite true they're not always one and the same. It's also true that, for me, they aren't mutually exclusive."

"Does that mean you have to love every woman you take to bed, or you have to take to bed every woman you love?" Annie's tone was deliberately sardonic.

David grinned. "You are getting better and better at verbal dueling, Annie."

"And you're as good as always about avoiding giving away any incriminating information about yourself."

"Incriminating." He rolled the word over in his mouth. "I suppose you've got a point there. I suppose I do fear that."

"Fear what?"

"Having you see me as . . . less than you might."

"I'm not the one who needs to put someone I care about on a pedestal, David."

He let out a long, low sigh. "That's not it, Annie."

"Then what is it, David? You're attracted to me. I know you are. And you've accepted my invitation to go away with me to Vung Tau. . . ."

"I thought it was understood that we were going there as friends. Strictly platonic. I didn't see this R&R as a heavy-duty romantic tryst, Annie."

"You talk about romance as if it were a dirty word."

He snubbed out his cigarette in the ashtray on the floor and started to rise.

"Let's not dissect our feelings for each other. I want us to stay good friends. The best of friends. I'm crazy about you, Annie, you know that. But I'd make a terrible lover right now. All of my energy is tied up in rage and in figuring out how I'm going to survive. Sometimes I'm scared I'll hold on to you so tight I'll suffocate you. I don't want that to happen. Maybe I'd better go."

"No. Don't." Annie sat up, dangling her legs off the cot. "I didn't mean to put you on the spot." She smiled.

"No more probing questions, I promise." She patted the mattress. "Come, sit down beside me."

He hesitated.

"I won't bite you."

He smiled crookedly. "Is that a promise?"

"I probably wouldn't be very good at it even if I tried," she teased.

He sat down beside her. "I've known you practically all my life, Annie, and yet it feels like I'm just beginning to really see you."

"I'm glad," she whispered, resting her head on his shoulder. After a few moments she began to hum an old Christmas carol.

"That's your grandmother's favorite," David reflected. "I still remember how she used to sit at the piano in your living room and have us all gather round and sing Christmas carols."

"And Hawk kept doing them to a rock beat."

David laughed. "I hope Hawk spends Christmas with your family. I'd like to think of him carrying on our tradition. Turner will be there, too, won't he?"

"Yes," Annie said. "He's bringing a couple of his teammates along."

"Oh," David said with a touch of disappointment, as if he thought Turner was bringing in scab workers. "Well, it'll be lively anyway."

"But it won't be the same," Annie said wistfully, memories of Christmases past blooming in the shadows, sparkling like fireflies.

"No," David agreed sadly. "It won't be the same."

Later that night David and Annie went for a walk. David stared silently up at the moon for a long time. "I wonder," he said, "whether the astronauts up there feel half as isolated as we feel down here."

"SILENT NIGHT, holy night . . ." In thick Vietnamese accents, the orphans sang the Christmas carol. Janice accompanied them on the piano, Sue Ellen on guitar. Meanwhile, in one of the offices, Annie was helping David get into his Santa Claus costume.

"Wait. You need an extra pillow," Annie decided.

"Santa is plump, not obese," David argued.

"Oh, stop being so disgruntled, Nickel. You make a darling Santa Claus." She gave him a little pinch on the behind.

His scowl deepened. "Watch it, kiddo, or this here Santa might just lose his Christmas spirit."

Annie giggled as she stuck another pillow under the red jacket. "There, that's better. Now the beard."

"It's a good thing Hawk and Turner aren't here right now. I'd never live this down. You tell them, kiddo, and your life won't be worth a plugged nickel."

"I'm not the one who can't keep secrets from the boys," Annie quipped.

"Okay, okay. For your information, we didn't always tell each other everything, either. I was just teasing you. I suppose we all have our little secrets."

Annie smiled. "Well, don't worry, Nickel. All your secrets are safe with me."

"I know that." The bantering tone disappeared from his voice. He observed her with gentle eyes. "So I'll tell you another one."

Annie waited expectantly.

"I don't mind playing Santa for those kids out there. They deserve a chance to make a wish."

Annie smiled softly. Embarrassed, David quickly looked away, concentrating on attaching the fluffy white cotton beard. It wasn't an easy task with one arm in a cast.

"Here," Annie said, "let me help."

She moved closer and reached up to his face. A touch of moistness in his dark eyes made them glitter, especially in contrast to the white beard. He looked incredibly appealing. Impulsively she tilted her head up and kissed him full on the lips.

He stared down at her with a lopsided smile.

"Sorry. I've always wanted to kiss Santa Claus," Annie said demurely.

David grinned. "How was it?"

She laughed. "Fluffy."

David's palm glided over the beard. "You're right." He looked down at her, his eyebrows raised, a half smile playing on his lips. Suddenly, he looked up at the ceiling.

"What is it?" Annie asked, puzzled.

"No mistletoe."

Annie looked up, too. In the same instant, David slipped off the beard and sought her lips, pulling her gently to him. The stuffing under his red jacket got in the way and they both giggled, but their mouths clung, swallowing each other's laughter.

When they finally parted, David exhaled deeply, his breath lightly caressing her face. He grinned wryly. "You're getting damn good at that, kiddo."

Her eyes sparkled. "See what a little practice will do."

ANNIE LET THE TEARS slide from her eyes, and David had all he could do not to cry as well, as Tai walked up the aisle on his own two feet and climbed onto Santa's knee.

"Ho, ho, ho." Santa's voice quivered a little, his hos huskier than the ones that had gone before. "And what do you want for Christmas, Tai?"

The solemn little child with the beautiful, beguiling face lifted his eyes to Santa. If he knew it was David, he gave no hint of it. Nor did he answer Santa's question.

Tai looked to be mulling it over and David didn't rush him, despite the impatience of the other orphans to have their turn on Santa's lap.

Annie edged a little closer to the tiny boy. Was this too much for Tai? Was he frightened?

David gave her a reassuring smile. Gently, affectionately, he repeated the question to the boy on his lap. "What would you like Santa to bring you for Christmas, Tai?"

Phil was about to snap a shot, but Jessie, who was standing just a few feet behind Annie, gave the photographer a little shake of the head. Phil lowered the camera.

Tai's eyes shifted from Santa to Annie. Annie smiled encouragingly. Tai studied her smile thoughtfully although his own expression remained solemn throughout.

Annie wondered if he wanted her to rescue him from a situation too perplexing and confusing for him to handle. As the question shot through her mind she took a step forward.

That was when Tai smiled back at her, a smile so touched with ingenuous innocence and spirit it seemed to create an electrical field throughout the large room.

Tai's eyes met Santa's once again. He still wore the smile as he murmured his one-word wish. "Life."

David's mouth sagged, and he, who hadn't cried since he was a small boy, felt his cheeks grow wet. He shot Annie a tortured look.

But Annie was still smiling. She understood. She stepped closer to David and Tai, resting one hand on each of them. "Jessie's told Tai that there's going to be a photo of me and him in next month's *Life* magazine. Along with the two pieces she's done, one on the orphanage and one on women in Nam. I believe, Santa, that Tai would like you to bring him a copy of that magazine."

Tai's dark almond-shaped eyes held an expectant look. The pained expression left David's face. His gaze rested on the fair-haired woman and the dark-haired child. And then he reached out his one good arm and managed to enfold them both. "Life," he whispered. "Yes, life."

It was a most unusual children's Christmas party. Not only did the children receive gifts from Santa, sing

Christmas songs, and play good old-fashioned American parlor games like musical chairs and Simon says, they also got to use flush toilets. Since the plumbing at the orphanage was primitive at best, it took some doing to get them to stop flushing the toilets. They kept pressing the levers and watching in awed fascination as the water whirlpooled and then disappeared. Next came the baths.

Many of the children had never bathed in real tubs before and none of them had ever taken a bubble bath. However, once they got over their apprehension of the bubbly, foamy water—the bubbles courtesy of Nanna who'd sent Annie a dozen bottles of flower-scented bath salts—the children took to the water like ducklings, shouting, laughing, and merrily splashing each other. Everyone had a great time.

Annie had also rounded up a handful of nurses and doctors to give the children checkups. Medical care was no easier to come by at the orphanage than decent plumbing. The medical team gave the nuns what the children needed—from antibiotics to antiseptic ointments—all individually labeled with the appropriate child's name. Of course, it was strictly against the rules to hand out military medical supplies to Vietnamese civilians, but no one at the party was walking around with a rule book.

Once the children were all dressed and cared for, they gathered around long tables in the gym to chow down hot dogs with all the trimmings and glasses of Kool-Aid. Tai sat between Luong and Annie, but today he did not need any coaxing to eat. Dressed in a bright red flannel shirt and real American Levi jeans, Tai bit into his hot dog voraciously just like a typical American kid. Annie grinned as Tai chewed and sipped his Kool-Aid at the same time. He let the straw go and gave her a shy but happy smile. Even those weary sad eyes of his, still oddly serene and indecipherable, seemed fresh and young today. She wiped a drip of mustard off his chin and thrilled to Tai's easy acceptance of her touch. She thought it was the very best Christmas gift she could ever receive.

Several times she caught David watching her from across the table. She wondered if he still felt she was getting too emotionally entangled with Tai. But then she recaptured the image of Tai sitting on Santa's lap earlier and she decided that David was as emotionally entangled with the tot as she was.

When lunch was over, Annie helped the children get seated for the Bob Hope show.

"Are you sure you can't stay?" Sue Ellen asked her.

"No, I'd love to, but I'm going to try to lasso David into coming back to the hospital with me and playing Santa for the boys. It'll give them all a good chuckle."

"Especially the boys from David's unit."

Jessie, who was standing close by, said, "You really think you're going to talk David into making a fool of himself in front of his boys?"

Annie laughed. "It's good medicine to play the fool every once in a while. It gives you a little humility."

"Good point. That argument will win him over all right," Sue Ellen said, grinning. Then she pointed toward her office. "You better hurry. Santa's ducking into the proverbial phone booth and in a couple of minutes he'll be Clark Kent again."

Annie waved goodbye to the children and paused for a moment to promise Tai she'd see him in a few days. When she got to the office, David had already unfastened the black belt from his waist, discarded the two pillows from under his red jacket and was about to step out of his matching red trousers.

"Hey, do you mind?" He pulled the trousers back up quickly, clasping them with his uninjured hand.

"I'd rather you wouldn't," Annie admitted.

"Why not? I've done my good deed. My part's over. My duffel bag's empty, all the gifts are gone."

"I have a refill."

"For the kids?"

"No. For the boys up in the hospital."

David raised his hand and took a defensive step back. His trousers dropped.

"Nice legs," she quipped as she tossed him his wide black patent leather belt.

"No way, Annie. I'd be the laughing stock of Long Binh if I showed up at the hospital dressed like this."

"No you wouldn't. You look . . . adorable."

Using his good hand he struggled to get his trousers back up and temporarily fit the belt around them. He wasn't having an easy time of it but he wasn't about to let Annie help him.

"Come on, David. Those boys deserve a laugh or two."

"Why does it have to be at my expense?" he asked stubbornly.

"Laugh along with them and it won't be."

He groaned.

"Please, David. Must you give me a hard time about everything I want you to do for me?"

He groaned even louder, but this time Annie detected a hint of acquiescence in his groan.

"You're impossible, Annie."

"I know," she said contritely.

"You're crafty. You're a tease. You're . . ."

"Hard to resist?"

He laughed. "It's getting harder all the time." He sang the words as if they were the ones from the Beatles' hit.

Resignedly, David grabbed one of the pillows and stuffed it back up inside his ample red jacket with the fluffy white cotton trim.

Annie's blue eyes sparkled as she watched him. "Well now, aren't we having a merry little Christmas after all?"

Annie had learned long ago that life was utterly unpredictable. Her mother's death had taught her that happiness could change to tragedy in the blink of an eye. But nothing brought that lesson home more sharply or more frequently than Nam. She and Santa walked into the hospital hand in hand, laughing, joking, full of Christmas spirit. Even though David had grumbled about playing Santa for the boys who were laid up, Annie saw that once he had gotten with the "program" he secretly took great pleasure in giving them their laughs. It was Christmas, after all.

The mood in the hospital was up. An American philanthropic organization had donated money to set up phone lines to the States. Nurses were going through the wards asking GIs if they'd like to place a call home. Annie and Santa pitched in.

"Hiya, Dad? Is that you, Dad? It's me. Billy. I'm just calling... Merry Christmas, Dad. I... I love you..."

"Nancy, it's Carl. Yeah, it's really me. Nancy... God, it's so great to hear your voice. I miss you, baby. I'll...be home... soon."

"What do ya say, slugger? Got a big kiss for your big brother? Sure, I'm okay. Is... Mom there?"

There wasn't a dry eye in the place. And for all the physical, spiritual and emotional hurt these boys were suffering, for this brief moment in time, they were *home*. Annie and David felt closer to home, too.

They were about to head to the last ward on the floor, when Annie bumped into a nurse who was rushing over to an emergency in ICU. One of David's boys, Kevin Downy, was still in ICU.

Even before they got there, Annie and David were sure the emergency was Kevin.

Sadly, they were right. The surgeon hadn't thought he'd make it through the first night. But Kevin Downy was a rugged hillbilly kid from Arkansas and he'd clung tenaciously to life. The ICU staff thought it was a miracle that Kevin had survived, and they, like Annie and David, were sustained by their faith in miracles. Now it looked like the miracles were running out.

David, still in his Santa garb, slumped into a chair just outside the swinging doors of the ICU. Annie brought him a cup of coffee but he waved it away. She sat down beside him.

"They're doing everything they can," she said softly.

"He's going to die."

Annie didn't reply.

"He was a great kid." Already David was talking about him in the past tense. "I remember when I first took over the unit. He had the thickest Southern drawl and he talked so fast, none of the Yankees could understand a word he said. I actually had to translate."

David yanked off the white beard, stood up and paced restlessly back and forth, compelled to talk about his dying friend. "He was a real comedian and he told these great stories. And he'd get the funniest mail. He came from a big family, thirteen brothers and sisters, dozens of aunts and uncles. Every one of them wrote him and they were all comedians." His voice choked and he stopped pacing and stopped talking for a few moments.

He slumped down in the chair before he began again. "What always amazed me about old Kev was that he somehow held on to his exuberant innocence even after having seen almost a year of combat."

He glanced over at Annie for a moment. "His DEROS date comes up in three weeks." David reflected bitterly on what those initials stood for—Date Eligible for Rotation from Overseas Service. It was a pretty cold way of talking about freedom. But, of course, eligible didn't guarantee you'd make it. "Kev talked all the time about that flight back home. He always said that everyone in his family believed he'd come back in one piece, and most of them were a lot brighter than him, so he'd take their word for it. That's what he always said."

Annie didn't know what to say. There was nothing she could do for Kevin and there was no way she could ease David's pain. Even though death had been all around

them since they'd been in-country, there were some losses
that broke not only the heart but the soul. When the nurse
came out of the ICU and gave them both a sad shake of
her head, Annie was almost relieved to see David shut his
eyes. The desperate grief reflected in them had been awful.

The worst part for Annie was having to leave David
alone. But her shift was starting and she was expected
back on her ward. Besides, her own feeling of loss galva-
nized her into wanting, more than ever, to give her all to
the boys still struggling to survive.

The impact of all that was wrong and hateful about the
war clutched Annie's heart. She looked down at David in
his Santa Claus suit hunched over in sorrow outside the
ICU in Long Binh. It was a Christmas Day vision that
would be indelibly imprinted in her mind.

She stood rigidly for a moment, staring at him, her
hands clenched. She wanted to console him, to ease his
pain. But no words formed in her mind. And she felt
wretched and powerless, knowing a profound change was
taking place in David. She could almost see him losing a
vital part of himself, severing it with his own will.

He finally lifted his head and met her anxious gaze.
"Go on, Annie. I'm okay," he said. But his eyes were
empty, his voice cold and distant, a disembodied sound
detached from the man himself. And then, before she
made the move to leave, he rose from his chair, brushed
past her and strode out the swinging door marked Exit.

Annie watched until the door came to rest. Then she
turned her back to the exit and started for her ward, her
heart hammering painfully.

She hadn't gone more than a few steps when the nurse
who'd given them the sad news about Kevin came back
out of ICU and called to her.

Annie stopped and turned.

The nurse, a sweet looking brunette named Donna, was
holding a tattered photograph in her hand. She held it out

to Annie. "I thought . . . maybe you or the captain might want to . . . mail this snapshot and a letter back . . ." She didn't finish the sentence.

Annie's hand trembled as she took the photo from Donna. It was a snapshot of Kevin in a tux, dancing with a pretty blond girl in a ruffled strapless gown. They were looking into each other's eyes, smiling at each other, the kind of smile that broadcasts the sharing of a private joke. Love was written all over their faces. A couple of all-American high school sweethearts.

Slowly Annie turned the worn snapshot over. There, written in a bold, confident hand were the words "Kevin and Susie forever, Prom Night, June 3, 1967."

Annie ran her finger across the photo before she pocketed it and Kevin's last letter home. Her eyes met Donna's for a moment. Then Annie headed back for her ward. With each step she took, the words *Kevin and Susie forever* flashed before her eyes.

She willed herself not to cry. She was going off to administer care and comfort to a dozen wounded boys. She couldn't cry. She had to be strong. But still the words echoed in her head; *Kevin and Susie forever* . . .

And then she flashed back to her own prom night, to David whisking her away from her date, leading her out on the dance floor, looking so incredibly handsome and cocky in his tux, the two of them doing the hottest twist ever seen at Beaumont High.

David and Annie forever, Prom Night, June 7, 1964 . . .
"Let's twist again like we did that summer . . ."

Chapter Twelve

A time to love, and a time to hate...

Long Binh, December 30, 1968

For Annie, as the year rolled to an end, there was none of her usual upbeat excitement and anticipation about the start of a new year. The wonders of the world beyond Nam seemed very far away. For the first three-quarters of 1969, she'd still be here, living on nerve ends, trying to cope with the seemingly endless bombings and casualties and trying even harder to cope with her own despair, grief and frustrations.

Growing up, Annie had always looked forward to New Year's Eve, especially to making fervent and occasionally inspiring New Year's resolutions. She'd always given them a lot of thought.

When she was a kid she'd resolved to study harder in school, keep her room clean, and not to pay attention to being teased unmercifully by Turner, Hawk and David.

As an adolescent she'd vowed to stop being boy crazy, to encourage her father to date, and to model herself after Jackie Kennedy who was so cool, so classy, so elegant.

By her late teens, she'd turned her attention to more global and humanitarian concerns. She'd vowed to work for world peace, to lend her support to the civil rights movement, to speak out against the escalating war in

Vietnam and, on a more personal note, to give up her
crush on the elusive, unattainable David Nichols. She did
march in opposition to segregation and the war in Vietnam that year, but she couldn't shake her crush on David.

And as this new year approached, Annie had no resolutions in mind, except to survive the year and hold on to
her sanity. The V.C. had once again stepped up the rocket
attacks on the perimeter of the base and there was a new
rush of casualties coming in from the field. Annie was
working her last shift before her three-day break, but the
hospital was so busy she'd offered to put her time off on
hold. It wasn't only that she didn't want to leave the hospital understaffed, she was no longer looking forward to
her little sojourn with David in Vung Tao. Ever since
Kevin Downy's death, David had spent all of his time
either holed up alone in his hooch or sipping beers alone
at a table at the Officers' Club.

Annie wasn't even sure David was still planning to go
to Vung Tau. And if he did join her, she had the feeling it
would be like spending the three days with a ticking time
bomb. She no longer thought of what it would be like *if*
David blew, but what would happen *when* he blew. One
thing was certain. He would not be alone in feeling the full
impact of that explosion.

As it turned out, Annie didn't have to cancel her leave.
A group of nurses who'd been stationed in Da Nang got
transferred to Long Binh to manage the overflow. Besides, Annie's head nurse, Georgia Nowicki, insisted Annie take the time off.

"You haven't had more than a one-day pass since
you've been here," Georgia said.

"I can take my leave in a few weeks."

"No, Annie. You need a break. Oh, I know you're a
trouper. But we all need a little distance every now and
then. You've still got a fair amount of time to put in. And,

to be perfectly honest, we can't afford to have you cracking up and getting shipped out before your DEROS."

Annie believed that her time for cracking up had come
and gone, but she didn't argue. She understood Georgia's concern, having seen a few nurses suffer break-
downs. It wasn't a pretty sight.

Since the nurses sent over from Da Nang were man-
ning her ward, Annie was temporarily shifted to the POW
ward to finish out her day shift.

Annie's first stint on the POW ward had been the
toughest. She'd been torn by ambivalence. No one liked
working that ward—Annie included. That was why there
was a general rotation, all doctors, nurses and corpsmen
having to put in time there.

As a nurse, her goal was to save lives. But extending
that to saving the lives of the enemy was hard to come to
grips with. One of the corpsmen working with her that
first shift had tried to help by telling her that she was really
doing her country a big service by keeping the POWs
alive. Some of them were high-ranking and could give out
vital information that might well save the lives of
hundreds of GIs. It was one way to think of it, but Annie
discovered after her first stint on that ward, that what
really motivated her was her growing recognition of the
fact that those men labeled *the enemy* were simply hu-
man beings and her patients.

This time, Annie accepted the POW ward duty with
reasonable goodwill. When she got there, she was assigned to a newly admitted POW who'd been brought in
with severe phosphorus burns. An armed GI stood on
guard at the foot of the patient's bed.

After Annie checked the burn victim's vital signs and
got an IV started, she turned to the GI.

"Relax, Soldier. This poor kid's half unconscious and,
believe me, he's not going anywhere." Behind Annie's
professional air of efficiency, she felt a tug at her heart.
The burn victim was so young.

"Is he gonna make it?"

Annie frowned. "It looks bad."

"We got a captain coming over to interrogate him in a couple of hours."

"I don't think this boy's going to be in a position to tell you much."

The GI cursed under his breath.

Annie gave the soldier an understanding nod and then turned her attention back to the POW who was still in his torn and tattered NVA uniform. Carefully, meticulously, she cut off the uniform and began cleaning his wounds. Once or twice he came to briefly and groaned in pain. Annie stared down at him, a rush of sadness enveloping her. He looked a little like Luong, and she guessed this poor kid wasn't much older than her young friend from the orphanage. Maybe he was fourteen or fifteen at the outside. Back in the States a kid his age would just be starting high school, maybe trying out for a letter in track or football, listening to the Beatles and the Rolling Stones on FM radio.

It seemed incomprehensible to Annie that this mere child could have information vital to the safety and well-being of American troops. Incomprehensible, but she knew it was far from impossible. If the boy was bright and had had some education before being drafted, he could well command a position of importance in the NVA. Still, this boy was suffering. And she couldn't keep herself from feeling some of the same concern for him that she felt for her other patients.

The POW regained consciousness and Annie advised the GI guard to call over to Army Intelligence to get someone to speak to the boy on the double. She knew the chances were he wouldn't stay conscious for long and Annie wasn't sure he would ever come around again.

A captain and a translator arrived ten minutes later. The captain brusquely dismissed the GI guard, ignored

Annie and began a very harsh, confrontative interrogation.

Annie was appalled. "Excuse me, Captain, but this patient is very weak. Could you go a little easy—"

"Don't tell me what to do, Lieutenant. Why don't you just go about your business and leave me to mine?"

"I'm sorry, Captain, but this patient *is* my business. His blood pressure is dropping rapidly and he's not going to be of any assistance at all if you continue..."

The captain waved her off, but Annie held her ground. She also took firm but gentle hold of the boy's hand. Despite the stoic expression on his young face, she could feel him trembling. She made eye contact with the boy and whispered to him in a soothing voice. He probably didn't understand what she was saying, but she hoped her tone would convey a message of comfort.

The captain was growing increasingly irritated as the POW remained mute. "We're not going to get anywhere at this rate."

"How about if I ask him the questions, Captain?" Annie suggested, feeling the boy's grip tighten on her hand. She sensed that she was his lifeline and she accepted that responsibility.

"You?" The captain looked from her to the Vietnamese translator. From the look on his face, he clearly didn't like the idea.

"Captain, you better decide fast," Annie said in a low voice.

Reluctantly he agreed to give her a try, and for the next fifteen minutes Annie, prompted by the intelligence officer and aided by the translator, carried out the interrogation, her tone firm but gentle. The translator followed her lead, shifting to a more neutral, soothing tone of voice. The boy answered Annie's questions, and his translated responses seemed to satisfy the captain.

The captain had many more questions he wanted asked, but at the close of fifteen minutes Annie came to an abrupt stop. The boy was fading fast. "That's it," she said quietly.

The captain started to protest, but Annie stopped him with an intractable gaze. "Can't you let him die in peace."

The translator stepped away from the bed. The captain stared at her, but he shut his mouth. Then, without a word, the captain did a formal about-face and marched off, the translator hurrying after him.

Annie stood beside the young boy, still holding his hand, occasionally stroking his brow gently and continuing to whisper words of comfort. While the boy appeared well schooled in not revealing his emotions, and was weak from his injuries, his fear was palpable. Once, when Annie turned to talk to the nurse who'd come to replace her on duty, a cry escaped his lips and his grip tightened on her hand.

"It's okay," she murmured. "I'll stay with you. I won't leave you."

Only after the boy's grip eased in death did Annie realize she was being watched. She let out a small gasp of surprise at seeing David standing just a few feet away.

David stared at her, silent and unmoving, his heavy-lidded eyes veiling his thoughts.

Annie extracted her hand from the dead boy's and gave David a weary, tentative smile. David's unyielding expression remained unchanged. As she approached him, she could see the rigid muscles pronounced along his jaw. In response, a pounding pulse hammered in her throat.

When she was standing directly in front of David, she reached for his arm, wanting to guide him out of the ward so that they could talk. He was like a stone statue, immovable, implacable.

"Come on. Let's get out of here," she coaxed.

He didn't move.

"Please David . . ." Her voice held a pleading note, the strain and tension of the last hours showing on her face.

His gaze flicked down over her. "You really are a saint, aren't you, Annie?" His tone was low and contemptuous.

"David..."

"No. Really, Annie, I've said all along that you were really something, but even I underestimated you. Why, you coo to Charlie just as sweetly as you coo to our boys." He glared at her hand on his arm. "That hand you were just holding so tenderly might have been the hand that held the gun that blew Kevin away. Now that crime is on your hands, Annie..."

"You're talking crazy..." Even as she said the words she regretted them. David was a tinderbox just waiting for her to strike the match.

"I'm crazy?" He laughed sharply. "Oh, yeah, I'm crazy, all right. I'm out in the trenches picking those bastards off, and you're here stroking their faces, whispering sweet nothings in their ears. But I'm the one that's crazy."

"If we're going to argue, let's do it in some place more private." She tightened her grip on David's arm, desperately wanting to get him off the ward, out of the hospital. Several corpsmen and nurses were watching them, as were the bedridden POWs.

"Move your hand, Annie," he said furiously, his eyes wild, dark as night. "I don't want that hand touching me."

Annie was stunned. David really was losing control. "Please..."

"I mean it," he snarled.

Horrified by his fury, Annie dropped her hand and let it fall limply to her side. Her insides twisted.

As he turned and started down the ward, she followed him.

She ended up racing after him through the compound. She wanted to talk to him, to bring him to his senses. When he reached the outside doors that led to his quarters, David came to an abrupt stop and swiveled around to face her. "Stop tagging after me, damn it. You've been tagging after me for years. Just leave me alone. I'm sick and tired of your sweetness, your goodness, your damn cheerleader pep talks."

His words should have routed her, but there was too much history between them for Annie to leave him now. She looked on his furious, trenchant pain as if it were a living, breathing demon separate from the man himself. So when he stormed down the hall and entered his hooch, Annie followed.

He didn't acknowledge her presence when she entered his room and closed the door behind her. Nor did he order her out.

She leaned back against the closed door. David flung open his locker, retrieved a bottle of whiskey from the shelf, took a big swig and then wiped his mouth with the back of his hand. Almost in slow motion he set the bottle back on the shelf of his locker and turned round to face her.

They were no more than eight feet apart. David stared at her, his expression hard and jagged. But in his eyes, Annie saw a vortex of anguish and confusion.

"Don't push me, Annie." His voice had a rough catch in it.

"Don't shut me out," she pleaded.

Her words made him wince. He shut his eyes tightly, his hands pressing against his temples.

Something drove Annie to his side. Maybe she was a little crazy herself. "Don't hold it all in. Talk to me, David. Please..."

When his silence broke, it was an explosive, violent break. Too late, Annie realized she'd pushed him too far. When she tried to step back from him, David grabbed her shoulder with his good arm and pinned her against the locker.

"What do you want from me?" he cried out sharply. And then, not giving her a chance to respond, he closed his mouth over hers, his teeth grinding into her bottom lip for a kiss that was hard and brutal and tasted of whiskey and bitterness.

Pressing her hands against his chest, Annie struggled for release. For a moment, she managed to break away from his lips. "No, David . . ." she sobbed out his name.

The harsh sound of his breathing rasped in her ear. He grabbed her with fierce abandon, a man possessed. Even the cast on his arm couldn't thwart his will. All of his raw grief, despair and fury was driving him on. His face was grim, his body taut as he pressed hard against her, his mouth over hers, his tongue probing deeply. And, as he ravaged her mouth, his hands moved over her hips, hiking up her uniform.

Annie gave up her struggle. She was terrified and she felt powerless to make David stop. And what made it all the more devastating for Annie was the sudden realization of how very much she wanted him. But not like this. Not with this anger and savagery. She wanted David to touch her body with tenderness. She wanted to feel the warmth of his love.

All of her strength drained out of her. Tears ran down her cheeks as he fell with her on the bed. He was on top of her, gripping her wrists. The fierceness in his eyes made her flinch. "What's wrong, Annie? What do you want from me? Surely you know, don't you? You've got all the answers."

"Don't do this . . . David. Don't do this to us."

"I warned you. You should have listened to me." His tone was low and forbidding. His cast made his movements awkward but no less effective as he grabbed a fistful of her hair and forced her mouth against his.

A deep uncontrollable shudder rocked through her whole body. That silent expression of utter despair breached David's wall of rage where words alone had failed. His attack abruptly ceased. His smoldering eyes raked her with a dazed look. And then, as the realization of his monstrous assault took hold of his senses, anguish and shame washed over him.

"Oh my God..." he whispered. "I must be crazy. I must..."

He rolled off her, sinking to his knees on the floor. He dropped his forehead to the mattress, avoiding her eyes.

Annie gently touched his shoulder. She didn't know what to say. She was badly shaken, and yet she knew her own trauma was nothing compared to his.

"How could I do that to you?" He lifted his head and looked at her, devastated. "How could I hurt you, Annie? You're the finest thing in my life. And I almost..." Horrified by his own brutality, he couldn't go on.

"It hurts. Oh Annie, it hurts...so much," David gasped as wracking sobs broke from him. He clung to her as he wept and she stroked his back and wept with him.

Even after the crying came to an end, David stayed on his knees, his head buried in Annie's lap. Gently, she traced the curve of his shoulder with her fingers. Then she threaded her fingers through his thick, dark hair.

When at last he lifted his head and gazed at her tear-streaked face, she could feel a breathtaking connection between them. Wordlessly, David rose and joined her on his bed. He took her hand in his.

"I don't know what's happening to me, Annie," he whispered. "I'm being chewed up inside." He stared down at her hand. "I didn't mean what I said before. I didn't mean any of it. Even as I heard myself talking, a part of me was saying, 'Who is this?'"

Annie pressed her head against his shoulder. "I pushed too hard. I..."

"No," he said firmly, cutting her off. "I need you, Annie. You're my sanctuary. And there I was, trying to destroy everything we had together."

"You could never do that, David. You weren't really striking out at me. I just got in the way."

Their eyes locked. Annie smiled, her lips parted. She leaned toward him, and his mouth found hers once more. This time his kiss was soft and gentle. Annie wrapped her arms around his neck and sighed.

They stretched out against each other on the narrow bed and kissed again. This time Annie pressed willingly against him and their kiss deepened. Afterward, David drew his head back, his eyes moist, his body trembling as he studied Annie's face. "What are we going to do?" he whispered huskily.

For answer, Annie clung tightly to him, her lips soft and yielding, her message clear. But even as she kissed him with mounting ardor, her breasts pressed hard against his chest, she could feel David pulling back.

She gazed at him with unmasked desire. Her face was flushed, her blue eyes luminescent. Her hands moved sinuously along the planes of his torso. But he stopped her hands and stared at her with earnest concern. "Annie...have you ever...?"

She smiled timorously at him. "No, but I don't intend to be able to say that later tonight."

He held her gaze, the strain raw but wildly sweet. With a feather-light touch he traced her bruised lips. "This isn't how it should have been. I would have liked to court you in the sunshine, take you for moonlight strolls, bedazzle you with my tenderness, charm and wit." His tone turned rueful and acerbic. "Instead, I present you with my worst self. I maul you, hurt you..."

She kissed his fingertips and whispered, "Then heal me."

His large hands cupped her face, framing it. "Let's heal each other," he whispered back, a mist clouding his eyes.

A wondrous sensation tingled through her body as she uttered a single word. "Yes."

With great tenderness, he smoothed back her disheveled hair and then began to unhurriedly unbutton her uniform. He was a little awkward using his left hand, but as he drew her shirt down over her shoulders, Annie shivered a little despite the afternoon heat. Her eyes rested on his face, mesmerized by his thick dark lashes framed against his cheeks.

When she was naked against the white sheets, David trembled at the sight of her, unprepared for the impact of her sheer physical beauty. Annie smiled at him without any sign of shyness. Rising to her knees on the bed she removed his shirt, letting her mouth rove across his broad bare chest. He stood up to rid himself of the rest of his clothes, and Annie watched him with open delight, her eyes traveling appreciatively down his body.

"Oh David, you're perfect," she murmured, with sweet, innocent candor.

David grinned with boyish embarrassment and pride. And then as he joined her on the bed, he drew her close. "I've wanted you for such a long time," he confessed. "But I was so scared, Annie. I thought the war had rendered me incapable of loving. The mere thought of it terrified me."

She smiled tremulously. "I'm scared right now. I'm scared I won't be good enough..."

"You'll be terrific, Annie. You're terrific about everything."

With tender abandon, they stretched out together. Annie sighed in pleasure at the feel of David's warm flesh on her own. She closed her eyes and he kissed her eyelids. Then he burrowed his face into her hair, his parted lips next to her ear. Annie's breath quickened in tune with David's, her fingers moving over his battle-hardened body.

As her caresses grew more intimate he cried out her name with longing. But, even as she urged him on, there was caution and care in his touch.

She gave him a questioning look. "What's wrong?" she asked.

"I love you, Annie." He said the words simply and sincerely. "I thought you should know that first."

Annie was deeply moved. She brushed her lips against his. "Thank you," she whispered. "I love you, too."

"Thank you," he whispered back. "Thank you for helping me back away from hell."

She was conscious of the trembling of his fingers as he began to kiss and caress her with fiery intensity. This time his awkwardness had nothing to do with his injury. Not only did she feel the passion connecting them, but there was a return of hope, a shedding of grief and bitterness. Freed at last, they made love with a passion that had been a lifetime in the making.

David was careful to use protection and when he entered Annie he was very gentle, easing himself in and out of her slowly, provocatively, careful not to overwhelm her. Annie responded to him without restraint, aware of a stretching sensation which very soon gave way to a pure consuming passion.

She urged him on, wrapping her legs around him. They moved in concert now, Annie's breath quickening as David filled her. She murmured his name in uninhibited pleasure, thrilling to the raging sensations coursing through her. When at last they united in a tumultuous finale, Annie experienced a surge of intense, all-consuming elation. For the first time in her life, she felt truly whole.

Later, as dusk fell on Long Binh, they made love again. This time Annie was bolder, more daring. David led her into new paths, teaching her new ways to please him, showing her how he could please her. Afterward, they lay spent in each other's arms. David started to doze, but when Annie shifted her position he awoke suddenly and fearfully, pressing her tightly to him.

"Don't leave me," he whispered in a choked, shaky voice.

Gently, Annie stroked his brow, wiping away the beads of cold sweat with her fingertips.

"I'm here," she murmured, running her fingers through his hair. "I won't leave you," she promised, holding him fiercely, protectively. Her eyes spilled over with tears as she thought of all the poor, dying soldiers she'd made that promise to. But this was different, this was a life-affirming promise and she sought David's lips, sealing that promise with a heated, lover's kiss.

Chapter Thirteen

A time to embrace, and a time to refrain from embracing...

There was an unreal quality about Vung Tau, the tiny coastal town of white rippling sands, banyan trees, blue skies and aquamarine seas. This little hamlet off the beaten track had somehow managed, at least so far, to escape the ravages of the war.

Except for the occasional helicopter overhead, it was almost possible for Annie to forget that the war existed, and she and David took full advantage of their time. During the day, Annie swam in the sea while David waded nearby, unable to join her because of his cast. They picnicked on the shore and took long walks together. Annie wore flowers in her hair and necklaces David made her of colorful seashells. In the evenings they danced under the stars to a transistor radio tuned into Air Force radio, laughed at each other's corny jokes, reminisced about the old days and, most wondrously, explored their love.

On New Year's Eve, Annie and David lay under the stars and listened to the waves rolling in to the shore. Annie studied her watch and did the midnight countdown. At exactly 12:00 p.m. she leaned against David and they shared a tender and provocative kiss.

"Happy New Year, Annie," David whispered.

"Happy New Year, David."

They kissed again and then Annie poured two small tumblers of absinthe.

"What shall we toast to?" she asked solemnly as they each took a glass in hand.

David pulled back to stare at her in the moonlight. Then he lightly touched his glass to hers. "To the world as it was meant to be, and to us as we were meant to be," he murmured with a low, bittersweet drawl.

They took sips of the absinthe, set the glasses on the sand, and then came together, two lovers lit by star-filled water. They savored the closeness and drew it out as long as possible. But later that night when Annie slept, she dreamed of David amidst frangipani blossoms, iridescent aquamarine seas, and yellow elephant grass that danced and swayed under the whip of military helicopter blades.

Her disturbing dream was cast aside when she woke up beside David the next morning, their last full day of leave. There was such joy and easy contentment on her face as she nudged David awake with tiny kisses planted down the side of his face, that David, normally a bit grumpy in the mornings, couldn't help smiling himself.

"I've got a great idea," Annie said as she cuddled up beside him, her fingers playing in his hair.

David wound his good arm around her and stroked her back in an idle caress while his eyes roamed her body.

"Not that," Annie said laughing. "Well, yes that, too. But—"

Before she could finish the sentence, his mouth moved persuasively over hers with confident ardor. She pressed harder against him, urging him on, putting all of her other ideas on hold. The excitement of David's naked body against hers filled Annie with heady desire.

The sheets rustled as they began to stroke and caress each other. Annie marveled at the things her body had learned to do and feel. She was all sensation as David nibbled her ear, her neck and shoulder, his hand capturing each of her firm, high breasts in turn. When his mouth replaced his hand, Annie's fingers cradled David's head as she arched against him.

While Annie knew she lacked the experience to make comparisons, she was convinced there could be no better lover than David. Somehow he managed to combine an earthy lust with an almost spiritual tenderness. It had taken him a long time to drop his guard, to still the warning voices inside his head. To cut through the barriers he had built. But now that he had put aside his defenses, he held nothing of himself back.

Annie responded in kind, giving herself fully and openly to David. And even while this was all still very new to her, she felt no awkwardness or anxiety. The man and woman who came together in Vung Tau were not the two kids who'd grown up together in Beaumont, Maryland. Annie knew she was no longer the pest, the tag-along, the kid sister. The experiences she and David had shared evened everything out. They were equals, bound together by the tides of war, joined at the soul.

On their last night in Vung Tau, their lovemaking took on a particularly desperate aura. Afterward, they lay spent and breathless side by side, not speaking, not touching. Tomorrow they would leave their paradise, and there was no way to talk about the future—it was too uncertain.

It was David who broke the silence. "Whatever happens, Annie... I hope you won't regret... any of this."

She pressed closer to him, her cheek resting against his chest. "These have been the happiest moments of my life, David. I never knew I could feel this wonderful. I've never felt so sure of myself, of you, of what I want...."

"Nothing is sure, Annie. Nothing is certain." There was a troubling edge to his voice.

"We still have a few hours, David. Let's not bring tomorrow any sooner than we have to." Her hand glided down his bare chest in a soft caress.

He studied her with quiet intensity, then gathered her to him, placing his lips against her silken blond hair, his hand stroking the gentle swell of her hip. "I love you, Annie. In one way or another I've always loved you."

Annie smiled tenderly. "I'd say it's fate, Nickel." She nuzzled against him. "My feelings about you were never exactly sisterly. From puberty on, Nickel, I thought you were the sexiest, grooviest dude in all of Beaumont," she drawled and gave a Scarlett O'Hara smile that made David laugh.

When the laughter faded, his eyes trailed to her face. "Oh Annie, I wish..."

She pressed her fingers to his lips, following them with a soft, inviting kiss. Taking his hand, she drew it between her thighs.

David's hand slid upward and he let out a long, ragged sigh. He brushed the lobe of her ear with his parted lips. "You're everything I could wish for, Annie. And you're right," he said in an urgent undertone. "Tomorrow will come soon enough on its own. Let's not rush it."

They made love again, desperately trying to ignore the ticking away of the minutes, doing their best to cling to their protected, private sphere of time. But it wasn't possible. Afterward, David stared up at the ceiling and smoked a cigarette. He wore a stark, private expression and Annie looked at him with a wanting so deep she felt like crying. When he finished his cigarette, he gave her a perfunctory good-night kiss. Rolling on his side to sleep, he turned away from her and Annie felt alone, desolate, lost.

On the morning of their return to the base, Annie suggested walking down to the water's edge one last time, but David said it would only make the ending harder.

"But this isn't an ending, David," Annie argued.

David smiled wistfully. He didn't want to argue with Annie. Not today. So, he gave in and they bade their farewell to the sea. Then they left Vung Tau to its slow winds, clacking birds, cawing monkeys and the sun's halo dancing over the waters.

On their way back to Long Binh they stopped in Saigon, rented scooters and took a brief detour to the orphanage to visit Tai.

Sister Mary Catherine greeted them at the door, her expression anxious and worried.

"Oh, I'm so pleased you're here. Poor Tai..."

Annie's skin went clammy. "What happened? Is he ill? Did he get hurt?"

David gripped Annie's hand supportively. "Tell us, please, Sister."

"Luong left with Jessie Morgan yesterday afternoon," the nun began.

"Left?" Annie broke in. "Left for where?"

"For Washington, D.C. The papers went through. For the boarding school."

"But...I just saw Jessie a few days ago. She didn't say anything about getting approval." Annie looked over at David. "She was complaining about all the red tape."

"Yes, I know," Sister Mary Catherine explained. "That was why Jessie was so surprised on New Year's day, when she found out that his papers had gone through. She got a wire from a friend of her father's, who interceded on Luong's behalf and pulled some strings." The nun's eyes spilled over with tears. "Luong and Jessie were so excited. I was so happy...for the boy. The school wanted him to come immediately so that he would be able to start the new term on time. They've arranged special tutoring and then, on holidays and vacations, he will live with a family named Powell in Washington, D.C. Oh, Luong's going to do wonderfully in the States. He's so quick, so bright. It really is marvelous."

Annie leaned heavily against David. "Yes, it's marvelous for Luong, but what about Tai?"

David squeezed Annie's shoulder. "It was going to happen at some point."

"But this was so sudden, so abrupt. Tai's had no time to adjust. He's all alone now."

"That's not true," David said soothingly. "He's got the Sisters and all the other children. He'll make new friends." But even as he tried to sound reassuring, he couldn't put his heart into it. David, too, felt for Tai. He knew all about isolation and loneliness and loss.

"He tried to run away last night," Sister Mary Catherine said softly.

"Oh no," Annie gasped.

"He almost made it to Saigon. We found him on the road. Since we brought him back here, he won't speak to any of us. And he hasn't touched any food since Luong left. He just lies on his cot, staring up at the ceiling. Oh, it's so sad," the nun said wearily. "He'd been making such wonderful strides. Now he's retreated both physically and emotionally." She looked expectantly at Annie and David. "Maybe you two will be able to reach him."

Annie felt herself begin to tremble as she turned to David, uncertainty clouding her eyes. David smiled at her as he said, "Come on. Let's bring him our gifts."

Tai looked so small and frail on his narrow white-sheeted cot. It was mid-morning and all the other children were outside tending to chores and lessons with the nuns. At first Annie thought Tai was asleep, but as she and David approached, his head shifted and his dark, troubled eyes came to rest on her.

"Hi, lazybones," she said with as bright a voice as she could muster. "Isn't it about time you got up and got dressed?"

There was no light at all in the small boy's eyes. He stared at Annie listlessly.

"Look," she said, kneeling beside him and holding out the jar of colorful seashells she'd gathered for him. "Aren't these pretty?"

David took out the conch shell he'd brought and held it against Tai's ear. "Listen. It sounds like the sea."

Tai seemed to focus on the sound. Annie touched his cheek. Tai accepted the caress, but his features didn't change. She opened the jar and removed a peach-tinged oyster shell. Then, taking Tai's small hand, she placed the shell in his palm. Slowly, the child's eyes shifted to the shell. He studied it for a long time then closed his hand around it in a protective, guarded gesture.

Annie smiled. "It's yours, Tai. They're all yours." She placed the jar on his bed and David laid the conch shell on his pillow.

"We're all going to miss Luong, Tai." Annie hesitated. "Maybe, some day you'll come to America too. And you'll see Luong again. It's possible, Tai. Anything's possible."

David gave her a quick, sharp look, his message clear. It was wrong to fill the child's head with impossible dreams. But Annie ignored David's disapproval. She refused to believe in impossibilities. She had to offer Tai hope. What else was there?

David muttered something about needing a smoke and went outside, leaving Annie alone with Tai. She stayed with the child for nearly an hour, talking to him, showing him little games he could play with the shells, trying to coax him to eat some of the breakfast he'd left untouched on a tray at the foot of his bed.

While Tai made no overt response to any of her overtures, Annie did note that after a while his eyes seemed less glazed, and a bit of interest came through as he watched her hands sift through the shells she'd spread out on the white sheet.

Only when she rose and started to leave did Tai act, whispering her name with heartfelt appeal. Annie dropped back down to her knees beside the bed and drew the fragile child to her breast and held him tight.

David was smoking a cigarette when Annie joined him outside.

"I think he's going to be okay," she said with a relieved smile.

David drew in a lungful of smoke, exhaling it through clenched teeth.

"What's the matter?" she asked immediately.

"You shouldn't deceive him, Annie. His only chance to get to the States would be adoption. And his chances for adoption are practically nil."

"Maybe Jessie..."

"Jessie can't rescue every lost waif in Nam, Annie."

"Maybe I..."

"Maybe you could what?" he asked sharply.

"Maybe I could write to the pastor of my church back in Beaumont. Sometimes, through the church..."

"Annie, let's face it. Vietnamese kids aren't exactly in high demand in the States. You're dreaming."

Annie gave David a wan look. "I suppose you're right."

"I'm sorry. I didn't mean to snap at you." But even as his voice softened, David's expression remained tense.

"How sorry are you?" she asked in a mere whisper.

He gave her a puzzled look. "What do you mean?"

"You've been so tense since last night. I just wondered if you're sorry about... our time together in Vung Tau."

He snubbed out the cigarette, and settled his hands on her shoulders, absently rubbing them. "Not if you don't build promises around them, Annie. I can't make promises I have no way of keeping. We've got to be realistic, Annie. We've got to accept that there's only now."

She turned away, her shoulders hunched as if he had wounded her.

He ran his left hand down her back. "Annie, listen to me. In another week this cast comes off my arm and I head back into... the boonies. If I think too much about it, I get sick. And scared. Scared out of my mind. So, I don't think. I just act. I just try to get through each moment and hope for another one to come along. But I'll tell you one thing. When I'm back out there, trying my best not to trip over concertina wire, not to step on a bouncing betty and get myself blown to smithereens, I'm going to hold on to the moments we've shared together for dear life. And in the dark of night, when I'm scared and alone in some godforsaken bunker, I'll whisper your name, Annie. And it will help me more than you can know."

Annie felt the hot, sweet rush of David's breath on her face as she wiped a tear from his cheek and kissed another one away.

"WELL, YOU LOOK rested," Sue Ellen observed, greeting Annie with a gum-cracking grin. "Good R&R, huh?"

Annie shrugged with feigned nonchalance. "Can't complain."

Sue Ellen grinned. "If you think it doesn't show, Scarlett, guess again."

Annie laughed and blushed at the same time.

Sue Ellen swung an arm around Annie's shoulder as they walked through the compound toward Annie's hooch. "So? Was it everything you dreamed it would be?"

Annie's blue eyes glistened. "It was . . . outstanding."

"Damn, but I'm jealous. It's mighty frustrating curling up with a pile of love letters every night."

Annie slapped the side of her head with her hand. "I never did get around to telling David my idea."

"Huh? What idea?"

"I've got a week-long R&R coming due in February. David hasn't taken his yet and I thought we could take it together and go to Hong Kong. Then I thought, why not make it a foursome."

"A foursome?"

"You're eligible for R&R, too. What if you came along and we arranged for Hawk to fly into Hong Kong from the States . . ."

"Hawk . . . ?"

"Why not? Nanna would cover the costs. She'd love to see Hawk get out of the hospital for a while. And it would give the two of you a chance to... have an outstanding time together."

Sue Ellen's face clouded. "It would be awfully hard for him to make the trip, wouldn't it?"

"I think it would be good for him. He's got to start the reentry process at some point. He's gotten way too dependent on the hospital. Sure, he's still going through intensive rehab, but getting a taste of functioning outside would do him good. Give him a chance to put what he's learning into practice. And the chance to see you would be a great incentive."

Sue Ellen's pace slowed. "I don't know. I don't know if he's ready."

Annie looked at her friend, puzzled by her reaction. "Are you ready?"

The tip of Sue Ellen's tongue glided over her bottom lip. She didn't answer right away. Her brow puckered. "I'm scared."

"Scared of what?"

Sue Ellen stared down at the ground. "What if he's... disappointed? What if I don't measure up?"

Annie narrowed her eyes in disbelief. "Are you kidding?"

"I'm not perfect, Annie."

Annie smiled softly. "Neither is Hawk."

"I'm not talking physical imperfections, here," Sue Ellen said with a scowl.

Annie's smile deepened. "Neither am I."

Sue Ellen laughed, but then her expression grew serious. "What if we're not... compatible? What if I've just been imagining he's looking for a serious relationship? What if he's just... filling in lonely hours? Maybe, when push comes to shove, he'll want to settle down with a sweet Southern belle?"

"Hawk hates Southern belles."

"He loves you."

Annie smiled. "Like a sister."

Sue Ellen absently rubbed her cheek. "I've got this thing about rejection. I hate it."

Annie laughed. "Who doesn't?"

"It's just . . . if it didn't work out in Hong Kong . . . and I had to come back here to finish up the year . . . it would be hell. Hawk's letters keep me going. If they stopped I'm not sure I could stick it out. And the thing is, I want to finish my stint. Some of the kids can't hack it and they quit. I don't blame them. I've felt like quitting plenty." Sue Ellen hesitated. "But then I think of the boys . . . like Kevin Downy . . . and others. I feel a responsibility." She shrugged. "Do you see what I'm trying to say?"

Annie swallowed hard. "Yeah, I see what you're saying."

Sue Ellen, never one to get sappy for very long, switched on a wry grin. "Okay, so now it's your turn to tell me a few things, kiddo."

Arm in arm, comrades in arms, they headed over to Annie's hooch for some serious girl talk.

A TAPE CAME for Annie the second week of January. She borrowed Sue Ellen's recorder to listen to it.

Hi Annie. It's your dad. Turner here thought it would be a fun idea to send you a Christmas-greetings tape. Well you know me, I'm not one for much gabbing into a machine. It feels kind of silly, but once your brother gets an idea in his head . . .

Nanna's here, too, and she'll say a few words. Maybe she'll do something from one of her old movies for you. Uh-oh, she's giving me one of her looks.

So, what can I say, Annie? I guess, the truth is, I keep hoping the war would just end and you'd come on home already. I say a prayer for you every morning and every night. Every time I read the papers or watch the news I feel sick inside. I guess I just can't stop myself from thinking how dangerous it is. Everybody's giving me dirty looks here. This is supposed to be an upbeat cheery message.

Hey Annie, it's me. Big brother. Don't pay attention to Dad. You know him. He's a regular worrywart. I know you can take care of yourself. And I gotta admit, kiddo, I score points when I tell gals my little sister is over there on the front. They think it's really cool, even the ones walking around with antiwar buttons. Go figure. So listen, where are you going for your R&R? I met a guy down in Florida who just got out of the Marines and he was saying that Hawaii is the place to be.

Okay, so enough about you. Let me talk about my favorite subject now. Me. Looks like your big brother just might make it to Fenway Park this spring. I'm in the running, along with these two big lugs breathing down my neck. Oh yeah, I forgot to tell you. I brought home two bums from my team for Christmas. And listen, these jokers here are dying to have a word with you. I don't get it. They saw some pictures of you around the house and they've been panting ever since. So, before you go and fall in love with some Army doctor or something over there, let the two of them make their pitch. But, if you want my opinion . . .

Hi there, Annie Magill. I'm Jeff. Jeff Walker. The best outfielder this side of the Mississippi. I just want to tell you that if you ever do come up to Boston to see a game or anything, I'd love to take you out for dinner. And dancing afterward. Don't pay any attention to your brother. I'm a cool guy. Good-looking, too. Hey, maybe I can send you a photo . . .

It's me again. Turner. Good-looking, my eye. Walker here's about five foot two, tips the scales at three hundred and has two left feet.

Hey Annie. It's not true. I'm six foot one, two hundred and . . .

Forget about Jeffie, Annie. I'm Russ Malone, but my friends call me Bear. You can call me anything you like. I gotta tell you, Annie, I took one look at those photos of you and, I swear, my heart started skipping beats. Tell her, Turner.

Bear's telling it like it is, Annie. But, as your big brother, I gotta tell you Bear's heart skips beats when he looks at girls' names in a telephone booth.

Not true . . .

Hello Annie, it's Nanna. I've shooed those unruly boys out of here, your father included, so I can have a few private words with you. I do feel foolish talking to you this way, but strange as it seems, it does make me feel a little closer to you.

I've been here in Beaumont for a few days. I'm planning to leave right after New Year's. I went over to Oakdale to visit Hawk on Wednesday and took him out for the day. I tried to talk him into spending Christmas, but he made some excuse, saying there was a big party at the V.A. and the fellows were expecting him.

He's going through hard times, but you know Hawk, he never lets it show. He talked about the letters he's been getting from your friend, Sue Ellen. He acts like it's just a pleasant diversion, but I can tell he's quite serious about her. He even offhandedly mentioned she might visit him when she finishes her tour of service with the Red Cross. I do hope this girl isn't leading Hawk on, Annie. And if she is serious, I hope she's prepared to cope with all of Hawk's problems. Not just the physical ones. I had a brief chat with your old head nurse, Glenda Wheeler. She told me that Hawk is experiencing a lot of emotional trauma. All the boys here are, but the most sensitive ones feel it the hardest. And for all Hawk's glibness, he's a very sensitive boy. He's going to need a patient, understanding and nurturing woman to see him through this, Annie. But I'm sure you know that from your own experiences and you wouldn't be encouraging Sue Ellen in this relationship if you didn't think it was a good bet.

Well, Annie, I have to admit this has been a sad and lonely Christmas. It just isn't the same without you and Hawk and David. How is David, Annie? You know I'm not one to pry, but I get the feeling from some of your letters that the two of you are going through a lot of changes. I hope everything turns out well, my girl. I love you, Annie. I miss you very much. And I'm very proud of you. So would your mother be—

Annie sniffed back tears as she turned off the tape recorder. Then she stretched out on her cot, closed her eyes and pictured Nanna at the piano, playing "Silent Night." Annie began to hum the tune, imagining herself back home. There she was, with Nanna, Dad, Turner, Hawk and David. She loved them all. And loving was one of the things she needed desperately to survive in this place.

Chapter Fourteen

A time to speak...

Life...February 2, 1969
The Women Who Will Not Be Forgotten
by Jessie Morgan, foreign correspondent

To be a correspondent covering a hospital in a war zone is an awkward role. When men are dying and young women are working desperately to save them, there is a dignity and intensity that mocks the reporter who arrives at will by air-conditioned jet and stands off to one side watching.

Much has been covered in the press about the men who are fighting over here in Vietnam, but little has been said about the women who have volunteered to come to this devastating battle zone to do whatever they can to help our boys. They are the unsung heroines—the military nurses, the Red Cross workers, the USO gals. Their stories are a remarkable and affirmative statement about humanity, integrity and courage.

First Lieutenant Annie Magill is a twenty-two-year-old triage nurse from Beaumont, Maryland, stationed at Long Binh in South Vietnam. She has been in-country since early September of 1968. When I first met Lieutenant Magill I was struck by her fragile gentility and seeming innocence. Fair-haired, delicately built, soft-spoken, and as lovely as a magnolia blossom, Annie did not look

*the sort to tough it out amidst the unbroken fury and
horror of Vietnam.*

*Annie would be the first to say she is no heroine. Others are quick to disagree. To the patients she treats and
sustains, with both her nursing skills and tender warmth,
she is a true angel of mercy. Her colleagues describe her
as dedicated, committed, "a ray of sunshine" in the
bleakest of worlds at the bleakest of times.*

*While Annie works amidst the throaty whine of artillery rounds and the reedy whistles of mortar barrages, she
never speaks of duty or bravery. She has volunteered for
service in Vietnam because that is where she feels she can
do the most good. She simply does what needs to be done
for young men who are in desperate need. She is a nurse.
That is, after all, her chosen calling.*

*Annie is a sharp critic of the war, but a fierce supporter of the American boys sent here to put their lives on
the line. She quotes Benjamin Franklin who once said,
"There is no good war and no bad peace." She prays for
peace every day.*

*On any given evening the hospital can shake and rattle
from the dull thunder of rocket attacks. Ask Annie how
she can function under such conditions and she shrugs.
"I'm constantly afraid," she says, "but I've learned to
push it aside." She says she's on an emotional pendulum
that swings from sorrow to rage. Her rage is directed at
the catastrophic toll of war, her sorrow at the seeming
inevitability of the arrival of the next medevac copter
bringing in more dead and wounded. Her tears come easily when she talks of the boys she's lost. And, tragically,
there are many of them.*

*Annie Magill describes herself as an ordinary nurse.
And, in the end, that is why I chose to write about her.
She is a perfect representative of the more than ten thousand nurses, Red Cross workers and USO women serving
voluntarily in Vietnam. Ordinary women all. Ordinary*

women made extraordinary by their acts of kindness, skill and valor.

I feel privileged to call myself her friend. Her strength, her humor, her gentleness and her open and genuine caring have touched me deeply. And in knowing Annie and others like her, I feel profoundly humbled, profoundly changed.

Now, hopefully, I will touch others with her story....

Copies of Jessie Morgan's article on Annie spread rapidly through the hospital and even the base. When Annie walked down her ward she saw, plastered on the walls, dozens of copies of the *Life* magazine cover that featured her and Tai playing cards together at a rickety table at the orphanage. At least ten doctors asked her out, one corpsman actually proposed marriage, and Sue Ellen and the other girls at the Red Cross center threw her a gala bash, which David couldn't attend now that he was once again out on maneuvers.

Annie was not thrilled by her celebrity status. She did not feel deserving, nor did she like standing out in a crowd. But there were some definite pluses, the biggest one being the impish delight Tai took in their fame. Tai had been making steady physical and psychological progress over the past month, but it was the *Life* article that really brought him out of his shell.

When she visited him, Annie couldn't believe the change. The minute she walked into the main room of the orphanage, Tai, surrounded by an awed and envious cluster of children, broke free from the group and ran to her.

It was a moment Annie would always remember, the very first time Tai ever came to her instead of waiting for her to make the first move. And as she felt his thin arms encircle her and hug her tight, tight, and his sweet, high-pitched voice excitedly whisper her name, Annie said a silent prayer of thanks to Jessie Morgan.

Sister Mary Catherine was beaming as she sat with Annie later that day.

"I never thought I'd hear that little boy laugh," the nun exclaimed.

"It's wonderful," Annie agreed. "And I've been thinking, now that Tai's become more than a...statistic, maybe you'll have better luck finding a family to adopt him."

Sister Mary Catherine sighed. "I suppose that could happen. But..." The nun let the sentence hang, her expression showing discomfort.

"What is it, Sister?" Annie asked. "What were you going to say?"

The nun's cheeks reddened. She couldn't quite meet Annie's steady, inquiring gaze.

"Please, Sister. Tell me what you're thinking."

The nun leaned forward a bit and finally looked directly at Annie. "Tai is a special child, Annie."

Annie smiled quizzically. "Yes. Yes he is. That's why I..."

"A special child with special needs." Sister Mary Catherine pressed her hands together.

Annie's smile grew fainter. "With love and care...why, you see the changes in him already. You said yourself..."

"Annie, we measure by different standards here."

"But..."

"He's suffered an array of infections, malnutrition. Shortly after he first came here he had several terrible bouts with malaria. He's very small for his age, Annie. And he's likely to always be undersized, with heaven only knows what complications from all he's been through."

"If he got to the States and was treated by a good physician, there's no telling..."

"I couldn't hide his medical history, Annie. It would take a very special family to be willing to undertake the kind of responsibility required to look after a child like Tai."

Annie refused to believe such a family didn't exist. Once again she started to object, but the Sister raised a hand.

"Tai has more than just physical problems, Annie."

"Yes, I know that, Sister. But, in that regard, surely you'll agree he's come a long way. You said as much already."

"Yes, that's true. You've been a lifesaver for that little boy, Annie, and I don't use lifesaver lightly. After Luong left, I feared the boy would never pull out of his depression."

"He's such a bright, tough kid. That he's survived all this is in itself remarkable."

"He brightens considerably when you're around, Annie. But there are times, many times, especially at night, when, in the darkness of the dormitory, I hear a high, keening sound. It's not always Tai, but very often it's to his bed I rush. I carry a candle, and stare down at him, and see his face contorted, as if in pain. He's fast asleep, ensnared by a nightmare. If I touch him, even in the slightest way, his whole little body stiffens and then contracts into a ball. It's terrible. When I manage, finally, to wake him his eyes are filled with terror. But once he's awake he says nothing. He refuses to acknowledge the nightmares in any way. I even spoke to an Army psychiatrist in Saigon about Tai's bad dreams. He said it would be a long time, if ever, before they abated. 'Is it any wonder?' the doctor asked. And all I could do was say, 'no.'"

Annie's throat was tight with pity for Tai. She gave the Sister a wan look. "It's so . . . unfair."

The nun leaned a little closer, her palms pressed together on the table. "Tell me something, Annie. What will you do when you get back to the world?"

Annie was surprised by the shift in conversation and it took her a few moments to answer. "I did my internship at a V.A. hospital close to my home town. I've thought of putting in for a placement there, at least until I finish my active service time. I was told, when I volunteered for Nam, that it could be arranged."

"And your . . . friend . . . David?"

"David?"

"Yes. What will he do?"

"I . . . I don't really know for certain. David refuses to talk about his plans for the future. Superstition, you know. If you talk about getting back . . . it may not happen."

"Yes, I understand."

"But, I suppose, in the best of all possible worlds he'd return to law school at the University of Virginia, and . . ." She let the rest of the sentence hang.

Sister Mary Catherine smiled. "Were you going to say, and ask you to marry him?"

A little laugh escaped Annie's lips. "I might have. Which is really dumb. David's never once mentioned marriage. Not to me. Not to anyone I know of, for that matter. Even if he hadn't enlisted and come to Nam, I doubt David would be thinking about marriage for years. He'd want to get through school, set up practice . . ." Annie stared off into the distance. "I never really thought seriously about marriage, myself. Until . . . recently. I don't know if I'm ready to get married either. It's such a big step."

Annie smiled more to herself than the nun. "I wonder what everyone would say. My brother Turner would be shocked. His good buddy, David Nichols and his kid sister? He'd think David had gone nuts. And Hawk? Hawk would rib poor David unmercifully. As for my dad, he'd probably be quite upset about it."

"Doesn't he like David?" Sister Mary Catherine asked.

"Oh, yes. Yes, he adores David. It's just . . . my dad hates the thought of losing me. Now that Turner's life is up north, I'm all Dad has left."

"Yes, I see. He depends on you."

Annie met the Sister's steady gaze. "My father was dead set against my decision to come to Vietnam. He's never really forgiven me for disobeying him. It's just that he's scared. My brother and I are everything to him. Especially since my mother died."

"How sad for all of you," the Sister said.

"Yes, I miss not having known my mother better. I was a small child when she died."

"And I understand your father's feelings about you being here. What parent wants to see his child going off to war, in whatever capacity? But, I'm sure he's very proud of you."

Annie looked down at the floor. "I don't know. He never says anything except how he prays the war will end and that I'll come home. He used to be so... warm and effusive about his feelings toward me. I remember when I was little and went to camp he'd write me the best letters." She closed her eyes. A moment later she felt the nun's hand rest lightly over hers.

"I didn't mean to make you sad, Annie."

Annie forced a bright smile. "Oh...you didn't. Really. I'm fine."

The nun studied her thoughtfully. "I suppose I was just...having a silly romantic fantasy."

Annie's expression showed surprise and curiosity. "A romantic fantasy?"

Sister Mary Catherine chuckled. "Nuns are not exempt from romantic fantasies, Annie."

"No, no, of course not..."

"Mine concerned you."

Annie blanched.

"You and David," the Sister hurried to amend.

"Oh." And then after a beat, "Oh?"

"Yes. You see I was just thinking. Well, if you and David were considering marriage, perhaps you'd thought about children as well."

Annie laughed. "I'm afraid your fantasies are a lot more advanced than mine. To be perfectly honest, Sister, I don't even know if David's my...boyfriend. I mean...well, here everything is so...intense, so...immediate. If David and I had never been in Nam...if we'd stayed around Beaumont, I doubt...well, I doubt we'd have gotten...together."

"But you *are* both here. And from what I see, the two of you care a great deal for each other."

Annie could feel her cheeks warm, and the nun smiled.

"I think you make a wonderful couple, Annie."

"Thanks."

"So, I'll tell you my fantasy. I thought to myself, wouldn't it solve everything if David and Annie got married and adopted Tai. What couple would be more perfect? What better environment for Tai to thrive in? Tai adores David and surely you know he loves you very much."

Annie listened to the nun in a daze. Finally, she found her voice. "That's quite a fantasy, Sister."

The nun smiled brightly. "Yes, it is, isn't it?"

"It's impossible."

"Oh?"

"I mean, David and I are light years away from even talking about marriage. And as for children, I don't even know how David feels about children. And the idea of adoption... Oh, I know David loves visiting Tai, but that's...here. It's not like he feels any long-term obligation or that he's making some sort of commitment."

"How do you feel about children, Annie?"

"Me? Why, I love children. I...love Tai." Annie looked at the nun speculatively, her blue eyes widening. "Do you really think I could do it?"

"Well, there'd be a lot of red tape..."

"No. I mean, do you think I would be...good enough at it? At being a mother? I'm so young. I haven't had any...experience..."

"Yes," the nun said at once. "I think you're a natural, Annie. And you love Tai. That's the most important thing."

For several moments, Annie stared pensively at the nun. Finally she said in a low voice, "It's a very nice fantasy, Sister. David and me and Tai..."

Sister Mary Catherine rose from her seat with a faint smile. "Sometimes, fantasies can come true, Annie," she reflected softly. "Did I hear you mention to Tai that you and David were taking an R&R in Hong Kong together later this month?"

Annie blushed, unable to look the Sister straight in the eye. "Well, yes, but..." She half expected the Sister to give her a lecture on morals.

Instead, Sister Mary Catherine merely smiled. "Then perhaps, you might feel David out."

"What?"

"About my little fantasy."

SUE ELLEN ROLLED OVER on the bed laughing. "You really thought Sister Mary Catherine said '...feel David up'?"

Annie grinned. "My eyes almost bulged out until I realized she'd said, feel him *out*."

"Oh Annie, I wish I could have been there," Sue Ellen said, sobering. "I could have used a good laugh earlier today."

"What's the matter?"

"I got a letter from Hawk this morning. He can't come to Hong Kong."

"Oh, no. Why not?"

"A prior commitment."

"Huh?"

"When's the last time you heard from Hawk?"

Annie had to think. "Not for weeks. I think writing to you wears the man out."

"Then you don't know about the new group that he joined."

Annie frowned. "No. What group?"

"Vietnam Veterans Against the War."

Annie had read about the group. A contingent of VVAWs had disrupted Nixon's Presidential acceptance speech at the Convention Center in Miami. One of the protesters, Ron Kovic, had been interviewed by Roger Mudd from CBS and had gotten national news coverage.

Annie wasn't really all that surprised by the news that Hawk had joined the organization. When he left for Vietnam, Hawk had believed in the American dream and gone off to war to protect it. But he'd returned disillusioned. Now he'd joined with other veterans in speaking out against the war.

"When did Hawk join them?" Annie asked.

"Not very long ago. I guess when he realized the peace talks in Paris weren't going to go anywhere, and our boys might not get out of Nam for years. Hawk thinks Nixon will pull some troops out just to appease the protestors at home, but plenty of troops will stay and others will come over. Hawk figures he's got to speak out, and he feels, rightly enough, that only the vets can really tell it like it is."

Annie didn't hide her concern. "He's not going to have an easy time of it. Especially being a vet. A lot of people are going to call him a traitor."

"And a lot of folks will cheer him," Sue Ellen countered. "I will," she added vehemently.

Annie smiled. "So will I."

Sue Ellen sighed. "He's been asked to speak at a couple of colleges and to attend a couple of rallies during the week we were planning to go to Hong Kong."

"You can still come with us," Annie said.

Sue Ellen laughed. "Three's a crowd, Scarlett. Anyway, a couple of kids at the center asked me to go with them to Bangkok for R&R. It's supposed to be very exotic.''

"Sounds like fun.''

Sue Ellen popped a piece of chewing gum into her mouth and stretched out on the handwoven rug on the floor of Annie's room. "I guess I'll have to settle for just fantasies about Hawk for a few more months.''

"Speaking of fantasies . . .'' Annie hesitated.

Sue Ellen rolled onto her side to look at Annie. "You wanna know what I think of Sister Mary Catherine's fantasy?''

"It's dumb. It's crazy. I'm sure David never . . .''

Sue Ellen laughed. "You could always pop the question, Scarlett.''

"Right.'' Annie's tone was thick with sarcasm.

"Why not? Gals are doing it all the time these days.''

Annie's spirits took a nosedive. "It's not that. I'm scared. I'm scared he'd turn me down.''

ANNIE WAS especially tense and worried about David's safety. While Tet, the Vietnamese New Year, had come and gone with relative calm, neither Annie nor anyone else could forget what they'd heard about the hell that had erupted during last year's Tet. The V.C. had struck at over thirty provincial capitals, countless villages and a dozen American bases. In Saigon, it had taken six hours to secure the American Embassy alone.

Was this the calm before the storm? Annie wondered anxiously. Was Charlie planning another major assault, hoping to catch everyone unaware by waiting until after Tet this year? These questions weren't on just Annie's mind. Everyone was jumpy. It wasn't spoken about—superstition again—but it was felt. You could see it in people's eyes, hear it in their voices.

Because of the secret nature of David's missions, Annie often knew nothing of his whereabouts. But he'd

promised that he'd be at the landing strip for their flight
to Hong Kong on February twenty-third.

The waiting was hard. Every time a medevac copter
landed, Annie held her breath. Would David be one of the
wounded? Or worse. Bad thoughts. Mustn't let those bad
thoughts in. Superstition again. Annie fought against the
thoughts, but they pursued her like typhoon winds—in-
sistent, powerful, unstoppable.

Her only respite came on her days off when she visited
with Tai. A new bond was forming between them. A part
of Sister Mary Catherine's fantasy had, indeed, taken
hold of Annie. Her maternal instincts toward the little boy
soared. She began imagining what it would be like to bring
Tai home to Beaumont. She envisioned him learning how
to ride, perhaps even learning, over time, how to breed
horses, and some day taking over her father's business.
Tai was a fast study.

Annie wanted to adopt Tai. She even spoke with Sister
Mary Catherine, exploring the possibility of adoption
even if she didn't get married. The Sister felt it would be
more difficult to get approval from the South Vietnamese officials, but not impossible. However, she also felt
that it might be too big an undertaking for Annie to
shoulder all my herself.

"I'd bring him home with me. My dad would help.
He'd teach Tai all about horses, hunting, Irish folklore.
And Nanna would visit a lot. She loves children. She was
so wonderful with us—Turner and me—when we were
growing up. She'd go wild over Tai."

"You were her flesh and blood, Annie."

"She was wonderful with David and Hawk, too. She's
always treated them as family."

Sister Mary Catherine looked uneasy. "Still, your
grandmother might feel differently about Tai."

"She wouldn't," Annie said vehemently.

The nun hesitated. "And your father?"

This time Annie wasn't quick to answer. How would her father feel about Tai? Would the child be a constant reminder to him of his daughter's defiance? Would he resent Tai?

Sister Mary Catherine rested a hand over Annie's. "And the community, Annie? How would your neighbors and friends feel about a single mother with a Vietnamese child? There's so much negative feeling about the war now. America is being torn apart. We'll all need time to heal. Time to forget."

"I don't want to forget. Besides, Tai is only a child. He can't be made to pay for the sins of others. He deserves a future. Look at Luong."

Sister Mary Catherine brightened. "Yes, Luong. I had a letter from him a few weeks ago. He's doing wonderfully at school. Just as I expected he would."

Annie squeezed the nun's hand. "Tai will, too. I know he will. I'll help him."

"And David?"

"I love David, Sister. In the best of all possible worlds we'd get married and raise Tai together. And have a few more babies as well. I'd like that. I'd like that very much."

Sister Mary Catherine placed her other hand on Annie's cheek. "Yes, I'd like that, too," she said softly. "I'll pray for the three of you, Annie."

ANNIE AND her triage group were unloading a dust-off chopper down at the landing pad when they spotted another one, billowing black, sooty smoke, looping in low and herky-jerky.

"Come on, scramble," someone shouted behind Annie.

With a half-dozen other people, Annie raced for the disabled chopper as it crashed. The pilot had shut down the engines, but he'd been hit bad. His co-pilot, injured as well, was dragging him off the chopper. A couple of corpsmen helped them both down and got them a safe distance away.

Annie helped unload the injured as fast as possible. The chopper was on fire and it was only a matter of time before it blew.

Smoke and dust got into everyone's eyes, and made vision impossible. They were clearing the landing area, certain they'd gotten everyone off the chopper, when Annie heard a plaintive cry from the wreckage. She shot a glance at the corpsman who'd been helping her move patients.

"Did you hear that?"

"What? No. I didn't hear anything. Come on, Lieutenant, we gotta move."

Annie spun around and stared at the crumpled copter with burning eyes. "Someone's still in there," she shouted.

Only the corpsman was close enough to understand her, the other hospital staffers were already well out of range.

"You can't do anything, Lieutenant. That wreck's gonna blow sky-high any second now. Come on."

"No way," she shouted at him, roiling anger and frustration driving her. She sprinted toward the burning chopper.

Annie choked on the smoke as she scrambled into the copter, searching blindly for the boy.

He was sprawled on a litter in the belly of the bird, unconscious now, that cry she'd heard probably the last one he thought he'd ever make.

She dragged desperately at his dead weight, her arms screaming with pain as she struggled to get him to the gaping door of the chopper.

As she reached the door she felt a hand on her shoulder and saw her corpsman. He gave her a fast, crooked smile and then reached up and heaved the unconscious boy over one shoulder.

Together they ran from the blazing chopper. Annie's lungs burned from breathing in the acrid fumes and the smoke. Her head swam and her ears rang with the crackling, snapping sound of the flames. Her eyes smarted and teared so that she could still barely make out where she was going.

Behind her the big bird's gas tank ignited in a tremendous white flash, the powerful explosion sending the hatch door, rotors, tail fins spiraling through the air like metallic confetti. She passed out cold a second or two after she stumbled to safety.

When Annie came to, about an hour later, she was lying on a cot in the hallway of the crowded hospital. The corpsman who'd assisted her in the rescue was at her side.

"How ya doin'?" he asked with a smile tinged with pride.

"How's the kid we pulled out?" Annie asked weakly.

"Okay, Lieutenant. It was touch and go there, but they say he'll pull through."

Annie smiled. "Good. That's good," she whispered.

The corpsman winked at her. "You sure got guts, Lieutenant. Either that or you're just plum loco."

"A little of both, I guess. Just like you."

He grinned. "Yeah, suppose so." He leaned a little closer. "Word's out that we're gonna get ourselves Bronze Stars out of this, Lieutenant. Won't our papas be proud of us then?"

Annie smiled weakly as she thought about it. If her father learned how she'd earned that star the last thing he'd be was proud. He'd be angry, and even more worried about his little girl. How could he ever understand the uncontrollable rage against allowing even one more senseless death, that had left her with no choice but to put her life on the line for a perfect stranger? How could she expect anyone who hadn't served here to understand?

David would understand her, Annie thought, closing her eyes. David would have done just what she'd done.

Waves of weariness, fatigue, loneliness and fear washed over her now that it was all over. She tasted the salt of tears on her lips. Oh how she ached for David's sweet, healing touch.

Chapter Fifteen

A time to gather stones together...

Dear Annie,

This morning I picked up Life *magazine and saw you and that little friend of yours you've written so much about on the cover. I can't describe the feeling that came over me as I realized "That's my girl." In a strange way, it was like I was seeing you for the first time. Suddenly, there you were, all grown-up. It took my breath away.*

Oh lass, all these months I've been so caught up in my own narrow, closed little world of fear and disappointment. I was so very selfish. I'm ashamed, Annie girl. Not an easy thing for a stubborn old dad to admit. I was so afraid of losing you that I couldn't see beyond that. I told myself you were foolhardy, naive and rebellious to go off to Vietnam. How wrong I was.

What can I say of a daughter who is so courageous and selfless, lass? To see it all in print, the danger, the long hours, the terrible sorrow that you have endured. More than endured, triumphed over. You are a remarkable young woman. I am proud, Annie—so very proud of you. My shame is in not allowing that pride to take hold of my heart sooner. Can you forgive your poor old dad, Annie? It's not that I'm not still afraid, but I can finally see now how my fear has held me captive and kept us apart in spirit.

You are my heart and my soul, my girl. I love you very much. And I am very proud to have you for my daughter, First Lieutenant Annie Magill.

Love,
Dad

Sue Ellen came over to Annie's hooch to pick her up. They were flying out together to the R&R center at Cam Ranh Bay and splitting up from there.

Annie was crying quietly as she stood by the small window.

Sue Ellen's first fear was that Annie had heard bad news about David. He'd assured Annie that he'd be at Long Binh on time for the flight to Cam Ranh Bay. But he hadn't shown up and there'd been no word from him.

Annie's bags were packed and ready beside the door. Sue Ellen called Annie's name out in a low voice.

When Annie looked up, Sue Ellen saw that she was holding a letter in her hand. So, it wasn't about David that she was crying.

"Bad news from home?" Sue Ellen asked softly.

A faint smile curved Annie's lips. "No. Not bad news." She handed the letter over to Sue Ellen.

When Sue Ellen finished reading the letter Annie's father had written, there were tears in Sue Ellen's eyes as well.

"Wow." Sue Ellen leaned against the wall. "That's so..." She sniffed.

Annie grinned and sniffed at the same time. "Yeah, I know what you mean."

Her eyes fell to the letter. "I feel so good about my dad coming round. But, it makes me worry that bad news follows good." She glanced at Sue Ellen with a look of pain. "I'm so scared something's happened to David."

"No news is good news in my book," Sue Ellen said, trying to inject a note of confidence into her voice. But the effort showed.

"I'm not going on R&R without him," Annie said firmly.

"That's dumb. It isn't gonna help you any to hang around this hole. He knows what hotel you're going to be staying in. What if he realizes he can't get back to Long Binh in time and heads straight over to Cam Ranh Bay, so he can catch up with you. Yeah, that's probably what he'll do. He might even be at Cam Ranh Bay this very minute waiting for you to get there."

"Do you really think so?" Annie asked expectantly.

Sue Ellen obviously wanted to believe it as much as Annie. "Yeah, I really think so." She paused, a quirky smile on her lips. "So tell me, Scarlett, did you decide whether to pop the question?"

"Forget it, Sue Ellen. I'm just an old-fashioned Southern belle. I want my man down on his knee, proposing in style."

"You can give him a little nudge."

Annie's expression turned serious. "He's not going to propose to me, Sue Ellen. Not now. That's for sure. And once we're back in the world . . . well, a lot of things can happen."

"He loves you, Annie."

"That's here. That's now. And David refuses to look past today." Her breath caught, her vision clouded. "Right now, even today seems questionable."

Sue Ellen donned an encouraging smile, refusing to allow Annie to give in to her fears about David's safety.

"Are you gonna say anything to him about your plans for Tai?"

"I don't know," Annie mused. "I'm afraid David might try to discourage me from adopting him on my own."

Sue Ellen hesitated. "Maybe…it isn't such a good idea, Annie."

Annie smiled ruefully. "So you're going to discourage me instead?"

"I was just thinking. What if David does want to get married when you both get back to the world. Maybe…he wouldn't want a…ready-made family. He might want to wait to have kids. He might only want his own."

Annie frowned. Sue Ellen wasn't saying anything she hadn't already thought about, herself. Without further comment she tucked her father's letter in her pocketbook to show to David and, in silence, she walked over to where her bags were piled on the floor.

Sue Ellen was a couple of feet away. "I'm sorry, Annie. I didn't mean to get you even more upset. I just want you to be happy. You deserve it. And I don't think there's a better matched couple on this earth than you and loverboy." She grinned. "'Cept maybe Hawk and me."

On impulse, Annie threw her arms around Sue Ellen. "You're the best friend a girl could ever have. I love you," Annie whispered.

Sue Ellen awkwardly ruffled Annie's hair. "Gee, Scarlett, what are people gonna think if they hear that?"

Annie laughed. "Since when have you ever cared about what people think?"

Sue Ellen giggled, dropped her duffel bag, put her arms around Annie and gave her a big, warm hug back. "Okay, okay. I love you too, Scarlett. Now let's blow this joint."

Sue Ellen swung her free arm around Annie's shoulder, and shouted out, "Civilization, here we come."

CAM RANH BAY, which passed as the heart of civilization in their corner of Vietnam, was a small wooden barracks and a few dingy offices. Sue Ellen gave Annie a nudge as they waited in one of the offices for their flight assignments out of country.

"Hey, they have air conditioners here," Sue Ellen whispered.

Annie was looking around distractedly.

Sue Ellen put a hand on her friend's shoulder. "Don't worry. He could have gone through the line already. When it's our turn, we'll ask that cute GI behind the desk if Captain Nichols has checked in yet."

Annie nodded absently as she surveyed the small, crowded room. A few dozen GIs were here waiting, just like them, for R&R flight assignments. The married soldiers would mostly be going to Honolulu for reunions with their wives, flown in from the States, courtesy of the military. The others would choose from Hong Kong, Bangkok, Manila, Tokyo, Singapore, Taiwan, Sydney, or Kuala Lumpur.

Annie had returned to watching the door, praying to see David, when Sue Ellen tapped her on the back.

"Okay, we're next." She rubbed her hands together. "Five whole days of shopping, sight-seeing, sunbathing, tranquility. I've gotta find Hawk something real kinky and funny. He's so worried that I'm gonna spend my whole leave partying and falling for some other guy." Sue Ellen smiled wistfully. "That good ol' Southern boy just can't get it in his head that I've lost my heart to him forever."

Annie smiled, pushing aside her personal anxiety for Sue Ellen's sake. "It'll sink in, in time."

A tiny frown marred Sue Ellen's perfect features. "Yeah, in time…"

The minute Annie approached the desk with her R&R papers, she asked the soldier behind the desk if Captain David Nichols had checked in yet. "He was supposed to fly out of here for Hong Kong today."

"No more flights out of here for Hong Kong today. There was one early this morning." The soldier checked a sheet of paper. "No Captain Nichols listed on it."

"When's the next flight?"

"Tomorrow morning at eleven. You can stay on base overnight, or spring for a hotel down at the beach."

The idea of spending another night in a hooch was too depressing. Annie opted for a hotel, and the soldier gave her a short list of choices. "You can catch a bus out front. It'll take you past all of them. Hop out when you see one you like."

Sue Ellen and her two friends stepped up to the desk next and learned that there was a flight to Bangkok leaving in less than thirty minutes.

Sue Ellen hesitated. "I hate leaving you alone like this."

"Don't be ridiculous. I'm a big girl. Go on with your pals. Have a great time. Buy me something sexy in Bangkok and I'll find you something hot in Hong Kong. When we do see our guys we'll knock their socks off. Now get going."

Sue Ellen gave her a brief hug. "He'll show up, Annie. Don't worry."

Annie managed a smile. "Have fun."

Sue Ellen winked. "Bet I won't be having as much fun as you."

THE NEXT MORNING Annie, dressed in a cheerful flower-print sundress, asked once more at the R&R center if David had checked in. There was still no sign of him. Despondently she boarded a civilian jet. Stewardesses cruised the aisles handing out drinks and cold washcloths. It would have felt wonderful to be heading away from Vietnam if only David had been sitting in the seat beside her.

The Hong Kong harbor was crowded: junks and tiny fishing boats hovered around large freighters like honeybees around a rose. When Annie landed, like the rest of the military, she was herded into a smoke-filled room for R&R orientation. Warnings were issued about the kind of "problems" GIs ran into on leave, and then pamphlets on the prevention of venereal diseases and brochures about hotels and sight-seeing junkets were handed out.

Annie had already booked her hotel, one of the swankiest in Hong Kong. She and David had planned to do this R&R right. Pure luxury for five whole days.

Glumly Annie caught a cab to the hotel. When she got to the desk, she gave her name and explained about her reservation.

The desk clerk, a pretty, dark-haired Eurasian girl, frowned. "Oh, I'm sorry...Lieutenant Magill. There must be an error. That reservation for a double room was canceled."

"Canceled? Who canceled it?"

The desk clerk shrugged. "I am sorry, Lieutenant. I do not have a record."

"Do you have a Captain Nichols registered here?"

"I will check." A minute later, the desk clerk shrugged again. "I do not see the name in our register."

Annie's frustration was mounting. "Look, I made this reservation weeks ago. No one could have canceled it."

"I'm sorry."

"Are you telling me you're all filled up?"

"Well...there is one suite available. But...it is the honeymoon suite."

"The honeymoon suite?"

"Yes. It is very beautiful. On the penthouse. Of course, it is quite expensive."

It wasn't the money that concerned Annie. It was superstition. Staying alone in the honeymoon suite sounded like a terrible jinx. But if she switched hotels, how would David find her if he did make it to Hong Kong?

"Okay. The honeymoon suite it is," Annie said resignedly.

The desk clerk brightened. "Yes, Lieutenant Magill. I am sure you will be most pleased with your decision." She motioned for the bellhop as Annie signed in.

"I'm registering in my name and Captain Nichols's. I'm expecting him at any time."

"Oh yes, Lieutenant Magill. Very good. Very good. No problem."

The lavishness of the honeymoon suite took Annie's breath away. It had been five months since she'd seen wall-to-wall carpeting, glistening polished-wood furniture, crystal chandeliers, gilt-framed prints on walls. Astonishment made her almost forget the bellhop who was waiting by the door for his tip.

Quickly she handed him a bill. "Thanks."

"Anything else, Lieutenant?"

"No, no thanks."

"Put things in your bedroom?"

"No. I'll do that myself."

The bellhop gave her a little salute and left. Annie immediately kicked off her shoes and pulled open the parlor drapes to reveal a spectacular view of the harbor.

Lost in thought, it took several minutes for Annie to notice the muted sound of running water. It was almost the sound of a hard rain, but the sun was bright over Hong Kong, the weather delightfully balmy.

Annie focused on the sound, realizing that it seemed to be coming from inside the suite. She looked toward the closed bedroom door.

Oh, no. It's the shower, she realized. The desk clerk must have accidentally booked her into already occupied rooms. Unless the walls were so thin she was actually hearing the shower next door. Annie hesitated and then, cautiously, approached the bedroom door. She knocked. No response. She gripped the doorknob, slowly turning it, opening the door a crack, peeking in.

She blanched. The suite *was* already occupied. Although Annie didn't see anyone, the bathroom door was ajar and she could distinctly hear the shower. And she saw a sexy black nightgown spread out on the king-sized bed along with a man's slacks and shirt. The newlyweds, she concluded, must be showering together. How romantic for them. How embarrassing for her.

Now what was she going to do? This was supposedly the only available space in the hotel. Only it wasn't available, either. Nothing was going right for her.

Annie closed the bedroom door carefully and looked at her bags in the hallway. Well, there was nothing for it but to haul them back to the lobby and tell the desk clerk she'd goofed. Maybe, if the clerk was embarrassed by her mistake, she'd somehow dig up another room for her in the hotel.

Annie hurried across the parlor, anxious to get out of the suite before she was discovered. It would probably be a toss-up who'd be more embarrassed. Really, Annie thought, how could the clerk have made such a foolish mistake?

The bedroom door opened just as Annie was hoisting her duffel bag. Too late.

"Hey," a male voice called out.

"I'm sor..." Annie spun around. The voice was familiar. Her eyes widened. "David..."

"Who were you expecting?" He wore only a boyish smile, and a skimpy towel wrapped around his waist.

"I...I thought...I saw the...nightgown on the bed..."

His smile deepened. "Did you like it? You look good in black."

"You bought it...for me?"

He chuckled. "Who else?"

Her duffel bag thumped to the floor. "I was so worried about you. When you didn't show at Long Binh, I thought something had happened to you." Her eyes narrowed. "When did you get here?"

"Yesterday."

"But..."

"I thought I'd surprise you."

"You did do that."

"I'm sorry, Annie. I didn't mean for you to worry. I was able to cut loose early and I thought I'd have everything all set here for when you arrived. I did a little shop-

ping, made reservations at a classy harborside
restaurant . . ."

"And you arranged with the desk clerk to keep your
arrival a surprise?"

"I know how you like surprises, kiddo." David let the
towel slide down his hips.

Annie laughed softly. "Oh Nickel. I do love your particular type of surprises."

"Then come over here and prove it."

She ran to him. Threw her arms around him. Held
fiercely on to him. Their lips met and she could feel his
lips quiver beneath hers. *Not so cool, calm and collected
after all, Nickel. Neither am I. Neither am I.*

His warm breath caressed her neck, his lips nibbling her
shoulder, his fingers attending to the zipper of her sundress. The dress dropped to the floor and he lifted her into
his arms.

He carried her into the lavish bedroom and settled them
both on the king-sized bed. He unhooked her white lacy
bra, and traced a line of kisses across her breasts. Slowly,
his mouth trailed down her body as he lowered her silk
panties.

David's caresses seemed part of a dream, a wondrous,
incredible dream from which Annie never wanted to wake.
What she wanted to do was give back to him all that he
was giving to her, to love him fully and with absolute ab-
sorption. Entwined in each other's arms, Annie felt
transported to a sunlit world of slow currents, deep places
and floating clouds.

Memories danced in her mind. A slender fair-haired lass
running along the banks of an estuary, chasing after the
three long-legged, broad-shouldered boys, almost but
never quite catching them; four youngsters diving into the
sun-sweet water of the river, laughing, splashing, having
races. A hand reaching out to pull the girl to shore at the
finish. David's hand. Always David's hand. Even then, all

those years back, there'd been a dazzling connection between them.

That connection had endured and matured. Now they floated together, their arms wrapped around each other, bodies curved and entwined to form a loving, healing whole. That evening they not only made love, they made magic.

Much later, Annie smiled playfully at David as her fingers trailed down his bare chest. "Any more surprises, Nickel?"

He nuzzled her neck, kissed the lobe of her ear, then kissed her mouth. "There was that surprise dinner I arranged. But I think we've missed reservation time."

"I don't need food."

"What do you need?"

"You. Oh you. Only you."

"Annie," he whispered. "I love you."

"I love you back. David, does it make sense to be so happy?"

"Here, with you, like this, it almost seems like Vietnam was some horrible nightmare."

"I know," Annie whispered, unable to keep her mind from flicking back over the weeks and months. *But it's only today that counts. Today is real, wonderful, exhilarating. Today makes tomorrow feel possible.*

She snuggled closer to David, kissing him again, wanting to eradicate his yesterday, obliterate those images of grief and violence, images that they shared, images that hammered and drained them both.

"Have you written anything to Hawk or Turner about us?" Annie asked softly.

"No. Have you?"

Annie laughed softly. "Not in any great detail."

"I'm never going to hear the end of it, you know?"

"I know."

David pressed his lips against her hair. "I don't mind." His warm breath caressed her neck. "You and me together, back in the world. It's all I think about, Annie. I can't hold back thoughts of tomorrow even though they spook me. I think about us being back home, horseback riding together through the woods, swimming down at the creek, smooching in the balcony of the Strand Theater."

Annie closed her eyes and sighed. "What's playing?"

"I don't know . . . I'm too busy making out with you to notice."

"Nothing about doctors or nurses."

"Nothing with John Wayne."

"Nothing sad."

"Nothing violent."

Annie giggled. "Something sexy."

"Mmm."

Annie toyed with David's short-cropped hair. "You'll have to let your hair grow long."

"And get some wide ties like they were showing in the fashion pages of *Life*."

"And I'll get my hair cut in the latest puff style."

"Never."

She laughed. "No, never."

"It's going to be strange. I feel so out of it."

"Yeah, what are the Jets doing, winning the Superbowl? I had fifty bucks on the Colts."

Annie gave his rear end an affectionate pinch. "Well, if you put money on the World Series next fall, you better bet it on the Red Sox."

David stretched languorously against Annie. "Won't it be something if Turner makes it all the way to the Series?"

"Yeah, it'll be something."

David smoothed back her hair. "Don't be disappointed in Turner, Annie. He's only trying, in his own way, to go forward. And it's only because he's so scared."

Annie touched David's cheek. "I know. I'm not disappointed in him anymore. Life is too short, too important, to waste it on disappointments. I love Turner. We all seek our own ways of grappling with pain and grief.''

David drew her close. ''And we all seek our own ways of finding joy. You are my joy, Annie. My light. My spirit. When we get home we'll leave all the pain and grief behind us. We'll leave it buried in Nam. We'll pick up the pieces of our lives. We'll forget,'' he whispered. And again, his voice a muted plea, ''We'll forget.''

''Vietnam is an undeniable fact of our lives, David. And it hasn't all been bad. We found each other. We found Sue Ellen and Jessie and...Tai.'' She held her breath, waiting.

But David's mind didn't rest on Tai. He was thinking about Sue Ellen. ''Wouldn't it be something if Sue Ellen and Hawk did get together?''

''David...''

''Yeah?''

''How do you feel about Tai?''

He gave her a crooked smile. ''He's a great kid. You've done a lot for him, Annie. You should feel good about that.''

''You helped.''

David shrugged. ''It was fun. It cheered me up.''

''Children are such resilient little souls. I can just picture Tai sitting up in the bleachers of Fenway Park cheering Turner on, waving his Red Sox banner, eating a ballpark hot dog, mustard dripping down his chin...''

''Hey, talking about hot dogs, I'm getting hungry. What do you say we go find ourselves a Chinese restaurant and feast on some egg rolls and chow mein?''

Annie tried to hide her disappointment at David switching the topic of conversation. ''That isn't real Chinese food.''

He laughed, swinging his long legs off the bed. ''Well, when in Hong Kong...''

He rose and yanked the covers off her. ''Come on, lazybones. We've got places to go, sights to see.''

"You going to see them in your birthday suit, Nickel?"

He grinned devilishly. "This is a strictly private showing, kiddo."

He reached for her, pulling her up and into his arms. Annie kissed him hard on the lips, and David responded with ardent pleasure. "Maybe we'll just call down for room service," he whispered. "What do you want?"

"You," she whispered. "Now and forever." Tears welled up in her eyes.

David brushed her lips with his. "You got me, kiddo."

Her eyes lifted and found his. "Do you mean it, David? Now...and forever?"

"As long as forever lasts."

Her tears fell freely. "Forever lasts a long, long time..."

FOR FIVE GLORIOUS days and nights Annie and David were lovers on holiday. In the mornings they shopped, picking up souvenirs. In the heat of the day they sought refuge in the less populated areas, picnicking on the unspoiled hillsides, admiring the vividly colored orioles and parakeets winging over them. David gathered huge bouquets of lady slipper orchids and lime-scented bauhinia blossoms and presented them to Annie. And each evening before dinner they took a ricksha ride through the narrow, crowded streets of Hong Kong, enjoying the atmosphere tingling with activity and excitement.

On their last evening they rode to gay and gaudy Aberdeen Harbor to dine on one of the lavish floating boat restaurants with its hanging banners and strings of lights suspended from its curved roof. They sat at a table overlooking the blue velvet water of the South China Sea, the lanterns of the restaurant splashing ripples of light on the water, the sun dropping below the horizon in an elegant fan of muted cinnamon.

Annie and David selected lobsters which were then cooked and served to them in a sweetly pungent sauce.

"Fantastic," Annie said, swallowing a bite of the succulent pearly white meat, but reflecting on far more than the food.

"Let's come back to Hong Kong sometime," Annie said dreamily, refusing to let her spirits flag. "I love this city. It's so alive, so exciting, so exotic." She leaned forward a little, her face animated. "I mean, snake shops, for heaven's sake. And this floating restaurant. I've never experienced anything like it."

"Yeah," David muttered, "our lives have been full of new experiences."

Annie knew he meant Nam, but she gave him a teasing smile. "Thanks to you, Nickel, I've experienced some incredible moments."

Her smile broke through his morose mood. He grinned and reached across the table for her hand, his index finger idly skimming her knuckles. "They have been incredible." He looked down at her hand in silence and then he met her gaze again. "I bought you something."

"Oh? What? What is it?"

His expression turned serious and compelling. "Annie, listen to me. I know we promised not to talk about anything heavy tonight, but I…" He stopped, closing his eyes for a moment. "I love you, Annie. And if I…make it…there's nothing in the world I want more than to pick up the pieces of my life. I wrote my father yesterday. I told him that I wanted to go back to law school, get my degree. I want…to live the good life, Annie. I want to live it with you. I want to marry you."

Annie's heart raced. "I want that, too."

He pulled out a tiny velvet box from his pocket. "Open it," he said, handing it to her.

Annie's fingers were trembling as she lifted the lid. Inside was an exquisite ring of white jade in a platinum setting. "Oh, David. It's beautiful."

She took the ring out, returned it to David, and extended her left hand. He slipped the ring on her finger and then brought her hand to his lips. He couldn't bring himself to look at her as he whispered, "If I make it, Annie, we'll bury all the horror and pain and the awful stench of war. We'll never look back. Never."

Annie tenderly stroked his cheek. "I don't think that's possible, David. Vietnam is a part of us now. We can't erase it or ignore it." Not only did she think it impossible to forget Vietnam, Annie believed that to forget it was to forget the unique and powerful bond between her and David that had been born of the war.

But a disturbing vehemence lit David's eyes. He seemed consumed by a desperate need to forget. He pressed her palm against his lips. "Oh Annie, it's going to be wonderful . . . if we can just get there."

Chapter Sixteen

A time to break down, and a time to build up...

Long Binh, June, 1969

The familiar sound of cracking gum came from where Sue Ellen lay, sprawled out on Annie's cot, flipping through the pages of a bridal magazine.

"This one is outstanding," Sue Ellen said, holding up a picture of a traditional Empire-style satin gown with long lacy sleeves and a high lace-trimmed collar.

Annie grimaced. "Too old-maidish."

Sue Ellen laughed. "A bride can't be an old maid, Scarlett," she said as she riffled through some more pages. "Okay, what about something with a gypsy flavor?"

Annie shook her head without bothering to look at the picture.

"I know. Wear a body stocking and throw a lace tablecloth over yourself. Everyone'll think it's the latest Paris original."

Annie gave a distracted shrug.

"Hey Scarlett, that was supposed to be funny. Where are the ha-has?"

"Huh?"

"No, not huh. Ha. Ha-ha."

Annie gave her friend a bemused look. "You're losing it, Sue Ellen."

"Me? Where are you, Annie? You're certainly not here."

Annie smiled. "Can you blame me? I was thinking about that big no-no—the future. Me and David and..."

"And? Don't leave me hanging, Annie?"

"And Tai. Me and David and Tai."

"You're really gone on that kid."

Annie laughed. "I'm gone on both those kids."

"What does David think about having a ready-made family?"

"He'll think it's wonderful . . . once I tell him."

"Annie..."

"I know. I know," Annie said guiltily. "But, I'm waiting for the right moment. When I broached the topic last time, David wasn't exactly gung ho on the idea. But that's because of where his head's at right now. He's focused on only one thing. Survival. And that's how it should be. It's so hard for him to talk about the future. He doesn't even want to think about it. I know he's scared it'll jinx him. I'm plenty superstitious myself. But, I know, once the danger and horror is behind us, David will come around and welcome Tai with open arms. You've seen them together."

"I've seen all three of you together at the orphanage," Sue Ellen said with a smile. "You do make a terrific looking threesome."

Annie gazed down dreamily at her engagement ring. "I can just picture Tai at our wedding, dwarfed between Nanna and Dad, all of them holding hands, watching me walk down the aisle. But my eyes will be fixed on David, standing there at the altar waiting for me, looking so outstanding in his tux." She gave Sue Ellen an impish smile. "David marrying me. Who says dreams don't come true?"

Sue Ellen smiled wistfully. She, too, was counting on her dreams coming true.

"All my life," Annie confided, "there's never been anyone for me but David. All the countless dreams and fantasies...and now it's really happening. Or it will, once we all get the hell out of here." She gave Sue Ellen an envious look. "Just think, you'll be on that Big Freedom Bird in a few weeks."

"A few weeks? You mean exactly three weeks, four days and..." Sue Ellen glanced at her watch. "Seven hours."

"And David's got six weeks, three days and probably the same number of hours," Annie reflected.

Sue Ellen swung around to a sitting position. "Once David's homeward bound, you'll only have five weeks on your own before you'll be catching the Bird to Paradise yourself."

Annie felt pangs of loneliness already. "I'm going to miss you, Sue Ellen. It's going to be so weird here without you."

"I'll be seeing you soon enough, Scarlett." Sue Ellen stretched back out on the bed and sighed. "I finally got up the courage and wrote the folks that I'd only be coming home for a short visit before flying down to Oakdale, Maryland, to see Hawk."

"How do you think they'll take the news?" Annie asked.

"They won't be too happy. But..." Sue Ellen hesitated. "Maybe I'll end up back in Queens faster than I'd planned. Good old Vinnie is still waiting in the wings."

"It'll work out for you and Hawk. You've got to expect these mood swings from him after what he's been through."

Sue Ellen frowned. "But he was really coming out of it. Working with the VVAW, finally getting ready to leave the hospital and get his own place. We were beginning to make...some serious plans." She swiped at her suddenly teary eyes. "It's so damn unfair."

"I know," Annie said sympathetically. "That seems to be the name of the game. But look at it his way. Hawk was told from the beginning that, down the road, there might be some physical complications from his wound. And it could have been worse.''

"Worse than six hours of surgery on his liver? Worse than ending up flat on his back for six weeks? Worse than feeling like his whole life was coming unglued again after having spent close to a year painstakingly gluing the pieces back together as best he could?'' Tears slipped down Sue Ellen's cheeks. For once in her life she didn't try to hide them. "Worse than resigning himself to being a cripple for the rest of his life? He's giving up, Annie. I'd do anything for him... if only he'd let me.''

When Hawk had first written to Sue Ellen that he was going to need some corrective surgery Sue Ellen had responded immediately that she'd chuck in the last few months of service with the Red Cross and hightail it straight to Oakdale to be with him. But Hawk wouldn't hear of it. He'd made it very clear to Sue Ellen that he didn't want her first glimpse of him to be lying flat on his back in a hospital bed. Now, even the thought of having her see him in his wheelchair troubled him. And, even though the doctors still held out some hope that he might one day regain a degree of mobility in his legs, Hawk seemed to be resigning himself to staying in a wheelchair for the rest of his life. And what was really getting Sue Ellen down was that, in his recent letters, he'd begun questioning what kind of life that would be for her.

Annie felt for Sue Ellen and Hawk, but she was preoccupied with her own problems. She and David had hardly had any time together since their return from Hong Kong. A few days after they got back to Long Binh, David's platoon had been transferred to a fire-base somewhere north, near Da Nang. Because they were involved in clandestine operations their exact location was top secret. David was only able to wangle a few one- and two-day passes down to Long Binh.

When Annie did see David, they both felt the pressure of having so little time to be together. Annie was nervous and David was tense, distracted, on edge. They found themselves clinging to each other, their lovemaking urgent and fiercely passionate. But there was no talk of the future. Instead they reminisced about their blissful moments in Vung Tau and Hong Kong, their happy times in Saigon. They tried to make each moment together precious. Wrapped in each other's arms, they did everything possible to seal themselves off from the horrors of the present.

Secretly Annie longed to talk with David about their future, so that it would feel more real to her. But David would have none of it. When she was alone, if not for the jade engagement ring on her finger, Annie would have thought his marriage proposal was nothing more than a figment of her imagination.

As for David, he was wholly focused on simply trying to make it through the day, his belief in the possibility of even the next day a bit shaky.

Hong Kong and Vung Tau seemed awfully far away and Beaumont, Maryland even farther. The real world was a fantasy, the nightmare of war was reality. And now, with their time in-country getting short, the nightmare had intensified. Annie knew that she, David and Sue Ellen all had short-time syndrome in a bad way. The symptoms were a magnified fear that something terrible would happen just before your DEROS date, anxiety about dealing with relationships back home and the terror that everything you'd dreamed about and hoped for on returning home wouldn't materialize.

And there was something else on Annie's mind. Tai. Deep in her heart, she knew that she could not leave Nam without him. Taking him was not an act of charity. Tai had become a part of her. To leave him behind would be to leave a part of her heart and soul. Sister Mary Catherine had given up trying to discourage her, and had promised to file all the paperwork for the adoption as soon as Annie gave her the go-ahead. But now that go-ahead depended on David.

Talking with David about Tai meant talking with him about the future, which David had clearly been avoiding. Still, when she'd seen him last, Annie had gathered her courage and broached the subject.

"Tai's doing so well now, David. You should see him. I'm really crazy about that kid."

"He's a great kid," David concurred. They were cuddled together on her narrow cot.

Annie felt encouraged. "I got a note from Jessie last week. She's back in Washington and she's been getting together with Luong. She said the change in him is incredible. And the family who sponsored him has decided to legally adopt him."

"That's great," David murmured absently.

"David?"

"Mmm?" He was breathing in the scent of her hair, clean, fresh, wholesome. It was an incredible scent. He slipped the bright green ribbon from her hair and idly twined it around his fingers.

Annie smiled at him, remembering the time so many months back—a lifetime ago it seemed—when she'd spied him slipping one of her hair ribbons into his pocket. Did he still have that red ribbon, she wondered?

"David, what would you think about the idea of my bringing Tai home? To Beaumont? I've been talking about it with Sister Mary Catherine. She thinks she could arrange for me…to adopt him." There, she'd said it. She held her breath, waiting for his response.

"You're joking."

"No. No, I'm not joking."

"Well, then you're crazy."

"I love him."

David pulled away, rolled onto his back and stared at the ceiling. "You're not making any sense, Annie. It wouldn't work out. I mean…where would that leave us?"

"I'm not putting any pressure on you, David. I'm not saying we rush into marriage just because of Tai. I'll move back in with my dad and look after Tai. You can return to

law school, get settled...whatever. And once you're...
established..."

"I couldn't, Annie." He shut his eyes. "I couldn't
handle it. Like I keep saying, all I want to do if I make it
out of this hole alive is...to forget." His heavy-lidded eyes
fluttered open again, but he didn't look at her. He kept on
staring up at the ceiling. "A lot of the short guys here are
collecting all kinds of...souvenirs. Reminders to bring
home with them. Not me. I don't want to bring home one
of those pottery dishes with dragons painted on them, or
even a snapshot. I don't want anything with the sight,
sound or look of this wretched place. To me, Vietnam *is*
despair, and I'm choking on it. All I want is to breathe
free again."

Annie could taste despair in the back of her throat. If
David couldn't tolerate even a piece of Vietnamese pottery for the memories it provoked, how would he ever
come round to accepting a Vietnamese child into his life?

"Are you saying that I have to make a choice, David?
You or Tai?" How could she ever choose when she loved
them both so much? They could be a family. They could
be so happy. Tai was an utterly innocent victim of war,
even more so than they were. Giving Tai a chance at a
better life gave some meaning to what they'd all endured.

But David didn't see it that way. Neither of them
wanted to argue. But when finally David drew her to him,
and they made love, for the first time Annie sensed herself holding back, unable to give herself fully to the moment or to David.

Short-time syndrome, Annie told herself later. Once
David got back to the world, he'd feel differently about
Tai. He'd come around. He had to. She couldn't leave Tai
behind.

ON JUNE TWENTY-NINTH, two days after Sue Ellen caught
that Freedom Bird back to the world, Annie was called
into the chief nurse's office. When she walked in, Annie's eyes immediately shot over to the tall, broad-

shouldered soldier standing at the window. He looked over at her, his expression grim, his body ramrod stiff.

Annie went cold. She recognized him. He was a sergeant in David's unit. She'd chatted with him a few times.

The sergeant attempted a smile of greeting, but it didn't quite come off. As her eyes met his, he dropped his gaze. He couldn't look directly at her.

Oh God, bad news, she thought, her chest constricting. *It's bad news. Okay, okay. Just let David not be dead. Not that. Please, please...*

The chief nurse's chair scraped across the wooden floor as she rose from behind her desk. "I'll let the two of you have a few minutes."

Annie heard the office door click shut. She felt as if the whole world had emptied, leaving only her and this messenger of ill tidings. She wouldn't cry. She wouldn't let herself. Crying would mean she already believed the worst.

The sergeant was giving her a soft, sad look.

Stop it. Stop looking at me like that. It isn't helping me.

In a rush he said, "I'm sorry to tell you that Captain Nichols is missing in action, ma'am." Gulp. "Lieutenant Magill." He kept shifting his cap from hand to hand. "The captain...he told us about you two...being engaged and all. I had a pass and I thought...well, I didn't want you to hear it...in passing."

"Missing in action?" She gave the sergeant a searching look.

He set his cap on the desk, clenched his hands, dug them in his jacket pockets, then pulled them out. "Yes, ma'am...Lieutenant. I'm afraid I can't go into specific details...because of the nature of our mission..."

"When?" *Missing in action. Missing. Lost. David was lost. Poor little lamb who's lost his way...*

"Three days ago. It's possible...he was picked up by Charlie."

"Captured?" *Prisoner of war? David a POW? Pow, pow, pow.* Annie's hand went to her stomach as if she were being punched.

"Maybe you wanna sit down, Lieutenant. Maybe some water. Really, ma'am . . . you don't look good."

She watched the sergeant move his lips, but she couldn't hear any words. There was such a terrible rumbling in her head.

"He's . . . short," she whispered. "Four weeks, two days . . . how many hours?" She strained to think. She counted in her head. Numbers were concrete, reassuring.

"Lieutenant, here's the chair now. You sit down. That's it, Lieutenant. Just sit down here and take it easy. I'm real sorry, Lieutenant." He knelt. "It could be worse," he said, and faltered. "Don't give up hope now, Lieutenant. Even if Charlie got him, the captain's one clever fellah. He'll figure a way to escape. Yeah, I'd put money on it, Lieutenant."

Annie nodded, looking down at her hands, feeling lost. The rumbling sound had stopped in her head. Now she could hear every sound in the room, magnified: the soldier shuffling his feet; his nervous breathing; the rustle of papers on the desk from the breeze drifting through the open window; her own heartbeat.

Finally she looked up at him. "It's all right, Sergeant. Sergeant Nelson, isn't it?"

"Yes ma'am. Roy Nelson. You want a cigarette, Lieutenant."

She nodded.

He pulled out a pack of Kools from his shirt pocket, tapped out two cigarettes, lit them both with a silver lighter, and passed one over to her.

She took a long, greedy drag of the mentholated cigarette, then let the smoke out in a whoosh.

"He talked about you a lot, Lieutenant. He was always talking about you."

She gave the sergeant a look of surprise. "Really? David's never been much of a talker. Not the kind of guy who wears his heart on his sleeve."

The soldier shrugged. "Out in the bush, we're all kinda exposed, if ya know what I mean? We're all kinda jiggy... ya know, tense. And lotsa times we're playin' a waiting game. It gets real boring. Even though we're scared. So we talk. We talk to keep ourselves from thinkin'. We all talk about our girls. Some of us that don't have someone special... well, we talk about the girls we met over here."

"Do you have a girl, Sergeant?" She could hear her own voice as if she were in an echo chamber.

"I did. Yessirree, I did. But..." He shrugged. "She got tired of waitin'. I don't blame her. But... I still carry her picture on me. For good luck, ya know."

Annie's expression turned thoughtful. "I was wondering, Sergeant. Did the Captain ever... show you a piece of... ribbon? Red ribbon?"

"Red ribbon?" He gave her a bemused look. "Say, now that you mention it, he did have this raggedy piece of ribbon strung through his dog tag. When we were in the bush he'd tie it around his leg, so the dog tag fitted into his boot. Ya know, so it wouldn't make noise. Ya don't wanna give yourself away out in the bush. Yeah, a red ribbon. I remember, 'cause it was kinda... different."

The sergeant's eyes trailed Annie's hair. Today she was wearing a ponytail tied with a bright yellow velvet ribbon. "Yeah, he's got that ribbon on him, Lieutenant. His lucky ribbon, right?"

Annie nodded her head slowly. "Yeah. Lucky." Her lips quivered, but she managed a soft smile. "His good-luck charm," she whispered.

"He'll make it, Lieutenant. That lucky ribbon has seen him through lots of tough times, take it from me. No reason to stop believing in it now."

ANNIE SPENT the next two weeks desperately clinging to her belief that David was alive and safe, but there was no change in his official status. He remained missing in action. MIA.

To fight her own depression, Annie wangled a two-day pass so that she could visit with Tai at the orphanage. As always, before she arrived, she stopped at the PX to pick up bars of soap, a supply of chocolate bars and as much fresh fruit as she could get, all of which were almost impossible for the nuns to come by.

Sister Mary Catherine greeted Annie at the gate, taking one of the shopping bags from her, not commenting on how drawn and pale she looked.

"Any word about David?"

"No. Nothing," Annie said, and then she added after a moment, "But I haven't given up hope." She was clinging desperately to that hope, it was all she had. Hope and Tai. One day... one day they would all be a family. She, David and Tai. It felt so right to her. And it would to David, too, once...

"Of course not."

"How's Tai?" Annie asked in a quavering voice.

"He's missed you."

"I've missed him, too."

They were walking slowly toward the main house, but now Sister Mary Catherine came to a stop. "Annie, there's something I have to tell you."

Annie's heart started to pound in her chest. "Is he sick? Is Tai sick?"

"Oh no. No, nothing like that. I'm so sorry, Annie. I didn't mean to alarm you. Nothing is wrong with Tai. It's just... I heard from Jessie Morgan last week. Did she happen to write you?"

"A few weeks ago. She wrote all about Luong and how well he's doing. Is it about Luong, Sister? Jessie said that he was doing wonderfully."

"Did Jessie mention that the Powell family is going to adopt Luong?"

"Yes. Yes she did. I thought it was terrific. The adoption didn't fall through, did it? Did the family change their minds?"

"No, quite the contrary. They're thrilled about it, according to Jessie. So thrilled, in fact, that they..." The nun gave Annie a measuring look before she finished the sentence. "The Powells have friends out in Minnesota who they've talked to about... adopting Tai. I imagine Luong must have had some part to play in it. He hasn't forgotten his 'little brother.'"

Annie's response was immediate and heartfelt. "Minnesota. No. Oh no. They can't. They can't have him. Oh Sister, they can't."

"Annie. Poor child. Please, I didn't mean to upset you so. You did tell me that David was against the idea..."

"He'll feel differently once he..." Annie stopped. *Once he gets home,* she was going to say. But, what if he didn't get home? What if... "I can't lose them both, Sister."

Annie grabbed hold of the nun's flowing sleeve. "I want you to file the adoption papers for me right away."

"Annie..."

"Please, Sister. I want to adopt Tai. I'm going home in six weeks. If it takes longer than that to make the arrangements I'll stay on in Saigon. But I am not leaving Vietnam without Tai."

JULY CAME with the heat and the heaviest rains: a thick, constant hiss drumming against the tin roofs of Long Binh. Annie felt adrift. Every day she checked on David's status. Every day she received the same report. MIA.

The adoption procedure was creeping along at a snail's pace. Sister Mary Catherine was doing her best, but she confided that it would help if Annie knew someone who could pull some strings. Jessie was the first one to come to mind, but she'd left Washington and was on assignment somewhere in the Middle East.

In desperation, Annie decided to write to David's father for help. She'd only written the Judge once before, shortly after learning that David was missing in action. She'd offered her sympathy, told the Judge how much she loved David, and that she believed he was alive and would make it back.

The Judge had written her back a formal, terse thank-you letter in response. He was a hard man. No doubt he felt that his son, like his wife, had bitterly disappointed and betrayed him by refusing to follow the path he'd set. Annie believed the Judge was terribly upset about David's disappearance, but he was not a man to admit to or share his sorrow. Annie held out little hope that the Judge would pull strings to help her, but she had to explore every last possibility.

Annie also wrote to her family about her plans to adopt Tai. Much to Annie's disappointment, neither her father nor Nanna was overly enthusiastic about the idea. They wrote to her with lists of concerns, both practical and emotional. Still, Annie hoped that once they met Tai, they would come around. How could they help but fall in love with Tai?

But Annie's biggest surprise came late in July, when she finally heard from her brother. It had hurt her that Turner hadn't written her after hearing about David, but Nanna had sent her a letter explaining that Turner had been devastated by the news. For once, Nanna said, Turner had been unable to suppress his pain and grief. Probably for that very reason, he'd been unable to write. Until now.

Dear Annie,

I suddenly seem to be looking at the world through blurry eyes. It's awfully hard to keep your eye on that fastball being hurled at you, when your vision isn't up to par. The thing of it is, the crying just came on me and I can't seem to get it to stop. I think about Hawk and David and you, and I feel scared inside. I never felt so scared and lost before, Annie.

Yesterday, I went to see Hawk. I hadn't seen him since his operation. I'd talked to him on the phone though, and I knew he was real down about the setback. And then there was the bad news about David. Like me, Hawk took it real hard. Only good thing was, it made us both realize how lucky we had it. Hawk and I talked a lot about David and, to tell you the truth, we did some crying on each other's shoulders. We're not giving up hope, though. So, don't you give up either, Annie. If we can put a man on the moon, we can find one missing soldier.

I spent the whole day with Hawk and his old lady. Sue Ellen is really something, Annie. I never saw two people so in love. She told me she plans to have Hawk out of the hospital within a couple of weeks. And Hawk's saying he's beginning to feel some sensations in his legs again.

I'm counting the days till you get back home, Annie. I feel like somewhere along the line we got disconnected—my doing, I know. But I want to be a part of your life again and I want you to be a part of mine. Most of all, I want you to know that I'm there for you, Annie. For you and little Tai. Dad told me all about your plan to adopt him and I think it's just great. A boy couldn't find himself a better, more loving, more giving mama. I can't wait to meet that kid of yours, Annie. He must be something. I already know you are, kiddo.

> *Your best and only brother,*
> *Turner*
> *xxxxxx*

Chapter Seventeen

A time to pluck up that which is planted...

Long Binh, August, 1969

It was another rain-drenched morning. Before heading over to the hospital to start her shift, Annie stopped by the Army engineers' office to check on David's status. It had become part of her daily routine, a part that filled her with trepidation.

She opened the screen door, nodding to the sergeant at the desk, who had become a familiar face. The sergeant rose as she entered the small, dank offices.

"I've been waiting for you to show up all morning, Lieutenant. I even sent a grunt over to your hooch to track you down. You must have just missed him." He broke into a wide smile.

Annie stared at that smile and she began to tremble all over. In a voice she could barely recognize as her own, she whispered, "Wait. I better sit down." Her legs had gone suddenly wobbly. She couldn't take her eyes off the sergeant's smile. It was the best, the warmest, the most comforting smile she had ever seen. *Good news. Oh, thank God, good news.*

The sergeant, a small, wiry man with close-cropped blond hair and a flamboyant handlebar mustache, came around to help Annie over to a chair. Then he rested a hand on her shoulder. "Captain Nichols is in a Tokyo hospital. He's getting shipped Stateside soon."

Annie closed her eyes and clasped her hands together to try to still the trembling. "How bad?"

"MFW. Multiple frag wounds."

"Yes, I know the initials."

He smiled awkwardly. "Yeah, right." He squeezed her shoulder. "He's gonna be okay."

Not only did Annie experience a rush of relief and joy, she felt a return of life, a calming of the raging storms inside of her.

Still, there were questions to be asked, details to understand. Confusion clung to her along with her happiness. "Why'd he remain on the MIA list after being sent to Tokyo? I don't get it."

"The report I got in says he was found in the bush outside of Da Nang about a week ago, by one of our mobile assault units. The captain was unconscious. No ID on him. Must have taken off his dog tag sometime before he lost consciousness in case Charlie tripped over him. All the boys in Nichols's unit know they've got to keep a low profile, if you follow my drift."

Annie was trying to keep her heart from racing right out of her chest. "Yes. I follow. Go on."

"The captain got medevaced over to the 95th Evac Hospital in Da Nang. He pulled out of the coma but there was...this memory loss. He couldn't even give his name, rank and serial number. So they patched him up and shipped him to Tokyo...to the psych ward."

"The psych ward?"

"Relax, Lieutenant. He didn't flip out. The docs just figured he needed some time and care to help him get his memory back. And it worked. That's how come we finally got the word on him."

"Then...he really is...okay now? He remembers...everything?"

The sergeant's eyes sparkled. "So it seems."

A soft laugh fell from her lips. Her cheeks reddened. "Thank you, Sergeant," she whispered.

"He's a real lucky guy, Lieutenant."

"Oh, I know. Thank God our boys found him..."

"No, I meant lucky to have a woman like you."

"Oh, Sergeant..."

"There's...uh...one thing, Lieutenant."

Annie's breath caught in her throat. One thing? One thing he hadn't told her? David wasn't really all right? She didn't want to hear and yet she found herself asking, "What is it, Sergeant?"

"He's pulled a medical discharge, Lieutenant."

Annie was finding it hard to breathe. "A medical discharge?" *The Army didn't hand out medical discharges for minor wounds. Only injuries that were incapacitating, permanent...*

"It's nothing real bad, Lieutenant. One of the frags got him close to his eye. His right eye."

"Did he...lose it?"

"No. They operated in Da Nang and were able to save the eye itself."

"How much vision loss?" she asked quietly.

The Sergeant hesitated.

Annie nodded. His hesitation was answer enough. He had to have lost all or most of his sight in that eye to rate a medical discharge. Still, she asked if she could see the report for herself, see it all in writing.

"It's...classified. Everything that comes into this section is classified, Lieutenant."

"Right."

"I really shouldn't have divulged..." He shrugged. "Anyway, once he gets back to the States, maybe they'll be able to operate on the eye again. It's pretty much patchwork out here, no offense, Lieutenant."

Annie rose from her chair. Her legs weren't shaky anymore. And her hands had even stopped trembling.

"Thanks for everything, Sergeant."

"My pleasure, Lieutenant. Hey, aren't you out of here in a few weeks, yourself?"

Annie nodded.

"Well then, you and the captain will be having yourselves a hell of a reunion, I bet."

Annie smiled faintly. As she left the office she was filled with a new apprehension. How was David going to react when he found out she wasn't coming home alone? The question she had once asked David played over and over in her head. *Are you asking me to make a choice between you and Tai?* It would be David's choice now.

Annie wrote David that afternoon. She knew that by the time her letter arrived Stateside, David would have made it home, too. It was a difficult letter to compose, the most difficult she'd ever written. She tore up what seemed like a hundred attempts, finally opting for something simple and forthright.

Dear David,

I love you very much and there are no words to express my joy at finding out you are home and safe at last.

Tai and I will be home soon now, too. I have not made a choice between the two of you, David. But I have made a choice nonetheless. I could turn my back on life and love. Or I could choose to live and love fully. I chose love.

I love you both, David. I hope you'll let us all heal our wounds together. Can you give love a chance, my darling?

All my love always,
Annie

"And this is a picture of your new great-grandmother, Tai. Nanna. She's very beautiful. Of course she's a little older now than when this publicity still was taken." She ruffled Tai's hair as he sat cross-legged on the floor beside her in her hooch.

"She got old man, Annie?" Tai gave her a devilish smile. He knew Annie didn't approve of the American GI slang he'd picked up from Luong.

Annie narrowed her eyes, but smiled. "Your great-grandfather died many years ago. I never knew him, but he was a very dashing young man."

"Dashing?" Tai's bright eyes registered his confusion.

"Oh, handsome, brave..."

"Like David?"

Annie tried hard to smile. "Yes. Like David."

David, who had not answered her letter. David, who was recuperating at the Oakdale V.A. hospital. David, who according to a recent letter she'd received from Hawk, was in an "understandably" withdrawn state of mind. "Give him time," Hawk had written. Sue Ellen had added a postscript to the letter. "Love is thicker than war. Keep the faith, Scarlett."

Annie felt a gentle tug on her sleeve. She reached for Tai's hand. "Sorry. I guess I was woolgathering."

Tai looked perplexed. "What is that?"

She tapped her index finger to her temple. "Thinking. I was just thinking," she said softly.

"You okay, Annie?"

She gave him a nod and smiled, but Tai was unconvinced.

"Don't worry, Annie. We be family, just like you always say." He hesitated, a tiny little smile curving his lips. "Okay, momma?" he whispered tentatively.

Momma. It was the sweetest word, whispered from the sweetest lips. Annie smiled gently at her child. Yes, her child. Her very own. Tai Magill. Her boy. She'd finally received unofficial word that the approval was being granted. No thanks, however, to David's father.

The South Vietnamese government had moved at a snail's pace. Every time Annie had thought she'd answered every question, filed every conceivable paper, provided every possible document, there was another official request.

To complicate matters, the adoption board had received a letter from the Minnesotan couple who were friends of Luong's adoptive parents, asking for an application to adopt Tai.

In the end, it was Annie's own family who had come through for her. Turner wrote to the adoption board on official Red Sox stationery, declaring that he would personally see to all of Tai's financial needs. Even her dad and Nanna, despite their private reservations, sent beautiful letters of support to the board. They lauded Annie and pledged themselves to Tai's welfare. Annie was deeply touched and appreciative.

Now she smiled at her son. It had been a long, hard pull, but here she was, showing him pictures of his new family. And as soon as she received the official adoption papers and Tai's visa and passport, he would be meeting them all in person. A shadow crossed her features. If only David would be there, too...

Tai gave her a soft, moist kiss on her cheek and bestowed a cheering smile on her.

"I love you, Tai." She hugged him against her breast and Tai wrapped his little arms around her neck. His breath smelled of the popcorn they had just shared. Tai adored popcorn and he delighted in the prospect of one day eating a giant bag of buttered popcorn in the Beaumont movie theater. He didn't care what movie he saw. All he cared about was the freshly buttered popcorn she'd told him about.

A tiny crease appeared in the smooth skin between Tai's eyes as he pulled his face away and looked at Annie. "We go home soon, yes?"

She smoothed back his black silky hair away from his brow. "Yes, son. Soon. And first thing we do when we get home is get you a real American haircut. What do you say?"

"No. First thing, I ride horse on Papa-san's farm. He say he teach me, right?"

Annie laughed. "Right, but I thought the first thing you wanted was buttered popcorn at the movies."

"That first thing, too. And see Sue Ellen and her old man, Hawk. Yes?"

Annie grinned at Tai's slang, thrilled that there'd be time enough to teach him proper English. "And we'll get to see Hawk's brand-new apartment." Hawk's and Sue Ellen's. Annie was truly happy for her two dear friends. Poor Sue Ellen had been a wreck when she left Nam. She was so afraid of her first face-to-face encounter with Hawk. But, as Sue Ellen had written later, the minute Hawk laid eyes on her, the connection was immediate and intense. All their doubts and fears had instantly evaporated. And in no time flat, Sue Ellen had wheeled him out of that V.A. hospital, and helped him set up his own apartment. A week later she'd moved in with him. The most wonderful news of all was that Hawk had continued to have sensations in his legs and he'd begun a whole new course of outpatient therapy. Annie firmly believed that it was Sue Ellen's love and fierce commitment to Hawk that was the secret behind Hawk's improvement.

Love, Annie believed, could conquer pain, despair and grief. Love could make miracles happen. Annie continued to cling to the possibility of miracles.

"What do you want to do first, Annie?"

Tai's voice pulled her back from her ruminations, but she hadn't heard his question. "What?"

"What do you want to do first thing when you go home?" he repeated.

When I go home . . . It would all feel and be so different, she thought. She could never return to the world she had left. So much had changed in a year, but nothing so much as her. Would she fit in, would she ever belong again?

And the truly burning question was, would being home have meaning without David there to share her plans and dreams with her? If only he'd written. All she could think was that he must have seen her adoption of Tai as a betrayal.

He'd been against it. He'd made that clear enough. Was she being utterly unrealistic to hope he would have a change of heart? And yet Annie knew that deep down, David loved Tai, too. They could be a wonderful family, the three of them. If only...

"Annie...you sad?"

"No." She turned her face away from Tai so he wouldn't see the quick tears which stung her eyes. To divert his attention, she grabbed up the photo of her father posing alongside his championship horse, Relay. "One day I'll take a picture of you standing beside your very own championship horse. What do you think of that?"

But Tai wasn't looking at the photo in Annie's hand. He picked up the one of Turner, Hawk and David at the beach. "What you call them again, Annie?"

It had become hard for her to bring out that photo. Hard to see again the happy, carefree looks that had once shone on the faces of those boys she so adored. Hard to look at Hawk, tallest in the group, standing in the sand on his strong, muscular, football-player legs. Hard to look at Turner, who bore no sign of the grief, pain and loss he could no longer escape. Hardest of all to look at David, so gay and spirited in that photo, his smile so open and full of mischief. David, her tender and passionate lover, the man who gave her life shape and color.

"The Three Musketeers," she whispered. "I call them my Three Musketeers."

"Tell me, Annie. Tell me stories about Three Musketeers."

"Not right now, sweetheart," she murmured.

Tai stretched out his hand and touched Annie's cheek. "You can tell later, okay?"

"Yes, later." Once again she hugged her child to her breast, tighter now, a feeling of intense attachment, love and need enveloping her.

ANNIE AND TAI ended up having to spend three weeks in Saigon, post-DEROS, waiting for the final adoption papers and Tai's exit visa. In all that time there was still no word from David. Annie's faith in that particular miracle began to flag. On her last day of mail call in-country, she received one final letter. It was from Sue Ellen.

Dear Scarlett,

This missive is to help prepare you for your reentry to the "world." If you think Neil Armstrong had it rough getting his land legs after diddy-bopping around on the moon, it ain't nothin' compared to what it's like for us "vets" in the good ol' U.S. of A.

First of all, except for your family and friends, don't expect cheering, flag-waving crowds giving you a hero's welcome home. My advice is to check out of your uniform and into your civvies before you even exit the plane. That way you may avoid getting rotten eggs and tomatoes pelted at you by the protestors.

Okay, that takes care of landing. Next. Be prepared for lots of funny looks when you start talking. Like, you might mention your butter bar and someone will tell you you ought to try the latest margarine. Tell someone you lived in a hooch for the past year and they'll figure you mean a loony bin. (Well, maybe they wouldn't be so far off!) Mention those notches in your short-timer stick and the rumor will spread that you've been in the poky for the last year. And, on the other side of the coin, you'll be hearing some lingo here you won't understand. Like everyone in the States is talking about The Hog Farm. That's what they're calling the farm up in Woodstock, New York, where they just held this unbelievable acid rock concert. I wanted to go, but Hawk's not up to that kind of trip yet. Anyway, Hawk's into country-and-western music these days. Ugh!!

Okay, next big topic around town. Diets. There's this new rage for dieting. Everyone wants to be Twiggy. (Hawk, thank the stars, likes a woman with some meat on her bones.) Anyway, there seems to be an endless array of diets floating around, and every gal you meet is likely to

be on one of them. I'm coming out with my own diet. The
stop stuffing your face diet. Whatta ya think?!

    Let's move on to habits. *You know, the quirky little*
habits we've picked up over a year in-country? Like,
tucking our pant legs into our boots after we strip to go to
sleep, so if we get some incoming we can slip back into our
clothes fast and make it to the bunkers. Or like buying a
dozen of everything at the PX because we never knew
when the supply would dry up. I almost flipped out the
first time I went into a supermarket in Oakdale. And let
me tell you, it took me weeks to get used to eating off a
china plate instead of a metal tray. No kidding!

    And now for a special warning, Scarlett. Be prepared
to freak out a little every time you hear a car backfire or
a crack of thunder. I still sometimes find myself diving
under the bed in a storm, reaching frantically for my hel-
met and flak jacket, terrified a rocket's gonna explode
right over me. Hawk says it'll pass. He should know.

    Okay, Scarlett, I know that the whole time you're
reading this letter, all you really want to read about is what
gives with loverboy. Well, here's the scoop. He's out of the
hospital and spending some time "on the road." He told
Hawk he needed to move around a little. He feels rest-
less. Hawk thinks he's got to do some private grieving over
his loss of the sight in his right eye as well as all the emo-
tional losses he's suffered. Like Hawk says, all of us who
make it home have our mourning time to do. So give lov-
erboy his time, Scarlett. He's running scared now, but
he'll come round. He loves you. And once he works things
through, he'll realize he loves Tai, too. Give that gor-
geous kid of yours a great big hug from me and tell him
that Uncle Hawk can't wait to meet him. It won't be long
now, Scarlett. What a time we're gonna have.

Your soul sister,
Sue Ellen

    Tai, conditioned to the tropical heat of his homeland,
shivered in the air-conditioned cabin of the jet. Annie

pulled a jacket out of her tote, but Tai shook his head. He didn't want to cover up the Red Sox sweatshirt that his Uncle Turner had sent him as a gift.

They were flying home at last, on the Big Bird to Paradise. In about forty hours, they'd be touching ground in Baltimore. Annie looked around at the other military passengers aboard the civilian plane. *We're all going home. We're going back to the world. We're leaving behind the calamities of a long-scarred exotic land where banyan trees and frangipani blossoms miraculously survive, somehow impervious to all the blood upon the soil. We're going home, but each of us, whether we want to or not, is taking a piece of Nam back with us.*

Tai's hand relaxed in Annie's and he drifted off to sleep. Just a few hours earlier, as they stood together in the Army discharge office, his little hand had squeezed hers in anxious fear. Would this large, powerful bear of a sergeant, sitting behind his gunmetal desk with the framed photo of Richard Nixon hanging on the wall behind him, decide at the last minute that Tai couldn't come home with her after all? Annie understood his fear and gave him many reassuring smiles as the sergeant checked through the adoption papers, Tai's passport and visa. Still, Tai did not breathe easy until they were on board and the plane had taken off.

Annie stared out the plane window as the jet engines droned their steady tune. She thought briefly of her flight in-country just fifty-six weeks ago. Unlike this subdued flight home, that one had been loud and boisterous to camouflage anxiety and fear. Well, now they had all faced their worst fears.

Annie would remember all of the pain, all of the horror and waste of what she'd seen in Vietnam, but she would remember the warmth, the closeness, the comradery and love, too. When she put all of the fragments together they formed a whole. Well, almost a whole. There was still one piece missing. One vital piece. David.

She envisioned David endlessly cruising the Interstates, grieving, searching, struggling to forget. How long would it take for him to work it out and come back home?

Annie feared that, if anything, David would now be more determined than ever to avoid all reminders of Nam. He had not only given Vietnam a year of his life and witnessed his men slaughtered and maimed. In the end he'd been permanently injured.

Had she been utterly naive to expect David to welcome Tai, an unending reminder of the horror of Nam? Had she been foolish to believe that the love she and David shared was strong enough, enduring enough, to conquer all the obstacles set against them? How awful to think of her darling son as an obstacle when she loved the child so much.

Would David ever be strong enough to forgive her for adopting Tai? Annie kept hoping that, now that David was home, he'd slowly come around. She could not stop believing in their love. She had to have faith that her love would heal David's pain and rage; that one day he would look with a smiling face at her and her child and see only love smiling back. She had to believe that the time would come when he would welcome that love.

When she looked at Tai, she saw beyond the devastations wrought by war. Her fragile son reminded her of the bravery she had witnessed, the amazing triumph of the spirit, unselfish acts of heroism, and the delicate, exotic flower blossoms that would not bend to the tides of war.

Unlike David, Annie felt a need to cling to memory. It was her memories of Nam that reminded her of how crucial it was to embrace and cherish life. And Nam had taught her about love. Love in all its complexities. Love for a man, a child, a friend. David, Tai, and Sue Ellen all held her heart inside of them. They, too, were Nam.

Chapter Eighteen

A time for peace.

Baltimore Airport, September 30, 1969

When it was Annie's and Tai's turn to step out of the plane, it was a toss-up who was squeezing whose hand more tightly. They took care climbing down the metal steps to the tarmac, both of them moving like strangers on an unknown landscape. Annie had a fleeting thought of Neil Armstrong. *One small step for man, one giant step for mankind* . . .

It was an Indian-summer day. The sky was cloudless. A fine, clear blue. A soft Atlantic breeze was coming in off the ocean. Annie, proudly dressed in her army nurse uniform, despite Sue Ellen's warning, felt the white cloth sticking to her skin. Tai would be warm in his sweatshirt, but he would undoubtedly welcome the warmth.

Annie's eyes anxiously swept over the waiting crowd. She tensed as if prepared for the pelting of tomatoes Sue Ellen had warned her about in that last letter. But the faces in the crowd were the faces of mothers, fathers, wives, sisters, brothers, fidgety children. They were the teary-eyed faces of family members here to welcome their loved ones home from Vietnam. Eager, anxious, joyful faces. As families reunited, the crowd began to shift into small clusters. Cries and shouts mingled with laughter. *We're home. We're home at last.*

Annie and Tai, hands clasped, started to make their way toward the crowd. Annie kept on the lookout for demonstrators. But there were none in sight. And she still hadn't spotted her family. Instead, several vets approached her, some merely smiling, a few wishing her a warm welcome. "You nurses are the best," one of them whispered.

Annie spotted Turner first. Turner. The dazzling star athlete. All grown-up. Leaner, even more handsome than she'd remembered. And something more. A richer character in his face. Her brother. He was waving wildly as he broke through the crowds, a big smile on his face. He was wearing a Red Sox sweatshirt to match Tai's.

For a moment Annie was too overwhelmed to move or speak. Tai tugged on her hand and pointed to the lean, blond man coming toward them.

"Yes," she whispered, a catch in her voice. "Turner." Then gripping Tai's hand even tighter, she ran with the child, meeting Turner halfway.

In one swift, athletic movement, Turner swept Annie under one arm and hoisted Tai onto his hip with his other. Then they were all hugging and laughing, tears streaming down the faces of brother and sister.

"Oh, kiddo. This is great, so great . . . I can't believe it. My baby sister. Oh Annie . . ." And then the words wouldn't come and Turner just held her tight, his cheek pressed to hers, their tears mingling. Tai observed them both with a big smile on his lips.

When her dad and Nanna got to them, there were arms everywhere, holding, squeezing, hugging. Nanna smoothed back Annie's hair, her ageless eyes brimming with pride. Her dad stooped down to shake Tai's hand, and then pulled him close and hugged him.

Annie saw that her dad looked older. There were deeper grooves on his ruddy Irishman's face. He pressed Annie to him and just let the tears come. "My girl. My girl. This is the day I've prayed for. Oh lass, it's so good to hold you." His warm, familiar Irish brogue, tinted with his acquired Southern drawl, filled Annie's heart with joy.

Nanna had lifted Tai into her arms. Annie was thrilled to see her child so surprisingly at ease in Nanna's grasp. The sweep of generations, great-grandmother and great-grandson. Nanna smiled at her. Her beautiful, loving smile. *We're home, Tai. We're home in the bosom of our family.*

Annie smiled back at Nanna, and then turned once more to search the crowd.

Nanna set Tai down and pressed Annie close. "David isn't back yet, Annie," she whispered softly, sympathetically.

"I...I was looking for...Sue Ellen and Hawk." It was true, in part anyway. "I was sure they'd..." And then Annie stopped and gave a cry of delight. "There they are. Look. Look Tai. Sue Ellen."

"And her old man," Tai said brightly. The whole family laughed.

Sue Ellen, Annie's gypsy soul sister, dark hair flowing, flamboyant, exuberant, looking more radiant than ever. She helped Hawk guide his chair.

Annie's eyes filled with fresh tears as she gazed at Hawk. He looked so similar to and yet so different from that boy she'd smiled coquettishly at that Thanksgiving day in '65. Now as then, he was wearing his brown hair long. But today he had it drawn back into a ponytail. He still wore love beads round his neck and his costume was more irreverent than ever—his army fatigue jacket plastered with antiwar buttons, his jeans decorated with American flag patches. Hawk. Her outrageous, endearing clown.

Sue Ellen gave Annie a quick hug. "You made it, Scarlett. Home, sweet home. Outstanding."

"Outstanding," Annie echoed, her smile falling on Hawk as Sue Ellen went to hug Tai and swing him in a big arc.

Annie bent toward Hawk and pressed her head against his shoulder.

"You look groovy, man," she whispered.

"And you're still the best damn looking nurse around."
Hawk's voice was husky and he swiped at his watery eyes.
"Now let me get a good look at this child of yours."

Sue Ellen deposited Tai in Hawk's lap.

"How's it going, slugger?"

"Okay," Tai said matter-of-factly.

"Okay, Uncle Hawk." He gave the boy a bear hug and
Annie leaned over and gave Hawk a full kiss on his lips.

"Hey," he quipped, easing Tai off his lap, "you think
I'm gonna take this come-on sitting down, kiddo?"

Annie kissed him again. "Oh yeah, big boy, and just
what are you-all going to do about it?"

He grinned up at Sue Ellen who was standing at his
side. Her black mascara was streaking down her cheeks
along with her tears. She grinned back, but her lips were
quivering.

"Show her, baby," Sue Ellen whispered. "Show her
what you're gonna do about it."

The small gathering—Annie, her dad, Tai, Turner,
Nanna and Sue Ellen—instantly grew silent, their collec-
tive breaths held, their eyes brimming anew with tears, as
Hawk carefully guided first one leg and then the other off
the metal footrests of his wheelchair. Quietly Sue Ellen
withdrew a pair of metal folding canes from her large tote
bag and handed them to Hawk. He clicked them into position.

Slowly, with great effort and concentration, Hawk
pulled himself up, using the canes for support. And then
he was standing there with them. Shaky, sweaty, more
than a little nervous, but standing. Standing and beaming from ear to ear.

"What a homecoming," Annie whispered as she looked
from Hawk to Sue Ellen. It was *almost* perfect.

Sue Ellen winked at her. "Whatta ya say I get a picture?" She pulled her camera out of her seemingly bot-
tomless tote.

Annie scooped Tai up in her arms and went to stand on
one side of Hawk. Turner went to Hawk's other side.
Annie motioned to Nanna and her dad to get in the pic-

ture, but they waved her off. "Just the youngsters this time," her dad muttered. Annie knew they just didn't want a picture taken of them with their eyes all red from crying. They needed a couple of minutes to compose themselves.

As the group moved in closer for the shot, Hawk dropped the canes and flung one arm over Annie's shoulder, the other over Turner's. "Okay, this is better."

Annie's smile was tremulous as Sue Ellen ordered them all to "Say cheese." There they stood, side by side, Annie and her boys. Her boys. But, one was missing. The picture could never be complete without David.

"One more," Sue Ellen demanded. "Come on, kids, show your pearly whites."

Annie was blinking back tears as Sue Ellen snapped the second shot. Relieved to hear the click, she started to move away when Hawk said, "Hold it, kiddo. We've got to get our pirate buddy in the next one."

Annie shot Hawk a confused look, and then she followed his gaze. It was David, wearing a black patch over his right eye, breaking through the crowd, coming toward them. He was smiling anxiously. Her warrior, her poet, her dreamer, her love. The boy of her dreams. Her dreams come true. Her hands began to quiver, her whole body trembled. Nanna took Tai from her arms.

"Get over here, man. We need a picture," Hawk ordered as David paused a few feet in front of Annie, his eyes glued to her. He was shaking, too. And waiting. Waiting for a sign from her.

"Hey, Nichols, wipe that hungry look off your face. This here's my sister," Turner teased.

Sue Ellen smiled. "Get used to it, Magill. It doesn't erase," she said. "Believe me, I know."

David held out his arms to Annie.

"Oh David," Annie cried, and Hawk, leaning his weight on Turner, gave her a little push.

It was all she needed. She rushed into David's arms.

Their tears mingled as they kissed. "Oh Annie, can you forgive me for being blind . . . ?" he asked.

"David, are you crazy? That doesn't matter..."

"I don't mean this bum eye, Annie. Even if they'd got both my eyes, I should have seen what you meant to me. I should have seen that I could never live without you. I do see, Annie. You're my love, my life. And I'm so sorry for putting you and Tai through so much. No one deserves happiness more than you..."

"We are happy now, David," she whispered, finding his lips once again. As they kissed this time, Hawk let out a loud whoop.

David shot Hawk a wink with his good eye, and then he did a classic double take. Stumbling back in shock, his eyes widened. "My God...you're standing."

Everyone laughed. Hawk laughed the loudest. "See what a good woman will do for a guy," Hawk announced, wrapping his free arm around Sue Ellen's shoulder.

David swept Annie back into his arms. "I see, all right. It just took me a little time, that's all." He pressed her close, his breath warm on her ear. "You were right, Annie. It's time to heal...together. All together." Slowly, he drew away from her and turned toward Tai, who was standing quietly, expectantly, at Nanna's side.

David smiled as he approached the child. "Welcome home, Tai."

Tai smiled back timidly.

David knelt down in front of the boy and stretched out his arms. Tai made no move. Instead, he regarded David closely. "You still gonna be my momma's old man?"

Everyone smiled as they watched David. David looked over at Annie. "If she'll still have me."

Tai shot Annie a look.

"I'll have him," she said softly, tremulously, fighting back tears.

"Okay," Tai exclaimed, moving into David's arms.

"One thing though, kiddo. I don't approve of you calling me *old man*."

"What you want me to call you then?"

David hugged the boy close, his gaze resting on Annie. "Dad," he said. "Call me Dad, Son."

Sue Ellen had them pose for another photograph. It was of Annie, David, Turner, Hawk and Tai. Annie and her boys. Her Four Musketeers. Her circle of love. She and David were kissing as Sue Ellen snapped the shot. It was a kiss full of hope, anticipation and promise.

"Hey Scarlett," Sue Ellen whispered to Annie as the entire clan gathered for one last picture that a returning serviceman's father offered to take. "Whatta ya say about a double wedding?"

Annie grinned. "Not if you're gonna wear a lace tablecloth over a body stocking, kiddo."

Sue Ellen laughed and threw her arms around Annie, giving her a loud smacking kiss on the cheek.

The picture was snapped, and then David swept Annie and Tai back into his arms.

Annie smiled radiantly through her tears. Sue Ellen had been wrong about one point in her reentry advice. She'd told Annie not to expect cheering crowds. But Annie *had* come home to cheers. Everyone who mattered to her, everyone she loved was there, cheering to beat the band.

To everything there is a season,
And a time to every purpose under the heaven;
A time to be born, and a time to die;
A time to plant,
and a time to pluck up that which is planted;
A time to kill, and a time to heal;
A time to break down, and a time to build up;
A time to weep, and a time to laugh;
A time to mourn, and a time to dance;
A time to cast away stones,
and a time to gather stones together;
A time to embrace,
and a time to refrain from embracing;
A time to seek, and a time to lose;
A time to keep, and a time to cast away;
A time to rend, and a time to sew;
A time to keep silence, and a time to speak;
A time to love, and a time to hate;
A time for war, and a time for peace.

Ecclesiastes

HARLEQUIN
American Romance®

ABOUT THE AUTHOR

When we asked New Hampshire writer Elise Title why she'd chosen to write about the sixties and the Vietnam War, she asked us to share her response with you, her readers.

"In 1969, I was one of the lucky ones. My husband had been passed over in the draft. So had my family and closest friends. While I was finishing school, I attended antiwar rallies and signed antiwar petitions, firm in my belief that the Vietnam War was wrong. And when the war ended in 1973, I cheered and joined in the great national healing process. Soon I'd even forgotten the words to the antiwar songs I'd sung so often with such heartfelt emotion.

"Years later, along with millions of other Americans, I witnessed on TV the dedication of the Vietnam Veterans Memorial. I was brought to tears watching the vets, the grieving widows, mothers and children searching that gleaming black granite for the etched names of their loved ones. Something else struck me, too. Among the mourning women on the screen were a few in uniform.

"I'd never honestly thought about the women who'd served in Vietnam. They were my contemporaries. Back in the sixties, while I was safe at home counting my blessings, they had gone to war. What terrible risks must they have taken; what horrors must they have witnessed? I found myself driven to understand the source of their courage. So I began reading books and articles, often written in their own words. Their experiences moved me to tears, to awe, to admiration, to love.

"These unique and remarkable women remain a haunting presence in my mind. I wanted to write a story that would show not only their valor and sacrifice, but one that would also capture their humor, their vulnerabilities, their passions and their loves.

"It is a time to sing their praises. And a time to remember the words."

ET